Joyride

ANNA BANKS

SQUARE
FISH

FEIWEL AND FRIENDS
NEW YORK

SQUARE
FISH

An Imprint of Macmillan
175 Fifth Avenue
New York, NY 10010
fiercereads.com

Our books may be purchased in bulk for promotional, educational, or business
use. Please contact your local bookseller or the Macmillan Corporate and
Premium Sales Department at (800) 221-7945 ext. 5442 or by
e-mail at MacmillanSpecialMarkets@macmillan.com.

Library of Congress Cataloging-in-Publication Data Available

ISBN 978-1-250-07998-5 (paperback)   ISBN 978-1-250-07905-3 (ebook)

Originally published in the United States by Feiwel and Friends
First Square Fish Edition: 2016
Book designed by Anna Booth
Square Fish logo designed by Filomena Tuosto

1   3   5   7   9   10   8   6   4   2

AR: 11.0 / LEXILE: 680L

To my husband, Jason,
who has been my partner in crime since high school

Joyride

One

Mr. Shackleford shuffles in the front door of the Breeze Mart, jingling the bells tied to a velvet string on the handle.

Please don't die on my shift.

Please don't die on my shift.

Please don't die on my shift.

He's one of my regulars—maybe even *the* regular—and one of the only customers to come in past 1:00 a.m., which is why I wait to sweep and mop until after he leaves. I glance at the clock; 1:37 a.m.

Right on time.

The other reason I wait to mop is because Mr. Shackleford is the human version of stale bread. He's moldy—seventy years old with a white flaky exterior, crusty around the edges, especially in the eyes where the cataracts congregate. On the inside, slow chemical reactions decompose what's left of something that used to be soft and pliable and probably pleasant (I say probably because where old people usually have frown lines, Mr. Shackleford has smile lines). The only thing that keeps him alive is the alcohol, due to what I imagine is a pickling effect. And due to the alcohol, he sometimes mistakes aisle four for the men's bathroom.

As he passes the front register where I've got my calculus splayed, he gives me a slight nod, which tells me he's fairly lucid—and the odds of him peeing near the beef jerky are slim tonight. He doesn't even fidget with the zipper of his camouflage pants, which is usually the first sign that I should direct him to the bathroom immediately.

I hear him scuffle down the last aisle and back again; this time the sound of a sloshing fifth of vodka accompanies him. I try to clear my books before he gets to the counter but I'm too late; he sets the bottle on my scrap sheet of graph paper, magnifying the graph lines I drew ten seconds before.

"Evenin', Carly," he says. I know he's been drinking, I can smell it, but his words aren't slurry yet. He appraises the books and papers in front of me. "Math. That's good. Math'll take you a long way in life."

He's gearing up for the Question of the Night, I can tell. No matter what stage of inebriation he's in, he goes all philosophical on me before he pays for the vodka. I know he thinks I fail at the answers, but that's okay. I live in the real world, not in an alcohol-induced euphoria. Last night, the question was "Is it better to be sick and wealthy, or healthy and poor?" Of course, I had to clarify a few things, like how sick and how wealthy and how poor. Very sick, very wealthy, very poor, he'd said.

So I announced that it would be best to be very sick and very wealthy. That way you could afford the best health care imaginable, and if you died, you could leave your loved ones something besides broken hearts and a funeral bill. In this country, to rise above healthy and poor is just an ideal. An ideal that most poor people don't have time to contemplate because they're too busy trying to put food on the table or keeping the lights turned on.

Like me and my brother, Julio.

Yes, it sounds like a pessimistic outlook on life blah, blah, blah. But pessimism and reality are usually mistaken for each other. And the realists are usually the only ones who recognize that.

Mr. Shackleford thumbs through his dirty camouflage wallet—which is always full of hundred dollar bills—and pulls out a twenty, probably the only one he keeps in that fat thing. I give him change, the same change every night, and he pockets the bills but leaves the seven cents in the got-a-penny tray in front of the register. I put his new bottle in a brown paper bag and gear up for the Question.

He tucks his purchase under his arm. "Is it possible to be truly happy without ever having been truly poor?"

I roll my eyes. "It's not only *possible*, Mr. Shackleford. It's more *likely*." Okay, so I like these debates we have. Mr. Shackleford is easy to talk to. He's not judgmental; I don't think he's racist either. Most people don't even say anything when they check out at my register. I know I look Mexican through and through—not even mixed Mexican—just straight-up Mexican, fresh from the border. But that's where they're wrong. I'm not straight from the border. I was born right here in Houghlin County, Florida.

I am an American. And so is Julio.

Mr. Shackleford has never treated me like anything but. He acts like I'm his peer, which is both a little weird and a little cool, that I could be a rich old guy's sixteen-year-old peer.

Mr. Shackelford purses his lips. "Money can't buy happiness." This is the root of all our discussions, and his usual comeback.

I shrug. "Being poor never delighted anyone."

He chuckles. "Simplicity has its merits."

"Being poor isn't the same thing as being simple." And surely he knows how hypocritical it sounds, coming from him. After all, he's about to hoist himself into his brand-new colossal pickup truck and drive away to his family's plantation house. He'll probably watch some TV before drifting off into his nightly vodka coma. Sounds like the definition of simplicity to me.

But he sure as heck isn't poor.

Besides that, things can get real complex when you're just poor enough to have to choose which utility bill to pay and which one to let go. When you can't send enough money along to your family without missing a few meals yourself. When school makes you buy a calculator that costs one hundred something dollars just to take a calculus class—and if you don't take the calculus class you don't qualify for the scholarship you've been working for since Day One.

Being poor isn't simple.

"How is it complicated?" he presses. He counts to three with his fingers. "Work. Eat. Sleep. The poor have time for little else. There is a kind of peacefulness in that simplicity. A peacefulness that the wealthy will never know. Why? Because of the drama, Miss Vega. Higher taxes. More ex-wives. A cornucopia of lawsuits. Lengthy, tortuous family vacations with stepfamilies of stepfamilies. Slavery to hideous fashion trends—"

The list continues to escalate in ridiculousness. Not to mention, I doubt Mr. Shackleford has ever found himself the victim of a fashion trend. In fact, it doesn't look like he's even acknowledged fashion since somewhere in the vicinity of 1972—and the extent of that acknowledgment appears to cover what was hot among rednecks back in the era of starched flannel.

"Surely this exhaustive list of rich-people issues has a point," I cut him off, unimpressed.

He grins. "I haven't heard your counterargument, Miss Vega." He pulls the package from his armpit and slides the paper bag off the bottle. Fixing his eyes on the cap, he slowly unscrews it. "I require of you a list to match my own. Prove that a poor person's life is so terrible." He takes a swig and waits for my answer.

And suddenly I don't want to talk about this anymore.

I know Mr. Shackleford is wealthy. Everyone does. And he knows that I'm not working the graveyard shift at a gas station because my family uses hundred dollar bills for toilet paper. This conversation has become personal. Hasn't it? I mean, his list is full of things that everyone already knows about the lives of the rich and famous. All the drama they create. It's public knowledge.

But the poor people list? That's a different story. The media rarely covers the glamorous life of poverty. It's this hidden gem of truth that only the impoverished get to polish. For the list to be genuine, it can only be created from firsthand experience.

So Mr. Shackleford isn't asking what I know about poor people. He's asking me about me. He's asking how bad my circumstances are. Mine, personally. At least that's what it feels like. And I don't like it. Before, it felt as though we were equals in these conversations. I doubt it will ever feel that way again. Have they been personal all along? Have they all been an attempt to . . . what, exactly? Get me to admit I'm poor?

Or am I being weird?

I just hope he doesn't want to make me his charity case or something. I could never take anything from him. How do you explain to someone that you were born with the need for self-sufficiency? And anyway, Mr. Shackleford should recognize this.

Just ask him if he wants help getting to his truck. Nooooooope.

"I have to get back to work," I say.

A glint of disappointment passes through his eyes, a reaction slowed by the liquor swimming in him. I've never spurned the Question of the Night before.

"Of course." With shaky hands, he finagles the cap back on the bottle and lowers it into the now-crinkled brown bag. "Some other time then."

No other time, I want to say. *Anything theoretical, but nothing personal.* Instead I take the bag and twist the top of it for him, as if doing so will keep the bottle from falling out or something.

"Thanks." He taps his fingers sloppily on the counter. I think he's going to say something else, and I'm gearing up to cut him off, but after a few seconds he says, "You have yourself a good night, Miss Vega."

"You too, Mr. Shackleford."

The jingle bells at the front door knock against each other violently when he leaves. I watch as he one-handedly fumbles in his pocket for his truck keys. I vacillate between going outside to help him or picking up where I left off with my calculus. Going outside might mean getting him out of here quicker, or it might mean another attempt at conversation suddenly gone awkward.

Calculus wins.

After about two minutes of not hearing the engine to Mr. Shackleford's truck roar to life, I glance up. And I wish I hadn't. But some things can't be unseen.

I swallow my heart as I take in the sight of Mr. Shackleford pressed against the side of his truck. His hands are in the air, shaking almost as badly as his knees, which lean in against each other in a need-a-restroom sort of way. The man pointing a rifle in his face is tall—or maybe the cowboy hat he's wearing is meant to make him appear that way. He's wearing an old blue T-shirt like a bandana around his face, nose to neck. I can't even see the guy's ears. Whatever he's saying to Mr. Shackelford, he must be whispering; I haven't heard a word of exchange yet. All I can see is the bandana moving—and Mr. Shackleford's corresponding responses—to the synchronization of a very serious conversation. And Mr. Shackleford's mouth quivers as he talks.

He could have a heart attack right here in front of the store.

On my shift.

The good news is, I'm short. I could easily reach the store shotgun just by lowering my arms behind the counter.

The bad news is, I don't know how to shoot a gun, and the chances of me taking aim before getting myself shot first are slim to none. Plus, I've never been robbed before.

Not that I'm being robbed just yet. In fact, the robber doesn't seem to be interested in me at all. I either pose no threat or he knows that Mr. Shackleford's wallet holds more money than my register does. I decide that this guy is either the world's stupidest criminal for turning his back on me, or I'm the world's dumbest clerk for not running out the back door and calling the cops. It's just that taking the time to run, to call the cops—that's time better spent on helping Mr. Shackelford *now*. Oh God.

Don't be a hero.

But I'm not being a hero. I'm just being a human.

I snatch up the shotgun and slide over the counter with it, which sends my homework sprawling to the floor with a thud. I almost bust my butt by slipping on one of the stray pieces of paper and I let out a pathetic little scream.

The robber whips his attention my way and that makeshift bandana hides everything but the surprise in his eyes as he takes in the sight of me: a five-foot-four-inch mess pointing the shaky barrel of a gun at him, hoping my finger is on the trigger—and at the same time, hoping it's not.

My legs involuntarily run toward the door, bursting through it, making the jingle bells angry. I'm not graceful, either, like in the movies when an organized SWAT team busts in on a hostage situation. I'm all elbows and knees, running like an ostrich in boots and coordinated as a dazed fly that just got swatted. Oh, but that doesn't stop me. "Get down on the ground," I yell, surprised that my voice doesn't tremble as much as my insides do. "Or I'll blow a hole in your . . . I'll shoot you!"

Since I obviously can't decide which part of him sounds the scariest to shoot a hole through, I go for directness. Directness is my specialty, anyway.

"Now, listen here," the guy says, and I swear I've heard that voice before. I scrutinize the eyes widening just over the rim of the bandana but I can't tell what color they are because of the blue fluorescent beer sign in the window right behind us. And there's no way I can form a face out of his hidden features. "Take it easy," he says calmly, as if I'm the one who's cornering a helpless old man against a truck. "I'm not here to hurt you. This is between me and him."

To my surprise and terror, I take a step *forward.* "I said get down. Now."

Wow, I'm going to die. What if this guy is allergic to bluffing? What if he makes me pull the trigger? I don't even know if the gun's safety is on. *Dios mio,* I don't even know if the gun *has* a safety.

The robber considers for several terrifying seconds, then raises his gun at my head, takes three intimidating steps toward me. I back away, hating myself for being a coward. I stop myself before I hit the glass door of the store. Cowardice has a threshold, I guess.

"Here's how it's going to go," he says gruffly. "You're going to leave the gun right there and go back in the store and stand over there by the chips so I can see you." He motions with the end of the gun.

"No."

This elicits a huff from beneath the bandana. "Unbelievable."

"You leave *your* gun here." If he thinks it's a good idea, then I do too. Still, I'm not sure what I'll do if he actually does put his gun down. Secure him with plastic zip ties from the boxes of candy bars that need to be stocked?

"You're a crazy little thing. Do you have a death wish or something?"

Oh God. He truly seems interested in the answer. "I . . . I don't want you to hurt Mr. Shackleford."

Rolling his eyes, he says, "Well, put the gun down and I won't."

I want to put the gun down. I do. I want to cooperate. I want to live. But this gun is my only leverage. "No." Did I say no? *Did I just say no?*

"Fine. Keep the gun. New plan." He uses the back of his hand to wipe some sweat off his forehead. "I'm going to leave. And you're going to let me."

"I'm calling the cops."

"Jesus, who *are* you? Look, you don't know how to shoot a gun, I can tell. And besides that, I definitely *do* know how to shoot a gun, so I have the advantage. If you fire at me, I'll shoot back. Understand?" When I hesitate, he adds, "When I start shooting, I'm aiming at the old man first."

"No!" I blurt. "Don't shoot him."

He nods. "I won't. As long as you let me back out of here. Just like this." He takes two steps backward, never dropping the gun.

"But you haven't robbed us yet," I say. Out loud. *Idiota.*

"Are you freaking kidding me? You *want* me to rob you?"

I raise my chin a little. "Well . . . It's just that . . . What did you come here for then?"

He shakes his head, then backs away more toward the end of Mr. Shackleford's truck, never lowering his gun. "You're crazy as a raccoon in daylight, you know that?"

I am crazy. He's right. "You should remember that, if you ever come back here again."

At this he runs, turning his back to me. Sprinting away, he pivots sharply and heads toward the side of the store. It takes me a second to realize what he's doing. Within a few breaths he emerges from the shadows pedaling my bike as if an angry boar were chasing him. The wheels wobble as he struggles to balance it, one hand gripping his gun and the other on the handle.

My.

Bike.

Right now I have the perfect shot. If I knew how to shoot a gun. And if the safety wasn't on. If it has a safety.

I take aim anyway, cradling the butt of the gun in my shoulder like some kind of hunter, and fantasize about blowing out the back tire of my bike. About this guy face-planting on the asphalt. About that stupid cowboy hat taking flight like a startled bird.

But his silhouette disappears into the night. And the moment is over.

I let out a huge breath and turn just in time to see Mr. Shackleford sink to the ground, wiping the truck clean of any dust with his descent. His legs spill out in front of him as he looks up at me. "You . . . You saved my life," he says. His voice shakes like he's freezing.

I did save his life. I know that. I saved us both.

If Julio found out I did anything like this, he'd kill me. Heroics bring attention. Attention brings scrutiny.

And scrutiny exposes secrets.

Two

The night did not go as Arden had reckoned it would. It was meant to be simple—relieve Uncle Cletus of his keys and hopefully scare him into never driving drunk again. An noncomplicated hoax turned into a catastrophe. Arden sifts through the reasons why.

Reason Number One: He didn't expect the girl behind the counter to be so ballsy. *She pulled a freaking gun on me. Who does that?* Isn't it in the employee manual to be submissive to gun-wielding robbers and be done with it? But no. This girl—what is her name, Carla or Carol or something—this girl pulled out a shotgun and gave him ultimatums. Maybe he should have watched her more closely in class before planning something like this. But everything she'd shown him screamed shy, insecure, unambitious. She wore a plain T-shirt and jeans every day. Never raised her hand in class, never spoke to anyone. No makeup, as far as Arden could tell. Shifted quietly between classes in a please-don't-notice-me sort of way. If he hadn't actually been scoping her out for this specific plan, he wouldn't have known she existed. Heck, she had three classes with him and he never even knew it before last Tuesday.

At best, he expected her to duck behind the front counter and let him rob his own uncle in peace. Maybe call the cops too, but he'd made sure Deputy Glass—the more competent deputy on duty—was busy with an anonymous intruder call at an abandoned house on the outskirts of town. That way, with a little efficiency, he could scare the bejesus out of Uncle Cletus without getting caught.

Not that Arden cared much about getting caught. His dad wouldn't allow the charges to stick anyway. Especially given the reasons behind it. Or maybe he would. Maybe this would be the last straw for his old man. Maybe this would be the one thing that his father wouldn't tolerate.

Reason Number Two: Arden's pretty sure he's stolen Carla/Carol's bicycle. It's a girl's mountain bike, nothing fancy, and it was parked near the entrance to the Breeze Mart. He would have made a run for it, but he was afraid she'd actually attempt to shoot at him as he made his way back to his truck parked about half a mile down the road. The bike was necessary for his mobility. For life and limb, even, because who knows what that crazy girl would do next? It didn't seem like she knew, either. Watching her thought process was fascinating. And frustrating, when he realized she didn't have any intention of backing down. He'd spent—wasted—all that time contriving a plan that ultimately failed.

With a scowl on his face, Arden skids to a halt in front of his red Ford truck. Gently, he lifts the girl's bike into the back of it, carefully laying it down so as not to scratch it. It's bad enough that he took it. It's probably her ride home for the night. He's hoping her parents will pick her up. And if not, Glass works Monday night patrol. He'll be the first of the two deputies to respond to the robbery—even with his counterfeit intruder call. That is, *if* that girl has the sense to call the cops. If she does, Glass will give her a ride home if she needs it.

Arden puts his truck into gear, steering off the dirt shoulder and onto the road. For once in his life, he buckles up and drives under the speed limit. He doesn't need to get pulled over tonight. Not when he's still wearing the robber's outfit and has the clerk's bike in his truck bed. Not when his curiosity has been piqued by this Carla chick. She has balls, that's for sure. But she doesn't seem to wear them when she's at school. *Why is that?*

Reason Number Three: Why did Uncle Cletus act like a dead body as soon as a gun was pulled? What happened to the sturdy old guy who used to tell him and his older sister, Amber, all those horrific war stories? About how he was a Vietnam prisoner of war and lived on one cup of rice a day, took regular beatings, and then ran this county as sheriff as soon as he returned from overseas. Seems like the toughest sheriff in the county's history would have reacted differently. Arden had been ready for an entertaining scuffle, but his uncle just dropped the bottle of vodka and retreated against the truck. Might have even pissed himself.

So much for alcohol being liquid courage.

Arden runs a nervous hand through his hair. Maybe his mom is right. Maybe Uncle Cletus has drunk himself into near death. Which is troubling. His uncle is the closest thing to a real father he's ever had. The only person he could ever really talk to.

Of course, if he was that close to me, I would have checked on him a lot sooner than this. Have I become so consumed with making Dad miserable that I've let Uncle Cletus suffer on his own?

Yes, he has. He knows it. Giving the new sheriff in town hell—the esteemed Sheriff Dwayne Moss—has been Arden's only objective for the past year. He was willing to give up the football team, the baseball team, his potential scholarship opportunities. All the things he knew his dad would want for him to continue after Amber's death. But the one thing he'd wanted to keep was his relationship with Uncle Cletus.

Arden tries to remember the last time he visited the old man and can't. And now he's just given him a heart attack with his botched-up convenience store prank. Shaved years off his uncle's life in a matter of seconds. If he even has years left.

From the looks of him, Uncle Cletus has been knocking on death's door and patiently waiting for it to answer. *I've got to go visit that old guy,* Arden thinks to himself as he pulls into his driveway.

And somehow I've got to get this bike back to its owner.

Three

I don't actually breathe until Deputy Glass pulls out of our sandy driveway. The fact that he insisted on giving me a ride home at all almost gives me an ulcer—at least he doesn't have his blue lights flashing when we pull in. My only saving grace is that no one in our trailer park is usually up at this time of night. Not even Señora Perez, who enjoys a late-night cigarette every now and then on the front steps of her trailer. That's the benefit of living in a community of close-knit, hardworking immigrants—everyone is so tired that they actually sleep at night. Which is a good thing, since this bundle of nationalities is tightly secured by a rampant grapevine of unreliable gossip. Even the Russians get in on it. Gossip, as it turns out, has no language barrier. If anyone was awake to witness me being escorted home in a cop car . . . The scandal would permeate the very air in various, frenzied dialects.

I'm surprised to see a faint light shining through the living room window. Surely, *surely,* Julio is not awake. I make my way quietly up the stairs and use my key to unlock the door, giving the handle a jerk. The chain catches; Julio has officially locked me out.

Does he know what happened tonight?

"Julio," I whisper between the crack in the door. "Let me in?"

I hear footsteps fall on the hollow floor of our living room, then the door is yanked shut from the inside. I bite my lip. I hear the chain being released and step back so the opening door doesn't knock me off the steps.

Julio greets me at the threshold with a tired smile. "Carlotta, why are you home so late? Did you have inventory tonight?" But he's already walking back into the house, toward the four-by-six area our landlord calls a kitchen. I bounce up the steps and shut and lock the door behind me. A fragile but definite sense of relief swirls through me as I realize I may be off the hook; if Julio had seen the cop car, he would have already been in ballistic phase. That's the one good thing about Julio—you always know where you stand with him.

"Uh-huh," I mumble, but I can't help but feel a little hurt. If he was awake and knew I was late coming home—I glance at the clock that dares to flash 4:37 a.m. back at me—why didn't he bother to check up on me? What if I didn't have inventory? I could be dead on the side of the road somewhere, and he wouldn't know because he's too busy . . . What *is* he busy doing, exactly? And do I really want to press the issue, given the circumstances?

Then I see a pair of worn-jeaned legs stretching across the kitchen floor, the booted toes pointed toward the ceiling. *Oh.* "Hi, Artemio," I call, setting my backpack on the counter.

Julio had told me he'd be having Artemio, one of my father's old friends, over before work to see if he could fix the kitchen sink.

Julio could hang drywall like a pro, but plumbing was entirely beyond his scope of construction skills. And our sink had been leaking for about three weeks now.

"*Hola,* Carlotta," Artemio says, his voice muffled under the cabinet. "You are very late. You sure she doesn't have a boyfriend, Julio?" He motions for Julio to hand him his wrench.

Julio looks at me. "She knows better than to have a boyfriend, don't you, Carlotta? My sister is smart, Artemio." The pride in his voice makes me perk up a little. "She knows boys are a waste of time. We stick together, don't we, Carly?"

It's nice to hear him say we stick together, instead of that he's stuck with me—which is how I feel. "Always," I say around a yawn. This situation does not require me, I know, but I'm hesitant to leave the room; Julio is not home often. Even now, he's already dressed for the day; he and Artemio carpool in the morning with some friends at work and will be leaving in about forty-five minutes. I might as well get a shower and change clothes too. But we have a guest. *Guests come first,* I can hear Mama say. "Can I make you some coffee, Artemio? Julio?" I flick my brother on his arm. "Did you make your lunch yet?"

Julio smiles. "We're fine, *bonita.* Go to bed."

Closing my eyes at this point would be stupid. Especially since I have to allot extra time to *walk* to school.

"You could skip school today," Julio says, seeing me yawn for a third time. "Get rested up for your next shift tonight. It's good that you stayed late. We could use the extra money."

Julio has always been on the school-is-not-important bandwagon, right alongside Mama. It's hard to disagree at this moment, with my eyelids sagging as if weighted down with iron. But someday my perseverance will make him proud. Someday I'll show him that it all wasn't a waste of time. Someday I'll hand him an upper-class paycheck that could only be earned with a degree.

And so I head to the bathroom for a cold shower.

～⌒・⌒～

I feel like slightly microwaved death.

Plopping down in the chair for fourth-period social studies, I set my books on the desk with the enthusiasm of a sloth. I offer a small wave to Josefina, who's already tucked neatly into her seat across the room. She's one of the girls who lives in my neighborhood, but we barely ever see each other except at school. She works too, cleaning houses on the weekend, so it's not like we'd ever have time to hang out—even if we did have more in common. She has four brothers, so she's into motorcycles and fixing cars and other things I couldn't care less about. The extent of our conversation is usually "Hi."

For which I'm grateful today. The few hours I normally sleep in the mornings between my shift at the Breeze and my first class at school were consumed by filling out police reports—and making sure Mr. Shackleford was truly going to be okay. Oh, and the joy of walking to school instead of riding my bike, thanks to the gunman I'm now convinced was high or psycho or both.

That dick. What, did he think I was going to pedal him down and shoot him? That a short stack like me would actually pursue a guy twice her size *on a bicycle*? Or did he just feel the need to take something, even if it wasn't cash? Klepto *enloquecido*.

What's worse, that was our last bike. Julio's got stolen a few weeks ago and we've been trading the one back and forth between us. And now mine got jacked—a fact that I haven't made Julio aware of yet. Thankfully, when Deputy Glass brought me home last night, Artemio had Julio distracted. Because Deputy Glass was a talker; he would have spilled the beans about what I did. And my brother would have nodded politely, thanked the cop, then made me call Mama to tell her how I had jeopardized the entire family by being a hero. By drawing attention to myself.

Earlier this morning, I didn't appreciate how lucky I'd been. Now, after my soda-induced stamina has kicked in, my brain can review the facts with clarity. And this is what I decide: I could have been so screwed. If Deputy Glass had walked me to the door. If Julio hadn't had Artemio there.

I push the thought aside and try not to dwell on things that could have happened but didn't. Taking out my school planner, I scribble in a note for Saturday: Go yard-saling. I've got at least ten dollars in quarters saved in my peanut butter jar. I was going to use the quarters for the Laundromat, but maybe Señora Perez in the trailer next door will let me trade some housework to use her washing machine. She keeps her place spotless, but sometimes she has odds and ends for me to do, like rearranging pictures or cutting the grass on her lot. I just have to catch her in the right mood, since she's already being generous in giving me the password to her Wi-Fi to use for schoolwork. But if everything turns out as planned, I'll find a cheap bike at a yard sale—if they're willing to negotiate.

I open my social studies book where my homework is tucked. Thank God I got that done before calculus last night at work. The other kids in my row pass their papers up, and just as I'm about to tap the shoulder of the guy sitting in front of me, he turns around. His gaze lingers at the top of the paper I'm trying to hand him.

"Hi," he says. "Carly, right?"

Somehow I keep my mouth from falling open. Arden Moss actually knows my name? And how disgusting is it that I even care? "Hi. Yeah." I hand him the stack of papers, which he accepts without taking his eyes off me.

"Heard you had a rough night." This throws me at first and not just because his eyes are ridiculously green. *I hadn't told anyone about the robbery.* Then I remember that Arden is the sheriff's son. Apparently confidentiality is not included in the sheriff's policy. Did the subject come up at breakfast or something? Did they casually discuss the most horrific moment of my life over their Wheaties?

I shift uncomfortably in my seat. I'm not sure why Arden would care or why he's acknowledging my existence. He might not be the school's star quarterback anymore, but he's definitely still on the tip of everyone's tongue. Now I know why. His green eyes, his honey-colored hair, the way his biceps bulge without flexing. He's mesmerizing, really.

And I don't have time for mesmerizing. "It was . . . interesting," I tell him. Maybe if I downplay it, he'll stop talking to me. "Not as bad as it sounds though." Which is a lie. I pointed a gun at a stranger who was pointing a gun at me. It doesn't get much more terrifying than that. Ask Mr. Shackleford. He actually messed his pants.

Arden's eyes seem to light up. "I heard you were brave. Talked the robber down."

I'm not sure what to say to this; I did in fact back-talk the robber like the *idiota* that I am. If I tell Arden that, he'll press for more information, I'm certain. It's too juicy to pass up. But the thing is, I'm not a good liar either. Señora Perez told me once that I'm "honest to a fault." And the way she said it, extreme honesty wasn't a good thing in her eyes. Of course, I'd just got done telling her that I didn't think her anti-wrinkle cream was working. But she *asked*.

Mr. Tucker saves me. Standing in front of Arden's desk, he clears his throat in a look-at-me sort of way. Arden whirls in his seat and hands the homework over to him. I notice that he doesn't have any homework of his own to turn in, but mostly I'm glad he didn't press the issue or infringe on Mr. Tucker's patience. After all, Arden isn't known for his adherence to the rules.

During class I can't help but stare at Arden's wide back. I'm a bit starstruck by our insubstantial conversation and I hate it. It was easy to ignore him before; he was Arden Moss, The Untouchable. I knew my place on the social ladder—crap, I'm not even *on* the social ladder—and I knew his. But now that he's spoken to me, I have to acknowledge that he's a real person—and I have to consider all the reasons why girls drool at the sound of his name.

So that's why I concentrate on his flaws. He's the sheriff's son. That's a flaw because the sheriff's entire platform this past election was getting rid of undocumented immigrants. Normally I don't care about politics and whatnot, but Julio wouldn't shut up about it, and since we're saving up to smuggle our parents back across the border, that's one cavernous rift between me and Arden.

Another blemish is that Arden Moss is prettier than me. So I'd spend my time being jealous of his flawless skin or something, and that's not healthy for anyone.

And who names their son Arden? It's an awfully girly name for a guy, I think. Maybe because it's so similar to "garden" and that reminds me of pink flowers and such.

So by the time the bell rings, I've magnified all his faults to the point where I'm actually disgusted with him. Which is way more convenient than being starstruck.

Four

Carly Vega.

Carly Vega.

Fearless Carly Vega.

Arden can't get her out of his mind. God, she would make the perfect partner in crime for so many reasons. She'd tried to convince him that the robbery was nothing to her, but her face told a different story; she's a terrible liar, at best. But the most important takeaway from the conversation in social studies is that she *was* afraid during his prank—and she took matters into her own hands anyway.

Which means that, one: She's fond of Uncle Cletus, and that wins her likeability points, and two: She handles scary situations with finesse, which wins her respect points.

He leans against the kitchen counter, sipping his coffee. Now he reckons all he has to do is convince her that she's perfect for the position of accomplice. That she has what it takes. More than that, he has to convince her of *why* she should cross over to the dark side with him. Right now she seems a bit uptight—proper, even. But he can tell her manners are false. They have to be. Her mouth says one thing and her eyes say another. Her lips spew boring politeness. But her eyes? The first thing he noticed about them is that they're the color of his favorite kind of coffee in the winter. But it wasn't long before he realized they're full of sarcasm. Mischief. And a little bit of pride.

She probably doesn't even appreciate what she's capable of. And Arden aims to change that.

"Good morning, sweetie," his mother says, startling him. The mug of hot coffee in his hand spills out, burning him. She stops then, the rustling of her silk robe hushing seconds later. Only a tinge of remorse glints in her hollow eyes. "Sorry," she says. She helps herself to a cup of coffee and sits on a barstool at the kitchen island, staring blankly at the refrigerator.

Arden remembers a time when she would have helped him soak up the coffee off the floor with a handful of paper towels, fussing over his minor burn and probably scolding him for his messy hair—all this while walking out the door to some social event or another. But all that changed when Amber got sick. And it stopped completely when she died.

From that day forward, everything that made Sherry Moss a mother seemed to dry up inside her and shrivel into the heavily medicated waif she's become. Arden throws the soaking napkins in the trash can. "Did Dad give you your medicine last night?"

"I think so. I don't remember." She takes a fistful of pills to help her sleep, Arden knows. But they mess with her memory too. In the very beginning, after Amber passed, she got Arden's doctor to write him a prescription too, when she found out he wasn't sleeping. But

Arden didn't take up her offer, flushing the pills down the toilet instead.

"Why don't you go back to bed?"

She gives him a small smile. It clearly says she doesn't feel like talking. She arranges that smile on her face often. "I'm going to check on your Uncle Cletus this morning."

Oh, she definitely doesn't need to be driving like this. "Cletus doesn't need your help. He's tough as a coconut. You should go back to bed."

His mother looks him straight in the eye then. "You want to talk about things that *should* be done, do you?"

Here we go. Deep down, the ghost of a mother in her occasionally feels obligated to bring up how he *should* rejoin the football team to make his father happy. How he *should* start caring about his grades again. How he *should* care about something, period. "Touché," he says, holding up his palms in surrender. He doesn't want to have this conversation any more than she does. In truth, Arden doubts she really cares, she's just trying to take the spotlight off what she perceives as her own failure. Or maybe she's just parroting his father's rants.

"You used to like football," she says more to herself than to him. She takes another sip of her coffee, as if dismissing the thought, the conversation, altogether. *The vacancy sign is definitely on now.* That's the mother Arden's used to these days.

But she's right, of course. He did like football. He loved it, lived it, breathed for it. And he kept his grades up too, because if he didn't, he'd get kicked off the team. Nothing Coach Nelson could do about that, especially after he'd fought so hard to get Arden on the varsity team as a sophomore. But football took too much away from him. His practices, his games. It was all time he could have spent with Amber. It was different when she actually came to his games. She'd sit beside his father and scream and shout when touchdowns were scored and refs made bad calls. She'd eat hot dogs and spill her drink when he landed the ball wherever he aimed.

But when she couldn't handle the pressure of being around people anymore, he should have stopped too. He should have been there for her. He should have seen the downward spiral she was trapped in. But he was too busy to notice.

It was only when she stopped wanting to go pranking on Sunday nights that he realized how skinny Amber had become. How inaccessible she really was. And how blind he had been. But by then it was too late.

He quit the team the Monday after her funeral. His father was angry—they nearly came to blows over it. But Arden's love for the game died with Amber. He kept on pranking though, in honor of all the times they did share together. And because it would piss his dad off more than anything else.

Explaining this to his half-sedated mother would be a wasted effort. She's incapable of understanding anything with depth anymore, and his father refuses to—which is nothing new. Open communication has never been a Moss Family Tradition, but there used to be times when Arden could talk to his mother and she would truly listen. Those times are long gone, and he's accepted that. It doesn't even make him angry anymore.

Besides, he has more important things to worry about today than reconstructing burnt, debilitated bridges with his parents.

And her name is Carly Vega.

He grabs his truck keys and plants a kiss on his mom's

forehead. "Have a good day," he calls over his shoulder as he leaves. He's surprised by how much he really means it.

His mother doesn't respond.

✦

Arden wanders around the outside picnic tables with a tray of cafeteria food that resembles rice mixed with mashed potatoes and topped with fish scales. He usually skips out on lunch and goes to Taco City a few streets down from the school with his friend Luke. But today he sent Luke away on his own. Because today is a special day. Today he has found a sidekick.

Luke doesn't qualify for the job. He's a yellow belly. Last time he accompanied Arden on one of his sprees, he got them caught and charged with trespassing. They'd planned to put a bunch of Butterball chickens into Eddie Revell's coop after relocating the live chickens to the back of the farm for safekeeping. Except one of the live roosters pecked Luke on the leg. He screamed, which set off the dogs to barking, which alerted Revell that something was amiss, which made him get his freaking shotgun out and hold them hostage until the cops came. Luke had frozen, wouldn't budge, and Arden wasn't going to let him take the fall by himself.

Luke swore off going with him after that, which was a good thing, since Arden vowed to never take him along again.

Looking for her purple T-shirt, Arden finally spots Carly at the farthest side of the picnic area. She's sitting alone, all her focus on the calculus book in front of her. She appeared to be studying the other night too, when he first approached Uncle Cletus outside the store. He'll have to cure her of that do-gooder stuff.

He stands over her, blocking the sun from her face. She looks up. Her mouth smiles, but her eyes are full of what-do-you-want-now. Arden is delighted. Without asking, he takes the seat opposite her and settles in for the big talk.

"Hey," he starts. "I heard your bike was stolen during the robbery. Do you need a ride home today?" Offering her a ride accomplishes a few things; he can find out where she lives so he can return the bike, and it opens the conversation with a little bit of hospitality. To set the right tone, he gives his most charming smile. He waits for the usual enchantment to light up her face; girls can't resist his dimples.

Well, girls who aren't Carly Vega. She narrows those espresso eyes at him. "I didn't report that my bike was stolen. So how is it that you 'heard' that?"

Awesome.

Five

Arden leans in, spreading his palms flat on the table between us, hovering over his lunch tray like he's protecting it from some unknown evil behind him. His eyes say it all. Bulging with guilt and surprise and what looks like a plea to keep my voice down. Arden Moss is full of secrets.

He arranges his expression into one of diplomacy. Neutrality. I can tell he's gearing up for an explanation. I can tell he has experience in giving explanations.

But I don't need an explanation. I need something to throw. "You," I hiss.

"Yes." His Adam's apple becomes more pronounced as he swallows.

I expect him to say more. To start confessing his excuses and justifications and maybe top it off with an apology. It's the least he could do, after all. But he doesn't. He just sits there watching me.

This is what I get? *This?* The offer of a ride home and a one-word confession? Unacceptable. Was he making fun of me in social studies? He had to be. He already knew what happened at the store. He already knew how it went down. He already knew I was terrified.

Because he's the one who terrified me.

Oh, how he must have choked down his laughter when I'd said it was no big deal.

My fists clench and unclench. Once. Twice. Again. I glance around us. People are watching us. Talking about us. Wondering among themselves why Arden Moss is sitting with me, conversing with me, attesting to my existence. They're probably trying to remember my name. I can practically feel their disdain.

"You're losing your temper again," Arden says, eyeing my hands. "I'm guessing you're not going to let me explain."

"Oh, were you *trying* to explain? Because to me, it looked like you were just sitting there like the steaming pile of crap you are." *Calm down calm down calm down.* This isn't worth the attention.

Nothing is worth the attention.

Arden doesn't even flinch with my insult. Why would he? He's Arden Moss. "You told me in class that it wasn't as bad as it sounded. Why are you all of a sudden acting as if I ruined your life?"

Seriously? "You. Pointed. A gun. At me."

"The gun wasn't loaded."

And he stole my bike. And he made fun of me. And now he's drawing attention to me. All good reasons to dot his eye for him.

But none of them are as bad as what he did to Mr. Shackleford. Because of Arden, my only friend lost the last sliver of dignity he had left. The way the old man's shoulders hunched in defeat, the way he stood pressed against his truck so no one could see the back of his pants. Who wouldn't be embarrassed? But Mr. Shackleford? He is especially proud. And especially destroyed by what happened.

Because he's a man who once stood for something, I can tell. I'm not sure what that something was, and I may not ever know. All I do know is that a man like him stands for things. Like my *abuelo* did before he died. I never met him, but Mama said he owned his own food cart in Mexico City where he sold lunch and dinner to construction workers. She said he kept his counter clean, his supplies organized, his money all faced the same way in the little tin box he made change out of. All he had was that cart, but he stood for what it gave him: freedom. Freedom to feed his family, to care for their needs. Freedom to work for himself, to earn a respectable living instead of turning to the local cartel.

Mr. Shackleford comes from a different country sure, but the same generation as my grandfather. The generation who stood for what they believed in. I mean, why else would he drink so much? He must have had something good, something valuable, and somehow he lost it. His wife, maybe. Or his child. Those would be the obvious answers. But there had to be something else, something even deeper than that. Mr. Shackleford is a thinker. He believes in things like wisdom and respect and decency. And then the times changed and left him and his ethics behind.

I think Mr. Shackleford lost his proverbial food cart, the way my grandfather did. And like my *abuelo,* it broke him.

I'm infuriated that an entitled ass like Arden Moss could snatch away his dignity.

"And you pointed a gun at me," Arden is saying nonchalantly. He scoops up a glob of white stuff from his tray and waves it at me. "You don't see me about to pop a blood vessel over it, do you? But let's not dwell on the past—"

And I lose it. As if from a distance, I watch my hands as they tuck themselves under his tray and flip it over onto his lap. The unidentifiable contents splatter everywhere. A bit of it even makes its way into his left nostril. He stares up at me, still holding his spoon midair. His jaw is in danger of falling off.

An eruption of whispers sprinkles around us. Kids stand up on tables to get a better view. It seems like the whole world is waiting for Arden's reaction. Even I hold my breath, and I hate myself for it. I shouldn't care what he thinks. I shouldn't care what our audience thinks. These kids should mean nothing to me. I don't even know most of them, and I've been going to this high school since freshman year—I'm a junior now. I've had more important things to worry about, things these kids will never understand.

And maybe I don't care what each individual thinks, but I do feel the pressure of the mob. I feel it in the warmth of my face, the way the heat of mortification seeps down my neck and into parts that are covered by my T-shirt. The attention closes in on me like a predator. And I care. I care very much.

Then I make myself remember Mr. Shackleford and the way he wouldn't look me in the eye after Arden's little visit and I get pissed off all over again. I regain my breath—my words. "How about now?" I say to Arden. "Popped any blood vessels yet?"

Suddenly, my hands are on my milk carton and splashing the remainder of it in Arden's face. "And *that's* for Mr. Shackleford!"

Oh. My. God. I can't believe I just did that.

The spectators ease in, and I know that most of them heard what

I just said. If they know Mr. Shackleford, they might investigate things further. He might fall prey to small-town gossip, and be even more embarrassed about what happened. I've made things about a thousand times worse. Anger creeps back in, dispensing any shame I might have felt about painting Arden Moss with his own lunch. Everyone's faces start to disappear. All I see is Mr. Shackleford, disgrace sagging down his features. He is the real victim here.

Arden slowly sets the spoon on the picnic table. Milk trickles down from his eyebrows, to his cheeks, tracing his neck to the collar of his T-shirt. Then, incredibly, he nods, as if in acceptance of what just happened.

It almost gives me an eye twitch, his steady composure. Especially since I'm toeing the line that separates rational from cray-cray, in public, and at Mr. Shackleford's expense. "Okay," he says finally. "I think we've officially established that you're impulsive. But don't worry. That can be a good thing." He seems to say this more to himself than to me. "Wait, where are you going?"

The lunch crowd is already parting a path for me leading to the cafeteria door and some of me wants to take them up on their walk of shame. To hold my head up as I pass, to show them that I'm not who they thought I was. But the truth is, I *need* to be who they thought I was. For Julio. For my parents. I need to be the girl who is nobody, who doesn't warrant even the shadow of a second thought.

But I'm not that girl anymore, and I can never be her again. Thanks to Arden Moss.

I turn and leave the picnic area the back way and head toward the school auditorium where the band practices, leaving the crowd—and Arden—behind to watch me go.

Six

Arden stares at the back of Carly's head in American Lit, wondering how he's going to revisit the very important subject of her becoming his accomplice now that it's evident she hates his guts.

I'll just have to get her alone.

He concedes that approaching her at lunch was a bad idea. He knew people would be curious, but he thought the attention would die down after it was apparent they were just talking. He never dreamed that before the conversation ever really started he'd be wearing his lunch and drowning in Carly's milk.

She has a right to be angry, and so he can't fault her for her reaction. Sure, it surprised the hell out of him, and even embarrassed him a little, which doesn't happen often. And then there was the inconvenience of having to shower in the locker room and change into his phys ed clothes for the rest of the day—and they aren't exactly fresh either. Plus the questions his friends had asked about the ordeal. "Dude, she turned *you* down?" and "Did you give her the

Prince Charming smile?" and "Have you ever been rejected before?" and "Why are you interested in her anyway?"

That last one got under his skin. But who is he to judge? A week ago, she didn't even register on his own radar. He can't imagine he ever would have looked twice, let alone spoken to her, which is a shame, because look what he's been missing out on. Look what the *world's* been missing out on.

This county will never know what hit it. Which is why he's got to try again. And he knows just exactly how to do it.

The bell rings and he follows her out of the classroom, keeping a safe distance—no telling what she'd do if she discovered him stalking her. But stalking her he is.

And what a weird—bordering on creepy—concept it is to stalk a girl. He'd never had to worry about things like this. He could have his pick here at Roaring Brooke High and he knew it. But none of the girls here offered anything that interested him—at least, not for more than a night.

And along came Carly Vega. The girl who pointed a shotgun at his head, dumped his lunch in his lap, then publicly shunned him all in the space of forty-eight hours. Arden grins, watching as she pulls her thick black hair into submission with a rubber band, wadding it into a sloppy bun on the top of her head. And he's not the only one watching. From across the hall Chad Brisbane pretends to be busy with his own locker, but his eyes are trained on Carly too.

Arden scowls as he watches Chad's gaze drizzle down the length of her, lingering on what Arden has to admit is a shapely rear, even though she tries to hide it with those off-brand jeans. He recognizes that too-familiar interest flickering in Chad's eyes. Chad is one of Arden's good friends. And up until now, Arden never minded that Chad was Roaring Brooke's most infamous man-whore.

But that was pre-Carly.

Arden makes his way to his friend and shoulder-checks him into the locker. The impact slams the door shut. Chad smirks up at his friend. "You're lucky I was done here anyway, Moss."

"Is that right?"

Chad winds the dial on his lock and takes up stride next to Arden as they walk down the hall. "Haven't seen you in weight lifting lately, Moss. You sure you want to go a round with me? I can throw up two thirty all day long."

Arden laughs. "Two thirty? I reckon that'll be handy when your mom needs help getting out of her truck."

Chad nods at Carly, who has made her way ahead of them already, and follows her with his eyes. "What's with you and her? Any drama I should know about?"

Arden shrugs. He's sure Chad either witnessed or at least heard about what happened at lunch today. Otherwise he wouldn't be looking twice at Carly. "Just that she's not your type, Brisbane."

Brisbane cocks his head. "From what I've heard, she's feisty. That's definitely my type."

"Incorrect."

"So you're going after her, huh? Even after what she did to you today?"

Arden is torn. He doesn't want to give the wrong impression about his intentions toward Carly, but at the same time, he doesn't want to have to deal with these kinds of issues either. Now that he's shown her some attention, others will too, he's sure. And if she's constantly getting distracted by potential love interests, how will he train her to be the ultimate sidekick? He doesn't have much of a choice here. "Yeah, I'm going to try again. She'll warm up to me after a while."

"Those grabber green eyes not working for you anymore?"

Arden shrugs.

"But you're officially asking me to step down."

"Yep." Only, he's not asking. And he doesn't have time for this back-and-forth with Chad. Carly is about to walk out the double doors at the end of the hall and he needs to get to his truck before she disappears altogether.

"Afraid of a little competition?"

Arden purses his lips. "You owe me, Brisbane." After Arden had quit the football team, he'd talked Coach Nelson into letting Chad replace him as starting quarterback—and that was after the coach had promised the position to someone else. But Chad's future rides on getting a football scholarship. He needed that kind of attention from the college scouts. And without Arden's help, he'd still be a second-string running back, nothing too impressive.

Chad grimaces. "Whatever. Alright, little buddy. I'll stay away from the missus."

"You're a tramp, you know that?" Arden calls over his shoulder as he breaks into a run to get to the parking lot. Squinting in the sun, he sees Carly walking out the front entrance of the parking lot and onto the sidewalk in front of the school. Thankfully she's heading west, away from downtown and into the less busy part of Roaring Brooke.

He hops in his truck and pulls out of the parking lot in time to see Carly turn down a dirt road in the distance. *Even better.* It's a shortcut through the woods between the main road that runs through Roaring Brooke and the county road that leads to the interstate. The only downfall to this route is that now he'll appear even more creepy, stalking her down a deserted trail and all.

But he's got no choice. *Why, with Carly Vega, am I always down to no choice?*

By the time he reaches the cutoff, she's already made it halfway down the road. He slows down, letting the truck idle beside her. She whips her head in his direction, startled. Until now, Arden would be hard pressed to imagine anything could startle this girl.

Just as he'd suspected though, her surprise morphs into something that looks a lot like rage. "You've got to be kidding me," she says, stopping abruptly.

"I have your bike," he blurts. Putting the truck into park, he hops out and shuts the door behind him. "It's in the back." He shoves his hands in his pockets because fidgeting in front of Carly is out of the question.

"Great. Get it out."

"Not until you talk to me."

She takes a step forward. Arden thinks she just might have the longest eyelashes in the county. "You're a jackass, you know that?"

"I'm not really. Just let me explain." It's a weird feeling, to plead with a girl. She takes another step toward him. He's disturbed that he notices she smells like honeysuckle on a humid day.

"There's not an explanation on the planet that will excuse what you did last night."

God, but she's amazing when she's angry. "What if I told you Cletus—Mr. Shackleford—is my uncle? That I was just trying to scare him out of driving home drunk?"

Carly's mouth drops open. And he knows he's got her.

Seven

I step away from him, shaking my head. "You're lying."

"I'm not. He's my great uncle. His name is Cletus Shackleford and he's my mom's father's brother." Arden fills the space I'd created between us. His wide back blocks the sun, saving me from the inconvenience of squinting up at him. "He lives at Eighty-Six Weston Road, but only uses up two rooms in that whole big house of his. His wife was my aunt Dorothy. She died when I was a kid, but I remember she used to make the best biscuits and gravy every Sunday."

I blink. Mr. Shackleford had a wife and her name was Dorothy. He lives in a big house. He used to have someone to fix him breakfast on Sundays. These added dimensions of him make what Arden did that much worse. I choke down an emotion I can't name. "Why would you do that to him?" I whisper. "He was so scared."

Arden sighs. "How well do you know my uncle?"

I shake my head. On top of what Arden just told me, all I know is that he comes into the Breeze Mart every night for a new bottle of vodka. That we have philosophical debates. Everything else I imagined, made it all up in my head as if Mr. Shackleford were a character instead of a real person. I didn't even know Arden was his nephew. Maybe Mr. Shackleford drinks because he lost Dorothy.

Then I remember what Arden said. *I was just trying to scare him out of driving home drunk.* "He drives himself back and forth from the Breeze Mart," I say. "Nothing's ever happened to him." Still, I feel the anger dissipating as a bigger picture of the situation comes into view. And I want to find fault in the bigger picture. But I can't.

Arden says what we're both thinking now. "It's only a matter of time." Which could be true. I have no idea where 86 Weston Road is—I'd always hoped Mr. Shackleford lived close. But I never in a million years would have called him out on driving drunk.

Because I'm a coward.

"And my uncle is stubborn," Arden is saying. "It takes drastic measures to get through to him sometimes."

"You scared him. He . . . He messed himself. He was embarrassed." I try to sound more informative than accusatory, but it still makes me mad.

Arden scratches the back of his neck. "I know. I didn't mean to do that. I didn't think he would . . . I swear, Carly, I didn't mean for that to happen."

And I believe him. His eyes are big. Sad. I swallow. "Have you checked on him?"

"My mom went over there last night. Helped him get cleaned up. Said when she left, he was sleeping like a baby."

I nod, feeling relieved that Mr. Shackleford had somebody to check on him. Feeling guilty that I've been so nasty to Arden. Feeling speechless because of all of the above.

Arden keeps his eyes fixed downward. He kicks at a rock embedded into the dirt road in front of him. "Look, I'm sorry I scared you in the process too. I didn't expect for you to . . . do what you did."

Me neither, is what I want to say. But Arden's not finished. He looks up then, meets my gaze. "And I wanted to say that what you did was brave. And . . ." He runs his hand through his hair. "Sorry. I didn't realize until just now that I suck at having a serious conversation."

It's true, he does kind of suck at it. All broken sentences and half explanations. In fact, he says more with his eyes than he does with his mouth. And if he was trying to say these things to me at lunch earlier, he totally blew it. All I heard was "I'm a jerk." But now I'm hearing something different. Now he's struggling—more than that, he's trying. And I want to come to his rescue. "So stop being so serious."

He lets out a breath that could resemble a laugh if it matched his expression. "I will. As soon as I say what I need to say." He pauses again and I think I'm going to go mad with anticipation. At the same time, I'm a little flattered that Arden Moss has something important enough to say to me that his tongue is tangled in knots. "Thank you," he blurts. "Thank you for trying to help my uncle. For protecting him. It meant a lot to me. It *means* a lot to me. I know it doesn't seem like it, but I do care about him."

I'm about to tell him he's welcome—because what else should I say?—but he continues. "And at lunch today, I completely screwed that up. What I was trying to say was that . . . Actually, I think I've said enough for now." The corners of his mouth lift up into a cheeky smile, not the kind of counterfeit, purposeful grin I've seen him use on girls. This one makes him look like a boy who's just been given a slingshot and something to aim at. "Well, now that I've made this way awkward for both of us, can I give you a ride home?"

Ah. And here is my opening to end whatever thing Arden and I had between us for this past forty-eight hours. Arden doesn't do serious conversation. I don't do complicated. "Oh no, that's okay. I don't live far from here. Like, two minutes on my bike, max." Hint hint.

His smile falters. "It's not a big deal at all. It's the least I could do."

This is true. But it's not happening. Julio would pass away directly if a boy brought me home. I can hear him now. *You're going to get distracted, get pregnant, and then we'll never get Mama and Papi back here.* "No thanks," I say, to both scenarios.

This perplexes Arden, I can tell. "Are you still mad at me? Honest to God, I didn't mean to insult you or scare you or—"

"Can I please have my bike back?" I know it's rude and abrupt, but I can't help it. I don't want to drag this out any longer. Like he said, it's already way awkward for us both. Why continue bumbling? It's time to part ways.

He sighs in resignation. "Alright." Walking to the truck bed, he reaches in and gingerly lifts out my bike as if it were made of porcelain—and as if it weighed as much as a pillow. I try not to notice his triceps flexing. "Here you go."

It's only been a day, but I've missed my bike. We've been through a lot together. Riding in the rain, two flat tires, pedaling away from a rabid fox. My bike and I? We are friends. "Thanks," I tell him. "See you in social studies." I loop both arms through my backpack and center the weight of it on my back.

I'm about to hop on the seat of the bike when Arden says, "Does that mean we'll actually get to talk in social studies?"

Seriously? "Um, I don't know about you, but I have to pay attention in class or I'll be totally lost." So I'm good at directness *and* evasion.

"You don't like me." Okay, so Arden's good at being direct too. Crap.

"I didn't say that."

"You don't have to. When you get on that bike and leave, you have no intention of ever speaking to me again."

I nudge the kickstand in place and cross my arms at him. The weight of my backpack makes my shoulders feel more squared, which I appreciate. "We're not friends, Arden. We're only talking right now because I was at the wrong place at the wrong time last night. If that hadn't happened, the rest of the school year would have gone by without you even looking in my direction."

Guilt flashes across his face but is immediately replaced by determination. "That might be true. But last night did happen. We did, er . . . meet. And I like you, Carly."

Oh, heck no. Not distracted and pregnant. Not this girl. I actually feel my nostrils flare. "Did you already make your way through the entire cheerleading squad then?"

"What? No, that's not what I meant. I don't like you like *that*."

I go from one side of the spectrum of offense to the other. I feel like one of those revolving doors you see at fancy hotels. "Oh, I know. You're *way* out of my league, right? I'm not good enough to like in *that* way."

"Jesus," Arden says, stacking his hands on the top of his head. "I can't win."

Oh, now that's rich. "You can't win? *You?* Arden Moss? You've already won, idiot. You have everything you've ever wanted in life, all handed to you on a silver platter." It's not fair what I'm saying. It's not fair, and it has nothing to do with getting distracted or pregnant or cheerleaders. I'm lashing out and I know it. I want this to be difficult for him.

I want *something* to be difficult for him.

"Don't do that," he says quietly. "Don't play the rich-kid card on me. I deserve a lot of things, but not that."

Ugh. Why does he have to be so human right now? Why can't he just let me vent?

But then I remember that Arden is not good at serious conversation. What he says next proves it. "And if I recall correctly, I don't have *everything* handed to me on a silver platter. Today it was handed to me on a plastic lunch tray, remember?"

Oh, I remember. The image flashes through my mind before I can stop it. Arden, battered in cream corn and smothered in a delicate 2% milk sauce. And I giggle. "That was reflex," I explain without remorse.

He grins. "I'll bet." He purses his lips then. "We can be friends, Carly. We're not as different as you think."

Yes, we are. But he obviously can't be convinced otherwise, at least not right now. I nod. Pretending to agree seems like the only way he'll let me leave on my bike. And I've got to start dinner before Julio gets home. "Friends," I say, as if the word is foreign to me.

"Friends." He grabs the door handle of his truck. "See you in social studies."

"Okay then." I turn around and start pedaling, trying to stir up a symbolic dust cloud in my wake.

Eight

Arden pulls into the long dirt driveway at 86 Weston Road. Long rows of straggly azalea bushes stand guard on either side of the drive. When in full bloom, this driveway is a sight fit for any Southern gardening magazine. That is, if trimmed properly. From the ruts and holes in the red clay, it doesn't look like Uncle Cletus has even had his driveway smoothed over in some time, let alone paid anyone to clean up the bushes.

And why should he have to pay someone? Arden thinks to himself. *When he has a perfectly capable nephew with an abundance of time on his hands?*

Hating himself more and more, Arden takes the last curve and pulls under the vaulted, monumental carport in front. The grand stone steps that lead to Uncle Cletus's double front doors are covered with last season's leaves and this season's moss; Aunt Dorothy used to keep flowers in the concrete vases at the bottom of the stairs. Now the vases stand purposeless and forlorn and pathetic looking. Up top, two giant lion statues on either side of the front door show their teeth as Arden rings the bell. The elegant noise echoes through the house in an uninviting way, as if to say, "Why bother?"

Not surprisingly, no one comes to the door. Uncle Cletus used to keep a maid, Mrs. Beeman, who came a few days a week to tidy up and prepare meals. She would even play the role of butler and answer the door. It's been a long time since Arden has seen Mrs. Beeman. It's been a long time since the front steps have seen Mrs. Beeman.

Arden retrieves his check card from his wallet and finagles the lock by the doorknob, hoping that the deadbolt isn't set. One minute and a bent check card later, Arden strolls into the enormous foyer. The house smells like a decade-old dust ball mixed with cheese. Dust lies on everything like a second skin. Aunt Dorothy and Mrs. Beeman used to keep the house meticulous. Now it looks like it could be undergoing a remodel, with books and magazines and papers strewn about, along with clothes and shoes and paint cans and pieces of art that fell and were never re-hung.

To Arden's left is the "fancy" room where he and Amber were not allowed to play. That's where the expensive stuff is kept. Vases and tea sets and a grand piano and a china cabinet full of porcelain collectibles and a pink antique couch that had probably accommodated the butts of some very important guests in its day. Now a pile of decaying wood sits by the fireplace in a delicate brass basket.

Arden knows there's no use checking the dining room or the kitchen or the library or any of the bedrooms upstairs. Uncle Cletus prefers to drink himself to death in the ballroom. There he has the perfect setup. The ballroom is empty except for the one corner of it haunted by Cletus Shackleford. Him, his polyester couch, and his old television. It's the only place in the house he claims has enough room for all his "lofty thoughts."

Arden pushes his shoulder into the ballroom door, which creaks open. This room seems to get smaller and smaller each time he visits. As a child, he always thought it was as big as town, dignified and luxurious but decidedly boring. All shiny baseboards and brass mirrors and chandeliers that cast a kaleidoscope of colors on the floors in the summertime. To Arden, the only thing the ballroom was good for was inside rollerblade hockey. He and Amber didn't need to be worried about oncoming traffic of the street or weather conditions like they did at their own house. And the bonus was that if you wiped out, you just got marble-floor burn instead of asphalt embedded into your bloody knees. Now that Arden thinks about it, it was pansy hockey. Not manly at all.

His steps reverberate through the room that was designed to de-liver music to every corner. There's no way his uncle doesn't know he's here. He walks toward the couch facing the far wall, with the TV tucked into it. Two booted feet hang off the end of the sofa, and the channel is turned to some sort of hunting show. Arden hears the swish of a bottle being upturned. He wonders how productive this conversation with Uncle Cletus will be.

"Hey, old man," Arden calls. The boots don't move. Arden rests his elbows on the back of the couch, looking down at Cletus. His uncle's hair is disheveled, his flannel shirt exposing a stained wife beater, and he's actually wearing an honest-to-God polka-dot bow tie around his neck. Arden nods toward it. "What's the occasion?"

Cletus reluctantly draws his attention away from the TV and

fixes his gaze on Arden. "I was wondering the same thing about you."

Arden almost cringes. "If you wanted people to visit, you should come to the door when they ring the bell."

"Back door's always open. You know that."

"After what happened to you the other night, I figured you'd be smart enough to lock all the doors."

"What do you know about what happened?" Uncle Cletus sits up on his elbows, almost spilling the contents of the bottle, which smells like whiskey.

"Mom told me." As soon as he says it, Arden regrets it. Now Cletus knows that Arden knows he messed himself. He'd wanted to save his uncle from that indignity.

"Did she."

"Said some moron held you up for your truck keys, then took off on a bike instead."

This time Cletus sits up fully and motions for Arden to sit beside him. He takes a swig and waits for the burn to subside before saying, "That kid was a moron. Thought I was driving drunk. Said he was trying to help me."

"And were you?"

"Was I what?"

"Driving drunk."

"Now you sound like your mother. It takes a lot to get me drunk, boy. You know that."

Arden doesn't want to have this conversation. Not face-to-face. It was different when he was anonymously scaring him out of getting behind the wheel. But having a serious conversation with Uncle

Cletus feels wrong. What business did a seventeen-year-old boy have telling a seventy-three-year-old man how to live his life? At least, that's what his uncle would say. And Arden would have no answer. Time for a subject change.

"Mom said the clerk came out with a shotgun, threatened to shoot the guy's balls off or something."

Cletus chuckles. "That Carly. She's a spitfire if I ever saw one."

Arden would have to agree. "So you know her pretty well then?"

Uncle Cletus's mouth tugs into a scowl. "I know her parents don't have the sense God gave a billy goat. Letting a girl her age work alone at a convenience store on the graveyard shift. I can't help but check in on her every night. I've spent a fortune on vodka I'll never drink. Too bad that stingy old Bagget won't stock whiskey but he'll stock something as useless as vodka. But I guess when you're old enough, that'll be part of your inheritance."

Arden remembers being surprised when Cletus had dropped the bottle of vodka on the ground last night. Cletus hated vodka, said it tastes like tap water. Arden had just assumed the old man's taste buds had changed. He never guessed his uncle would buy vodka every night just to see Carly.

Cletus takes a sizeable gulp from the bottle, then points at Arden. "You'd learn something from that one, boy. She's a hard worker. A survivor. Gets things done. That girl doesn't know it, but she's going places in life."

Not what Arden wants to hear. Why is everyone obsessed with going places in life instead of just living life? "Maybe I'll come with you one night and meet her." Arden grins. "Sounds like my kind of girl."

Cletus wipes the excess liquor off his chin with the back of his hand. "She's way out of your league, boy. You won't be good enough for her until you get yourself straightened out. Hell, you might not ever be good enough for her."

This stings more than Arden expects. Even Cletus thinks he's wasting his life. His uncle is the one person who always thought Arden could do anything. What changed? His quitting the football team? What exactly has his mother been telling Cletus? And what's so wrong about slowing down and enjoying life? "I will eventually. Get straightened out, I mean." But the words fall as flat as they feel. Because to Arden, he is straightened out. More than he's ever been.

"It's been a year, Arden. It's time to let her go."

Arden balls his fists. "Amber has nothing to do with it." He can't keep the bitterness out of his voice. He comes here to check on his uncle and now all of a sudden he's under attack. And what if he's not ready to let Amber go? She would want him to move on, he knows. But she doesn't get what she wants. His bending to Amber's will ended when she took her own life.

"Everyone deals with things differently, son. But you don't seem to be dealing with it at all. Your mother says you don't sleep. That you're out gallivanting, stirring up trouble every night. Says your grades are crap. That's not going to get you into FSU."

Nice. He comes over here to check on his uncle and suddenly his baggage is getting checked. "Who says I want to go to FSU?"

"Things are expected of you, boy. You can't run from that forever. You could get counseling. Heard that helps some folks."

Arden isn't going to discuss expectations with his uncle. Not in a million years. "Sure," he grounds out. "Maybe we could go to counseling together. Me for Amber, and you for Aunt Dorothy."

Cletus opens his mouth to fire back but closes it again. Anger flashes across his face like a strike of lightning. He takes a long drag from the bottle, his way of hosing the fire in his temper. Then another. Each calculated sip would have scalded a lesser man's throat. But not a pro like Cletus Shackleford. When he's done, his face is calm again. "I can see why you think that. But we're different, you and me. I'm an old washed-up man who's done everything I've wanted to do in life. I've got a bank account to prove it." He waves his hand in a grandiose gesture of the room. "A big, useless house and more land than you could hunt in decades. I was married to the woman of my dreams for forty-three years."

"You tell me all the time that wealth doesn't matter. That material possessions are just more things to take care of. Now you're telling me to go to college so I can get *stuff*?"

"I'm telling you that you only think you're happy doing what you're doing. You used to have drive, son. I don't care if you're as poor as a church mouse when you get to be my age. Find something that matters to you. Even when it's gone." At this, his uncle's eyes glisten with threatening tears.

Arden swallows. This house has eighteen rooms. Eighteen rooms full of expensive furniture. Expensive carpets and tapestries and paintings and antique décor. But this house is empty. Empty without Aunt Dorothy.

I don't want anything that matters, Arden wants to say. *I don't want anything else to lose. The pain isn't worth it.*

"I was thinking I could bring over Dad's pressure washer and get your steps in front cleaned up," Arden says. "And your azalea bushes need more trimming than your ear hair, and that's saying something."

Cletus huffs. "They could use a trimming, now that you mention it. The azalea bushes too."

Arden grins. "I'll be back this weekend. Anything else you need done?"

His uncle thinks for a moment. "I can't find my spare keys to the truck—had to have it towed home, did your mom tell you? Maybe since you're not going to be sleeping anyway you could swing by the Breeze Mart and check on Carly. I'm sure she'll be there even after what happened. Did I tell you that girl's a spitfire?"

"I'll try to make time for it," Arden says, delighted that now he actually has an excuse to see her again. He could tell she wasn't feeling the whole friendship scenario.

She'll get used to it after a while.

On his way out the door, Arden hangs the keys to his uncle's truck on the coatrack. It'll be a while before he finds them there. Especially because he's probably already looked.

Nine

I brace myself on the metal steps to the trailer; the door tends to stick when you open it and a few weeks ago I pulled too hard and found myself sprawled onto the broken concrete slab we call a porch. When I step inside, the aroma of whatever Julio's cooking in the slow cooker hits me like a spicy snake slithering up my nose.

Julio insists on doing the cooking because whenever I cook, I make things like hamburgers and pizza or pasta—what he calls American food. Which, of course, I'm proud of. It's something that's mine. Our trailer might be the tiniest version of Mexico you ever saw, but at least my cooking—and my bedroom—are the one place you can experience American culture. Or, you know, whatever American culture I can find at garage sales and thrift stores.

Since Julio won't be home for another hour or so, I set my backpack down and head over to Señora Perez's to see if her washer is available. I knock on the door and am greeted with an invisible wall of stale cigarette smoke when she opens it.

Señora Perez is in her usual pink matching sweat suit with a magazine rolled up in her hands. She's obsessed with keeping flies out of her house; that particular issue of *People en Español* probably has the guts of hundreds of flies on it. "*Que?*" she says.

I wouldn't call us friends, Señora Perez and I. We have an arrangement, one that benefits us both. I'm not even sure if Señora Perez has any friends, anyone who comes over regularly to gossip about the celebrity drama she's obviously so fond of. I never see anyone in our mostly Mexican trailer park coming or going from her door. Some say that she's not one of us, because she had an American husband who died a few years ago. I wonder what they say about me, and my taste for American culture. Either way, Señora Perez and I are not so different. Probably if we were both more friendly, we might be friends.

"I was wondering if I could wash a load or two in your washing machine," I say in Spanish. "I noticed you had some weeds that needed pulling in your garden."

Garden is hardly the word for the hodgepodge mess of plants Señora Perez keeps in the sunny part of her lot. There is a stone bench, around it some seasonal flowers, and then for some reason she planted bell peppers, which she doesn't even eat. Maybe her husband used to love them. She sells them to my brother for dirt cheap though, so who am I to complain?

She leans against the doorframe. I wonder how small she really is under those big baggy clothes. I wonder if Señora Perez is secretly sick, and that's why she's grouchy all the time. "I suppose. But you'll have to come back in an hour. I've already got a load washing. And bring your own detergent. I'm not a Laundromat here." With that she shuts the door.

I've got to find a cheap washer one of these days. I bought one a few months ago for fifty bucks but it broke after a week and Julio was so pissed for me wasting the money when we can use Señora Perez's most of the time. But Julio isn't the one who has to deal with Señora Perez. And *most* of the time doesn't cut it when you're out of clean panties.

I get back home just in time to answer the phone. I'm pleasantly surprised to find it's Mama. "Carlotta, what are you doing home this time of day? Shouldn't you be working?" Mama only speaks Spanish to me. Sometimes I wonder if she thinks I'll forget where I came from—even though I've never actually been there. I want to tell her that Julio is making sure that I don't forget.

"I miss you too, Mama."

"Carlottta, shame on you. You know I miss you. I miss you so much that I'm trying to get back to you. So we can be a family again. I just thought you'd be working since you're out of school."

I wince. "Sorry, Mama. I do work today. My shift doesn't start until ten o'clock tonight."

"Oh, my child, please tell me you're not still working at that convenience store?"

"I am."

"I thought you were looking for a different job that gives you more hours or at least better than minimum wage. We talked about this last week."

And the week before. I bite my lip before answering. "It's just that the Breeze Mart is easy. I can do my homework there and my shift ends in time for school."

I do miss Mama fiercely. I just wish we could talk about something else when she calls. But we have to get this business of work out of the way first. Money is, after all, the main thing that's separating us right now.

"Homework?" She makes a *tsk*ing sound into the phone. "Carlotta Jasmine Vega. We've talked about this. The most important thing right now is getting your family back. Then you can finally meet your brother and sister."

"I know." Of course I want my family back. Of course I want to meet my brother and sister. But keeping my grades up and getting a scholarship is the only way I'm making something of myself. And isn't that what they were trying to do when they came to the States? To make something better of themselves?

She wants me to find a job with more hours, to save more money, to get her here sooner. But more hours means less time for homework. Less time for homework means my grades get flushed. I'm not the kind of student who can pass without studying. I'm the kind of student who barely holds on by her teeth and almost cries when she gets an A. The Breeze Mart keeps me on the honor roll, in a way.

And without the honor roll, I'm not getting any scholarships. Without scholarships, I don't get to be the first person in my family to go to college. All I have to do is survive this thing called high school—and keep up my grade point average while doing it. One day, with a degree, I'll be able to provide for my entire family.

Besides, it's not like I'm *not* contributing to the family fund now. I keep ten dollars of my paycheck—a girl needs nail polish sometimes—then I hand the rest to Julio every single week. Bringing that up again is not going to win me any points. "I'll keep looking for a new job," I tell her obediently. What I don't tell her is that it has to be exactly like the Breeze Mart only with more pay or I'm not taking it.

"That's my good girl. When I get back, you can cut your work hours and I'll teach you how to cook. How does that sound?"

When I get back sounds delightful. "You need to teach Julio too. You should smell what he's got in the slow cooker right now."

Mama laughs.

Feelings of selfishness and guilt knead knots in my stomach, making me question whether or not I'm doing the right thing by not finding a better job. I've missed Mama's laugh. Her eyes almost disappear into her face when she smiles. It's beautiful. I know it's important to have my family back. I've been yearning to hug my mother since the day she was deported three years ago.

But it's important that we have security when they get here too. And an education can provide that security.

Mama chatters on then about the latest antics of Juanita and Hugo, my younger twin siblings (she was pregnant when she got deported), about her neighbor's daughter getting married, about a house down the street catching fire. Some things are new, some things are repeats from last week's conversation, but I relish it all, because the sound of Mama's voice soothes me. It always has.

With a frown, I remember the way Julio hung up the phone the day he got the devastating news that my parents had been in a car accident. My father had rear-ended another vehicle, and though no one was hurt, it was a major ordeal because he didn't have a driver's license—or insurance. What's worse was that they were stuck on a traffic-jammed bridge and had nowhere to flee. The responding cop picked them up and called Immigration as soon as he found out they were here without proper documentation. We didn't even get the chance to say good-bye in person. My parents didn't want to risk the Department of Children and Families taking me from Julio, so they didn't mention that they had kids at home. And besides, that was the rule: If you get caught, you don't give any names. You just suck it up, and go back to Mexico.

And then you try to get back again.

"Has Julio mentioned how much is in the fund?" Mama asks, drawing me away from my bitter line of thought.

"Julio never tells me how much we have." And I don't want to know, mainly because I know that however much we have to pay *El Libertador*—that's what the guy calls himself to keep his real identity a secret, I guess—to get my family across the border will make me sick. Thousands of dollars each, but how many thousands I'm not sure. And that's just ensuring they get across the border. Getting them across the Chihuahuan Desert safely is all up to us—unless we want to pay extra.

"Tell him to call his mama when he gets home from work, yes?"

"I'll tell him." Julio misses Mama too. It's evident by how much he tries not to show it.

"Your brother is a hard worker, Carlotta. You could learn a lot from him."

I know he's a hard worker. He works five days a week in construction and then washes dishes at a seafood restaurant on Highway 98 in the evenings and on weekends. Tuesdays are his only nights off. And even on his night off, he feels the need to prepare something in the slow cooker for us to eat and scrolls the Internet on the computer I borrow from school for odd jobs to pick up.

I want to be more like my brother. I do. And I'm trying to be—just in a different way. I can't wait for the day when I can come home to Mama and Papi and tell them I've got a high-paying job that will get us out of this trailer park and into a brick house on a real foundation—maybe even in a gated community. One day she'll see that all my hard work in school will have paid off. She'll see it, and Julio will see it. He quit high school to take care of me. One day I will pay him back.

"I am learning from him, Mama."

"Good. You're a smart girl, Carlotta. I'm sure you'll find a way to help out more. I love you."

"Love you too."

I end the call and place the phone back on the charger. It would be nice to have a cell phone, so I could talk to her more often instead of leaving it up to chance that I'll be home when she calls. It's not like I would waste minutes on it talking to someone else. Only two people call us. Mama, when she's really missing us—or she wants to know how much money we've saved up—and Julio's restaurant manager, who wants to know if he can work late or come in on his day off. But Julio won't even pay for cable, let alone a cell phone. Not when we have a perfectly working landline. He wouldn't even pay for that if it wasn't essential to our cause.

I walk to the couch and fold the clean towels in the laundry basket next to me, then I gather Julio's and my dirty clothes and get them ready to take to Señora Perez's. I wash the few dishes in the sink, then wipe down the counters. The closer to the slow cooker I get, the worse it smells. I open it up to get a peek.

Then I take a pizza out of the freezer and preheat the oven.

The phone rings again, while I'm opening the box of my dinner. I wonder what Mama forgot to say. But it's Julio who greets me on the other end. He must be borrowing a friend's cell phone. "Carlotta, do you work tonight?"

"Yes, I'm getting some things done, then I'm going to try to sleep before my shift. Why?"

"Make sure you turn the slow cooker off before you go to sleep. Does it smell good?"

"Nope."

He snickers. "Pick me up a candy bar at the store? I've been craving one of those nutty chocolate things. The ones with the red wrapper."

I gasp. "Spend money on candy? Julio, where is your head?" I'm only teasing, but this seems to actually get under his skin.

"They're two for a dollar still, right?" He sounds worried.

"Yes. I was just kidding. I don't care if you want a candy bar, Julio."

He sighs into the phone. "I'm not always going to be cheap, you know. When Mama and Papi are back, I'll buy you all the candy you want."

I feel bad now, because I didn't mean anything by it, and I would buy Julio a hundred candy bars if he asked for them. Next time, I decide, I'll keep my mouth shut. "Mama called," I say, changing the subject. "She wants you to call her."

"Did she get the money we wired her yesterday?" It's generous for Julio to say "we" since it's mostly his money we transfer to them each week.

"She didn't say." Both of them ask me money questions, but neither of them want to talk in actual numbers. I wonder if they think I'm too young to know about such things, or I wonder if they think they're protecting me from the big bad world of finances—or the lack thereof. I'd love to correct them on both accounts, but I can't think of a scenario in which I'd actually speak up and say this.

"Okay. I'll call her when I get home tonight. Get some sleep, *bonita*."

I hang up and pop the pizza in the oven, feeling guilty that I splurged on buying a few frozen pizzas this week instead of buying Julio any chocolate. I should eat Julio's slow cooker concoction—or whatever else he makes. I should be more grateful that he still bothers to prepare a portion for me at all.

I should be more grateful, period.

Ten

Deputy Glass pulls his cop car into the parking lot of the Breeze Mart. It didn't take much effort on Arden's part to persuade the deputy to come to the little convenience store on the edge of town to check up on Carly. "She was here all alone that night, you know," Glass says. "What kind of parents would let a girl her age work a shift like that?"

Arden is beginning to wonder himself. "Do you mind if just I go in? She's a friend from school."

Glass gives a reluctant nod. "Fine. But hurry up. Roger's on a call for a domestic downtown so I'm up next."

"Will do."

Deputy Glass lets Arden ride with him sometimes on slow nights. One of the few perks of being the sheriff's son. He gets to go on calls, which mostly consist of domestic disputes, reports of drunk drivers, and old people reporting the violation of noise ordinances.

Old people.

"I'll just be a few minutes," Arden says, shutting the door behind him.

The bells hanging from the door jingle as he enters. Carly is already waiting for him. "Why are you in a cop car?" she asks. "The sheriff's son gets his own personal taxi?"

"Nice to see you too," he says. He makes his rounds of the store, grabbing some gum and some chips and some beef jerky for Glass. When he circles back to the register, Carly has already dug back into her homework.

"I thought it would be nice to check on you," he tells her, chucking his purchases on top of her graph paper. "Heard you got robbed the other day."

She lifts her chin. "You heard wrong. Mr. Shackleford did. Of his dignity."

So much for trying to be cute. Nothing works on this girl. "Does the owner know you do your homework on the clock?"

She shrugs. "He doesn't care as long as I get my work done and my customers are satisfied."

"Well then, maybe you should put the pencil down and ring me up."

This pisses her off, he can tell. But he's tired of giving miles to someone who won't budge an inch. Carly uses her scan gun to ring up the items. He pulls out one of the twenties in his wallet to pay for it, which seems to irritate her more.

I'm never going to get this girl figured out. "You'd prefer I stole it?"

She bags it all up for him without asking and hands the plastic bag to him along with his change. "Have a good night, sir."

"Did I mention we could be friends?"

Her face softens. "We are friends. That's why I gave you half off on your gum."

"The sign said it was buy one get one."

"But the point is I remembered."

"Alriiighty then."

He grabs the bag then and turns to leave. Just before he pushes the door open, Carly says, "Arden?"

He turns, waiting to be blasted for something else. *What, is she going to dissect the way I walked to the door?* "Yes?"

"Thank you for checking on me."

"You're welcome."

He returns to the police car then, unsure whether or not progress has been made.

❧•❧

Arden is the first to social studies for once in his life. Even Mr. Tucker is surprised to see him, peering over his reading glasses from his desk to get a better look. "I'm not offering extra credit, Mr. Moss," he says, pressing his glasses back up his nose.

Arden grins, holding up his empty hands to show he hasn't even brought his book to class. "I'm not asking." *Not from you, anyway.* He takes a seat in the back row, which will give him a panorama of the class. And hopefully, the perfect view to study Carly.

He feels like a spider lying in wait for a precious, elusive fly to finally land in the intricacies of his web. A skittish fly with long black hair and the gift of impulsiveness and a penchant for retreating from him.

Carly is one of the first five to arrive to class, do-gooder that she is, and when she appears in the doorway her gaze immediately connects with Arden's. She gives him a confused half smile and takes her seat on the opposite side of the room from him. She even picks the opposite corner. Arden wonders if they're starting from square one again. *I knew she was full of it when she said we could be friends.*

How can I get this girl to talk to me?

His friend Jake takes the seat next to him in the back row and offers him a pencil and paper. "Nah, man," Arden says. "I take notes with my phone."

Jake snorts. "While you're 'taking notes,' you should look up the last video post on Mudslide. The guy has your same truck."

"Will do." Mudslide is a Web site dedicated to trucks and mudding. Arden uses it sometimes for ideas on how to get out of the giant mudholes he's put his 4 × 4 through—and his future plans to do the same.

As soon as the bell rings Mr. Tucker is on his game. "Homework, please." Arden has nothing to pass up so he gives the girl in front of him a high five when she reaches around for it. She smiles like she's just been given a hundred dollars. He'd usually take the opportunity to flirt—the girl is definitely his type, all big breasts and perfect teeth—but he notices that Carly is searching frantically in her backpack for something.

And Arden's hoping she doesn't find it. Then she'll know it's not the end of the world if your homework isn't turned in. It's just a grade. An expectation that others have of you. By not turning it in, you're showing them that they can't control you. That you're symbolically shunning their established set of rules and make your own.

But find it she does, and right in time. To Arden's surprise,

Mr. Tucker, the mascot of impatience, waits for her to dig it out and unfold it for him. Even gives her a little smile.

What's up with that? Surely my new accomplice isn't a teacher's pet? Gross.

But it becomes apparent that she is. During class, she sits up straight. Takes notes, probably verbatim. Smiles when Mr. Tucker makes a stupid joke. She even gets up to sharpen her pencil and *Mr. Tucker stops his lecture to let her do it.*

How have I missed this before?

Of course, when the bell rings, she's the last one to pack up, because she has to organize everything just right in her binder.

Oh geez.

"Carly, wait up," Arden calls. There are still a few students packing their things, and they exchange curious glances with each other. When Arden reaches Carly and offers to carry her backpack, Mr. Tucker gives him a disapproving frown.

"Oh, crap," he hisses to Carly. "Is Mr. Tucker your dad?"

She snickers. "Um. No."

"Then why is he looking like I've just invited you to my backseat instead of offering to carry your bag?"

Carly scowls. "Because even Mr. Tucker realizes for me and you," she gestures between them for emphasis, "to be chitchatting is weird."

Arden rolls his eyes. "You care too much what people think."

"I don't have the luxury of being careless."

"What's that supposed to mean?"

She shakes her head, as if conversing with him is a bother. "I can carry my own backpack. Thanks though." With that she stalks out of the room and into the hallway traffic.

He has to run to catch up with her. *That's probably why people are looking at us,* he thinks to himself. They've never seen me try so hard. *Everyone must see what Carly is doing is rejecting me, over and over.*

And deep down, maybe he does care what everyone thinks. Maybe just a little.

But obviously not enough to stop him from chasing after her. He snatches the backpack from her shoulders, which halts her in her tracks. She turns around, fuming. "Are you serious?"

"I figured out why people are staring at us," he says quickly. "It's because I've never been rejected like this before." This he keeps to a whisper. He hates himself for it too. That something like that would matter to him. *I guess I haven't completely freed myself from the expectation of others.*

She rolls her eyes. "You're really that full of yourself?"

"Look, I don't know how to talk to you, okay? I'll just be direct. I want to give you a ride home today."

"No."

"Yes, dammit! All I'm asking is to give you a ride home."

"I have a bike."

"Which we both know fits in the back of my truck." She crosses her arms, the makings of yet another rejection forming on her lips. He wipes a hand down his face, hoping to erase any frustration that might be showing there. "Look, if you agree to it, I swear I won't talk to you for the rest of the day."

It irritates Arden that this seems to appeal to her. "You promise?"

Oh my God, who is this girl? "I promise, or pinky swear, or whatever it is you chicks do."

"How can people actually think you're funny?"

"What'd I do now?"

"Where is your truck parked?"

"In the front lot."

"My bike is in front too. I'll see you at last bell." Then she walks away. No good-bye. No thanks. To Arden, it's hard to view this as a victory.

Hopefully this will all be worth the headache.

As he turns to go to his next class, he catches Carly out of the corner of his eye being rammed into a locker. The force is so hard she loses her grip on her backpack and it drops to the floor. The guy who ran into her—Ashton is his name, he thinks, because he tried out for the football team freshman year—simply keeps walking as if he didn't nearly just dislocate her shoulder. He's a big guy, bigger than Arden, and seems oblivious to what he's just done. Carly recovers quickly, throwing her backpack over her shoulder again and moving on.

Arden scowls. Has he ever done that to her? He wouldn't know. Up until just days ago, when he started planning his attack on Cletus, he hadn't been aware of her existence. *It could very well have been me who ran into her, and just kept walking.* She definitely acts like she's used to this sort of thing—she doesn't even bother to unleash her crabbiness on her assailant.

Why does it bother me that neither party seems affected by what just happened? And why am I walking toward Ashton like I'm about to do something? "Hey, Ashton," Arden calls out, passing Carly in his wake.

Ashton stops and waits for Arden to reach him. "What's up, man?"

Carly tries to walk by them, but Arden grabs her wrist before she can. He pulls her in beside him. "Did you know you just ran into Carly?"

Ashton has a solid eighteen inches on Carly. He glances down at her. "Carly?"

"It's not a big deal," Carly says quickly. "I was in the way."

Arden shakes his head. "No, you weren't." He turns his attention back to Ashton. "You ran right into her, man. She hit the lockers pretty hard. I think you should apologize."

Ashton shifts his books between his hands. Arden can tell he doesn't want to apologize. He probably doesn't even believe he ran into her—a rhino wouldn't notice running into a mouse either. But Ashton knows Arden outranks him in every kind of social status there is. And he's probably aware that Arden doesn't back down from a fight. Ever. After all, it's the best way to get suspended— and piss off his father.

Ashton looks at the small crowd gathering around them, then back at Carly. "If I ran into you I'm sorry. I didn't mean to."

"It's fine," Carly chokes out. "Really."

Arden nods to Ashton, an unspoken signal that all is well again. Having been dismissed, Ashton turns and walks away. And Carly melts wordlessly into the crowd.

Eleven

Something like wasps flutter in my stomach when I see that Arden is holding me to my word. He pulls around to the car pickup lane and hops out, already reaching for my bike. "You're sure?" I ask.

Because the truth is, I don't know why he's doing this. Why he's harassing me into friendship. I'm thinking he's feeling guilty for what he did at the Breeze Mart, and if that's the case, then I'm going to clear the air for good on the way home. I don't need Arden Moss's pity friendship.

Still, I feel that I should show a little pity for *him*, because of what he did for me in the hall today. I know he sees it as coming to my rescue instead of bringing more attention to me. And . . . it was nice to get an apology from Ashton. That's not the first time he's slammed me into the locker. The last time he did it, I had a nasty bruise on my arm that took weeks to yellow and disappear. I get that he's this big muscular beast and I'm small and slow. But maybe he'll be on the lookout for me now that something was said to him.

Now that someone like Arden said something to him.

So I guess I have to allow Arden to give me a ride home, as backward as that sounds. Still, my eye nearly twitches out of control when he opens the door for me. Because of what this looks like. Like he's wooing me. The last thing he wants is for people to think I'm rejecting him. The last thing I want people to think is that I'm one of Arden's conquests. One of his many, many, many conquests. Actually, the last thing I want people to think is that I exist at all. I'm supposed to be staying under the radar—trying to smuggle your parents back over the border isn't exactly considered a constructive pastime here in the States. The fewer people I know, the fewer I'm close to, the better. Because what will they say when my parents suddenly show up and we're one big happy family again? What questions will they ask? What answers will I give?

But here I am, mocking the radar that keeps me hidden. Here I am making faces at it.

I take Arden's hand as he helps hoist me into the truck. Lovely.

He cranks the engine and the faint smell of burning oil fills the cabin. The radio whispers country music at us while Arden adjusts his mirrors and backs out. I wait until we're just outside the school parking lot to begin my spiel. Deep breath. "You don't have to keep being nice to me," I tell him. "In fact, I don't want you to."

"I noticed."

Of course he noticed. I wasn't trying to be subtle. "You already explained why you did what you did. I get it. You don't have to, like, make it up to me, or whatever."

"Is that what you think I'm doing?"

"It's exactly what you're doing."

"Well, you're wrong. I bet you don't like to hear that, do you,

Carly Vega? Nope, I can tell by the way you're stank-eyeing me that you don't like to be told that you're wrong."

"Who does?" And really, who cares?

Arden shrugs. "Good point."

After a few seconds of silence, I start again. "Well?"

"Well, what?"

"Why are you all of a sudden interested in being my manservant at school? Any particular reason? Because just to be clear, I'm not going to sleep with you. Ever."

He shifts in his seat, leaning against the driver's door with one arm, steering with the other. "Have I asked you to? Have I even tried to kiss you?"

"Then what do you want?"

He runs a hand through his hair. The result is not unattractive. "I can't . . . I can't explain it. Not without sounding stupid. I want to show you something. Do you have some time this afternoon? As in, right now?"

Do I have some time? Let's see. "It's now two o'clock, my shift at the Breeze Mart starts at ten. I have two loads of laundry I have to take off the line and fold before I can eat some dinner and get some sleep before my shift. Um, no."

Maybe it's the look of pleading in his eyes, or the way his newly frazzled hair makes him look desperate. Maybe it's that I now feel indebted to him, even though I didn't ask for his help. Whatever it is, I feel I should follow up. "I mean, how long will it take?"

His eyes light up like I've given him a present. "Like half an hour, tops."

"Okay. Show me."

As soon as I say the words he maneuvers into the turn lane and does a U-turn. The exhaust on his truck sounds like a monster chasing after us when he presses the gas. Within five minutes we're pulled into the parking lot of Roaring Brooke's Goodwill. He cuts the engine and the monster hushes. "Stay here. I'll be right back." He hops out and crosses the street.

And like a stupid person, I stay and wait. Arden has now used ten minutes of his precious (my precious) half hour. Goodwill is in a small shopping center with a nail salon and a Mexican restaurant. Goodwill's half-off sale is drawing the most business by far.

When Arden comes back out, he's got a small plastic bag in his hand. He slams the truck door shut and presents me with its contents: A small black-and-gray knockoff purse. Fuzzy around the edges and worn on the straps, but all in all, in pretty good shape.

"What's this for?"

He grins. "You'll see. We have to make one more stop before the fun begins."

"Alriiighty then," I say. He recognizes mockery when he hears it.

He glances at me sideways. "You're going to love this," he says. "It's a huge stress reliever."

It's possibly the most convincing thing he could've said to keep me hanging. I don't get many opportunities for relieving stress—I just hope my idea of stress and Arden's idea of stress is at least similar.

He takes us down a dirt road and pulls off on the grassy shoulder, next to a fenced-in field full of grazing cows. In the distance, goats wander around a long wooden bin. A big white house with black shutters looms atop a hill. "Does someone live here?"

"I'm guessing yes. There's a box of ziplock bags in the glove box. Can you hand me those?"

I do as I'm asked, more curious than ever. I don't question why he has an already-opened box of ziplock baggies in his glove box, even though it seems to be proof that this entire afternoon was highly premeditated. How did he know I would come with him today? Or does he always keep domestic treasures hidden away in his truck? Does he have a slow cooker in here too somewhere?

He pulls out a bag and turns it inside out in his hand, then tugs it on like a sloppy glove. This makes me skittish. "You're not going to hurt a cow, are you?"

He looks at me, then at his plastic-wrapped hand. "I'm not even going to ask what you think I'm about to do." With that he's out of the truck. He's agile for being such a big guy, hopping the wooden fence in one swift motion. He doesn't make it far before he swoops down and picks something up off the ground. With deliberation, he slowly zips it up.

He brings his findings back with a satisfied smirk: A ziplock bag full of fresh cow turd. "Here, hold this, would you?"

"Seriously?" I press myself into the truck door. The handle jabs into my back.

"Don't be a baby," he says, dangling the bag toward me. "I made sure none got on the outside. I'm holding it, aren't I?"

"Which has what to do with me?" But I take the bag, using my index and thumb to hold the corner. I maintain it a safe distance away from me like it's full of leprosy.

"Now for the fun part," he says, starting the engine again. "Nothing like a stink pickle to up the stakes."

"Did you really just say stink pickle?"

We drive and drive. We're leaving town, going south, heading to Highway 98, the touristy part of the county. I realize that it will take longer than the half hour he promised it would. I knew half an hour was wishful thinking. But I owe him now. I hate owing anyone anything. If I can just get through this little field trip, then we'll be even. Then we'll never have to speak again.

"So what did your parents think about the whole robbery thing? Were they proud of you?"

I frown. With a longer drive comes a higher price: conversation. This is exactly why I never try to make friends. Eventually they'll want an explanation for my home life. "I live with my brother, Julio. And I didn't tell him."

A moment of silence. I can tell he's back and forth about asking the next question. "Where are your parents?"

"Dead."

"Sorry."

"What for? You didn't kill them."

"Geez, you know what I mean." I see his hands tighten on the steering wheel. "So why didn't you tell your brother?"

I shrug. "Nothing much to tell."

He looks at me then, all serious. I can tell he's going to press for more information. I cut him off. "Look, Julio has enough on his plate without having to worry about me. He works hard for the both of us. And nothing happened so . . . Why worry him, you know?" I bite my tongue. What Julio has on his plate is none of Arden's business. I feel a tide of heat fill my cheeks. I need to be more careful with what I say.

Another pause. "And what about you?"

"What do you mean?"

"Seems like you have enough to worry about too. Is there a night you *don't* have to work at the Breeze Mart? And obviously you care about your grades." His voice is tight when he says this.

"I get one night off a week." And I usually get called in for it. But telling him that would only add fuel to whatever fire Arden is building right now. "Some people have to work for their money, you know. Not everyone gets wads of twenties for their allowance."

"I knew you were looking in my wallet. Just couldn't help yourself, huh?"

Oooh, I've hit a nerve, I can tell. "You were practically shoving it in my face!"

"I was paying for my stuff!"

"You almost disemboweled your wallet on my counter!"

He closes his eyes and scratches one eyebrow furiously. "I usually don't carry around that much cash with me."

"So you were showing off."

"And what if I was?"

Yep. I got nothing. Except, my mouth drops open in an unattractive way. Arden Moss just admitted he was showing off . . . for me? Next up, world peace.

"It's just that you're so hard to impress . . . And it felt like I kept screwing it up . . ." He grimaces at me. "Can we just get on with our fun-having?"

I nod. Although now we seemed to have bogged down our fun-having with issues.

The rest of our ride is in silence. We pull into the huge parking lot of Destin Commons, a high-end shopping center on Highway 98 in Destin. "This is the best spot," he announces, parking us in front of a big name department store.

He retrieves his new knockoff purse, then gingerly relieves me of my bag of poo. With ease that can only be gotten from experience, he opens the purse and slides the turd pile in with perfect precision. Then he pulls out his still-engorged wallet and takes a five dollar bill from it. All the while I watch like a fascinated child. He tucks most of the bill into the purse, zipping the top almost shut, but leaves the corner of the bill sticking out, showing the denomination.

I swallow hard. A perfectly good five dollar bill, now smeared with crap. It hurts. It hurts bad. Julio would be cussing right now.

Without another word, he slips out of the driver's side and onto the sidewalk, the purse tucked securely under his arm, out of sight. He places it on one of the waiting benches with the fluidity of a pickpocket, then takes a light jog back to the truck. By this time he's grinning from ear to ear.

Shutting the door behind him, he points at a woman approaching the store who appears unaware of the purse sitting on the bench. She's enthralled with finding something in her own purse—her wallet? Her return receipt?—so she passes by the bench without looking down. I wonder if I've ever passed any purses with an easy five bucks sticking out of it. I resolve to pay more attention.

"Aw, that would have been funny," Arden says, disappointment thick in his voice. But the downer is short-lived. He leans forward, putting his forearms on the steering wheel. "Here comes our target. See that guy right there?"

"We have a target?" I shift in my seat. Having a target sounds so . . . conniving. "Why do we have a target again?"

The dude approaches the bench with a fast pace, eyeing the purse. Oh, this guy. He's all macho, wearing a name-brand sporty wind suit and pristine running shoes that I'm sure have never seen a genuine sweaty mile. He's balding slightly, and what's left of his hair, he's gelled into submission. He looks cocky. Too cocky to pick up a woman's purse. So he passes it, keeping his eyes trained on the door ahead of him. I'm relieved. Arden scowls. "I was sure he'd fall for that." He turns to me. "This guy is a complete jackass. He comes in here every Tuesday and demands a senior discount, even though he's not technically a senior yet. The store manager bows to his almighty will—moron—and lets him treat his cashiers like total garbage. One time, a lady in front of him in line dropped a twenty dollar bill from her purse when she was getting her wallet out, and this guy picks it up and pockets it without even telling her."

"And so you've stalked him?" I mean, to time something this perfectly, Arden would have had to study this man, his habits. I remember the incident at the Breeze Mart then. Arden knew Mr. Shackleford would be there at that time.

"I like to call it recon."

I watch as Mean Guy places a flat palm on the glass door. But he only pushes it halfway open. He pauses then, peering into the store longingly. With a self-loathing shake of his head, he turns and considers the purse again, his stature stiff with hesitation. Slowly, he lets the door close behind him. And he walks to the purse.

I have mixed feelings when he picks it up. On the one hand, I want him to get what he deserves. On the other, I so don't want to get caught doing this. I contemplate whether or not this could be a felony. Not that I know what constitutes a felony.

Arden gives me an anticipatory grin.

Mean Guy tests the weight of the bag, holding it by the strap with one finger and letting it dangle for a few seconds. I have no idea what he's hoping to discern by this. Apparently finding the purse an acceptable weight, he gingerly unzips it. And, oh my God, he opens it wide.

"Score!" Arden whispers next to me.

Mean Guy is overcome with disgust. His nostrils flare as he thrusts the purse into the bushes behind the bench. He stares at his hands as if they've become feet.

Against my will, the corners of my mouth tug up into a grin. Arden ducks behind the steering wheel and motions for me to get down. I follow his lead, my heart pounding. "He's looking around," Arden explains.

After a few seconds, Arden peeks up, looking through the steering wheel. "He's putting the purse back on the bench!"

"What? Why would he do that?" I poke my head up over the console. Sure enough, Mean Guy is arranging the purse, setting it prettily on the seat.

"He's setting someone else up. I told you he was a jackass. Look, he's going to his car to watch."

Sure enough, Sporty Spice gets back in his car, eyes on the bench. And we all wait. "We should go get the purse," I tell Arden. "Our target didn't take the bait."

He sighs. "I can't go get it. He'll recognize me, because I've said something to him before. Do you want to go get it?"

And risk Mean Guy thinking it was me who set him up? Uh, no.

Arden sees my hesitation. "Didn't think so. All we can do now is watch. Might as well enjoy the moment."

It doesn't take long for the next victim to approach. Of all the people in the universe, it's an old lady and a kid who is probably her bratty grandson. He's about five years old with a straight-up bowl cut and he's pulling her faster than her bony legs can walk. They're about to pass the bench without noticing our little present for them. I will them with my eyes to look at the purse, and at the same time, I want them to pass by it.

Look at the purse, you little punk! No, don't!

And suddenly, he does.

We can't hear what he's telling his poor grandmother, but we can see that he's excited. He's about to pull her finger out of its socket, trying to reach the bench. Trying to reach our putrid pocketbook. I'm dying seriously dying for that kid to pick it up and get himself a big whiff of turd pie.

This is wrong, my conscience screams. *And risky.* Even so, I keep watching.

Turbo Brat lets go of her hand then and Granny almost falls backward, which scares me a little. But she must be used to this kind of behavior because she catches herself just in time and with not a little grace. Meanwhile, Turbo Brat is picking up the purse and opening it. This kid deserves a trophy for being such a terror.

Arden snickers beside me. I giggle. But only a little.

Turbo Brat seems unconcerned with the money, and he doesn't seem to be assaulted by the smell just yet or maybe young kids are immune to that scent, so he actually sticks his entire hand inside and digs around—maybe for candy or other things that interest five-year-olds more than money—and as soon as I get done laughing, I'll die and go to hell like I should.

Arden is holding his stomach at this point. "His face," he chokes out. "Did you see his face? Oh my God—he's smelling his fingers—I can't even!"

I can't breathe. Seriously, I need air. I'm trying to roll the window down but Arden puts a hand on my arm and shakes his head. "Too . . . loud . . . ," he says and I think what he means is that we're laughing too loud so it also means that I can't roll down the window right now.

Turbo Brat starts to cry when he realizes what's on his hands and Grandma saves the day by producing a handful of baby wipes. She rips each one ferociously from the travel-size box and begins to devour his hands with them. After she's satisfied with her cleanup job, they proceed into the store with the purse in tow, probably to report the incident. The ruined five dollar bill still lies on the concrete in front of the bench.

I feel bad for Granny, I really do. But that kid just might have learned a life lesson today, so my sympathy only stretches so far. "Should we go get it?" I ask, finally catching my breath. Not that I'm volunteering. From across the parking lot, I see Mean Guy in his seat, covering his mouth with his hand. He's still watching.

Arden clears his throat. "I don't think we'll have to." He nods toward the storefront.

A boy on a skateboard is making his way on the sidewalk toward the bench. With a smooth agility, he jumps the board and skids it across the back of the bench, then lands with the poise of a tiger. Using his foot to flip up the skateboard into his hand, he bends down to examine the five dollar bill. He scrutinizes it for so long I wouldn't be surprised if he produced a magnifying glass. Picking it up, he pulls it to his face and sniffs it, and visibly recoils. Then he puts it in his pocket and skates away.

Arden leans back against the driver's side door. "Proof that one man's trash is another man's treasure."

"You really are Mr. Shackleford's nephew." It sounds like something he would say.

"He would approve of this exercise in wisdom. He's the one who thought it up."

"Be serious."

"No, he did! He used to take me and Amber to do it all the time."

"Amber? Who's Amber?"

"She was my sister. She died."

"I'm sorry."

"What for? You didn't kill her." With this, he smirks. It's getting harder and harder not to like Arden. "Well, my half hour is up. But on a scale of one to ten, how entertained were you?"

Ten. Hands down. "About a seven. And a half."

"Maybe next time we'll get that up to an eight."

"Next time?"

"Yes, next time. And the time after that."

"I didn't peg you for an optimist."

He scratches the back of his neck. "Come on, Carly. You don't think we had a moment today? A tiny sliver of a moment that gave our acquaintance status room to blossom into friendship status?"

I tilt my head at him. "I guess so." I mean, we watched people dig through a shitty purse together. We seem harmonious enough.

"Great. So, now that we're friends, I have a very important question to ask you. I'd like to know if you'd do me the honor of being my accomplice."

I wonder if everyone else notices how weird Arden Moss actually is.

Twelve

Arden waits at their picnic table, trying not to appear as antsy as he feels. Also, trying not to dissect why he thinks of it as "their" picnic table instead of "the" picnic table.

And where is she? She said this morning she would meet me here at lunch.

Arden's stomach growls. Waiting for a girl is an exhausting experience. All this *Will she show? Will she be pleasant? Will she be armed with whole or 2%?* business. But he's willing to go through all that again. He's willing to do what it takes to woo Carly.

He didn't realize until yesterday just how much he has missed having an accomplice. It's so much better to share the enjoyment of giving someone their comeuppance. Of course, Amber was the perfect sidekick in every way. Actually, compared to Amber and her creativity, *he* was the real sidekick. Carly will never be Amber, he knows. And it's not like he's looking to replace Amber—no one could ever do that. But Carly has undeniable potential. And loneliness has taken its toll on him.

Carly shows up late, about ten minutes later, hauling a heavy backpack, a rare grin, and a light lunch tray. Chocolate milk.

She takes the seat across from him, wasting the next two minutes carefully arranging her homework in front of her and her backpack on the bench beside her. She opens her chocolate milk with the finesse of a lunch lady. "What?" she says.

"Lunch is almost over." Arden's stomach growls again. "You might as well have stood me up."

"I had some questions about our assignment," she says. "You act like this is a date."

"It's a meeting."

She picks up her pencil and scribbles something in her notebook. Arden doubts it has anything to do with him. She doesn't look up when she says, "So I've thought about your, uh, proposal."

Not a good sign.

"And first I just want to say I did have a fun time yesterday . . ."

Yep, this is what he says when he's about to reject a girl. Nope, it doesn't feel good to be on the receiving end. Funny that he ever thought it was gentle.

"And being your accomplice in all this prank stuff sounds fun . . ."

She keeps saying fun. *Fun* is now the most neutral word in the world.

"But I kind of have to work for a living. Like, I have a job. It's this thing where they pay you to do stuff . . ."

Wait, what? *Is she mocking me?*

"Like, you exchange work for money, then you buy your own things. You don't even have to ask your parents. You should try it sometime . . ."

"Screw you."

She smiles. Hugely. Beautifully. Arden wants to hate that smile. It's evidence that she's entertained by his anger, after all. But the smile is just so . . . gorgeous. "I was just messing with you," she says. "It looked like you zoned out on me."

"Oh. Well. I didn't."

"But I really can't be your accomplice."

"Because?"

"Because of work."

"So what part were you messing with me about?"

She blinks. Her mouth tightens into a pout. "You said we would be doing things after school. At night. I can't. I have to work. At the Breeze Mart."

"What do you make there, minimum wage?"

"So?"

"I'm just saying, it doesn't seem like a job worth keeping."

"Have you ever had a job, Arden?"

"I've worked for my uncle a few summers."

She rolls her eyes. "I'll bet that was backbreaking. You probably overdosed on your aunt Dorothy's lemonade."

Maybe. "About as backbreaking as doing homework on the clock, I guess."

She folds her hands in front of her. "I need that job. It's not something I'd expect someone like you to understand. In fact, I need more hours."

"Here we go again. The silver platter talk. Let's skip that today, okay? I get it. I'm privileged and that makes me a bad person."

A glint of remorse flashes across her face, giving him hope. Until she opens her mouth again. "I don't think you're a bad person. I'm just not, well, in the same position you are. It's not that I didn't have fun with you. I did. I just have things that I *have* to do and they're more important than what I *want* to do."

Arden runs a hand through his hair. Obviously this is a bigger deal than he'd originally thought. He knew she was different from all of his friends but he thought it was by choice. Now he can see the differences as if a flashlight were shining on them in a dark room. All of his friends have their own cars, where Carly rides a bike everywhere—even to the next town over to work the graveyard shift at a dumpy convenience store. She wears T-shirts and jeans—something he thought was preference—and as far as he can tell, she only owns one pair of shoes, which happen to be filthy off-brand Converse. What girl would wear dingy shoes every day if she could help it? But it's not that she doesn't care about her appearance. He can tell Carly would be girly if she had the chance. Even now she has a complicated-looking braid in her hair and her nails are painted a deep purple.

How he missed these things before, Arden is not sure.

So, Carly Vega is poor. But, unless she's lying, she wants to have fun with him. She just has an obstacle in her—and therefore his—way.

There's got to be something I can do. "I'll pay you," he blurts. "I'll pay you for your company." Whoa, that sounded way wrong. And other people heard it. It's like the air actually gasped.

Tables of kids around them stop eating. Stop talking. He's in danger of a chocolate milk bath, he can tell. Carly's eyes flash with the ferocity of a starved predator. He wouldn't be surprised if she bared her teeth.

At this moment, there is no amount of salt that would make his foot taste better.

Carly rises from the bench seat. She gathers up her homework in a neat pile, tapping the edges straight, shutting her book with a deliberation so cool it could chill a deep fryer. She tugs at the strap on her backpack and eases it up, onto her shoulder, which is squared perfectly with the other despite the added weight.

"Carly, I—" Arden chokes out. *I what, exactly? I'm sorry* falls infinitely short of what it will take to get her to speak to him again. Miles short of what it will take to make it up to her. Years short of what it will take for everyone to forget that he said that today.

Carly turns and walks away. Before she opens the cafeteria door, she wipes her feet on the floor mat, as if symbolically. And then she's gone.

⌒⌒·⌒

Out of the corner of his eye, Arden feels Deputy Glass glance at him. Once. Twice. Again. Arden shifts in his seat, slumping even farther down. "Aren't cops supposed to keep their eyes on the road?"

Glass takes it in stride, bringing the car to a halt at a stop sign, then slowly turning right. Classic patrol driving. "You're quiet tonight. Having girl problems? Thinking of that little Mexican girl?"

"Why does she gotta be Mexican?"

"Uh, because apparently her parents are Mexican?"

"I mean, how do you know they're not like Puerto Rican or something?"

Glass shrugs. "So what if she is? So what if she isn't? Is there something wrong with being Mexican?"

According to the mighty Sheriff Moss, that's a big unofficial yes. He might center his campaign around deporting undocumented immigrants, but the truth is, he doesn't care if they're documented or not. Glass knows it. Arden knows it. Sheriff Moss treats racial profiling like a hobby.

And Arden knows Glass doesn't feel the same way. So what Arden says next is unfair. "Why does she have to be anything? Why couldn't you just say 'short girl' or 'girl with the long eyelashes'? Who cares what race she is?"

Glass grins wide, exposing a rarely seen dimple and the fact that he's not as old as he looks in that nerdy uniform. If Arden had to guess, he'd say he's only about twenty-four, maybe twenty-five years old. "Girl with the long eyelashes huh? That 'short girl' has Arden Moss squirming in his little ol' panties, eh?"

"It's not like that." Arden turns to face his friend, feeling a deep scowl embedded into his expression. "I insulted her today by accident. And now she won't talk to me about it. Not even to let me apologize."

Glass gives him a charitable shrug. "Your specialty is girls. You'll figure it out."

"Not this one," Arden grumbles, but Glass is turning up the radio. Dispatch issues a call for domestic violence. The address is close to them.

Glass rolls his eyes. "Copy that," he says into the mouthpiece on his shoulder. He rolls his eyes at Arden. "It's Rose again, beating up on Henry. This'll be her third offense so I'm going to have to take her down to the station. You want to come or you want me to drop you here?"

Glass knows Arden hates coming to the station; there's always the chance he'll run into his father there. But tonight, he doesn't want to be left alone with his own thoughts. Tonight, he could use some entertainment drummed up by someone else for a change. "I'll come."

Glass nods and flips on the blue lights, which illuminate a hedge of rosebushes outside the window. People dread the sight of the flashing blue lights. Those lights may mean a hefty speeding ticket or possibly jail. That's what they mean to Arden too. But there was a time when Arden loved them. It meant that his father had come home from work—back when his father was just a deputy. Back when Arden actually wanted his father to come home.

He and Amber would sit and wait at the front window, waiting for Deputy Moss to arrive at the end of his shift. As soon as he pulled into the driveway, he would turn on the blue lights—which were actually blue and red back then—and Arden and his sister would squeal, "Daddy's home!" and run to the door to greet him.

Arden nearly laughs aloud at the idea of looking forward to seeing his father. They say kids can sense someone's character. Arden guesses that doesn't apply to one's own dad. He never saw the real Dwayne Moss coming.

They pull into the driveway of a familiar residence—the Walkers, starring Rose the Wife, Henry the Husband, and Caden the Toddler. Caden is outside on the walkway, happily holding on to Henry's hand. Henry is a walking stick of a man, redheaded and freckle-faced, with disheveled hair and a swollen red nose that might have been bleeding before they arrived.

When Deptuy Glass opens the door to get out, Arden rolls down his window to listen in. He's not allowed to get out and actually take part in calls. But he's allowed to observe, by policy. Anyone can, in fact. It's one of the most well-kept secrets of the county.

Henry extends his hand to shake Deputy Glass's. He nods toward the yellow vinyl-sided house, where the light is on in the living room, and the front door is wide open. "Rose is in the bedroom crying her eyes out. She feels real bad about it this time," Henry says. "If it weren't for my little man here, I wouldn't care none. But I've got to raise him right, you know? What goes in might come out one day."

Deputy Glass nods. "That's right, Henry. That's right. You know what's going to happen now, don't you? I can't do anything about that. It's her third time."

Henry hangs his head and nods. Arden can't tell if he's sniffling because he's crying or because he's sucking up more blood that might be oozing out. Probably both.

Glass disappears into the house and when he reemerges, he has Rose Walker in submissive tow, hands cuffed behind her back. She's in her pajamas, which are mismatched Tweety Bird pants with a Mickey Mouse tank covering her muffin top, all accentuated with hot-pink bejeweled flip-flops. Her runny mascara and mussed-up hair will make a classic mugshot. Deputy Glass allows her to kneel down so that Caden can throw his chubby little arms around his mother's thick neck.

"Mama's got to go away for a little while, but Daddy will take care of you, okay, little darlin'?" For what it's worth, it does appear that Rose seems more remorseful this time. Probably because she's going to jail.

"Daddy has boo-boo," Caden announces. "Mama hit Daddy."

"Mama loves Daddy, okay?" she says. "We just get mad at each other sometimes."

Arden rolls his eyes. *Way to teach your son that domestic violence is the norm.* Arden's quite certain little Caden would understand if Rose said something more accurate like, "Mama isn't supposed to hit Daddy. That's bad." But instead, she splits the blame between them. Glass calls it classic abuser syndrome.

If only Henry would grow some balls and say it himself. But everyone in this yard knows that will never happen.

Glass opens the back door of the car for Rose and helps her in. "Hi, Arden," she says. "How's your mama doing these days?"

Arden grinds his teeth. "She's doing." The truth is, she isn't doing, not much anyway. She's awake half the night and sleeps during the day and in between she apparently fusses over Cletus. She must miss having someone to fuss over, now that Amber is gone. *At least Cletus is good for something.*

"Well, that's good."

Arden's not sure what's so good about it, but Rose isn't really interested in talking pleasantries. As soon as Glass gets in the driver's seat, she starts in immediately, pressing her face against the metal, netlike barrier between the front and backseat. "You know that hag May's going to fire me over this," she says. Arden perks up. Rose works as a waitress at Uppity Rooster Café on Highway 98. Has for as long as Arden can remember. His aunt Dorothy was best friends with the café manager and owner, May Haverty.

"You really want that to happen?" Rose continues. "I support us, you know. Henry hasn't had a job for six months now. Who's going to feed my Caden if I'm in jail?"

At this Arden is surprised. The Walker house is in a good

neighborhood. It's a nice house. They even have their lawn cut regularly by a lawn care service. At least, they have a sign advertising a lawn care company stuck in the ground by the sidewalk. The Chevy truck parked in the driveway looked new. *How much could Rose possibly make as a waitress?*

"You make good money there?" Arden says. Deputy Glass looks at him as if he's grown double D breasts. Arden shrugs. He usually doesn't take to talking to the backseat guests, but this could be pertinent information. Arden turns around to face the husband beater.

Her chin raises slightly. "I make enough to pay the bills, feed us, and then some. I make sure my little Caden doesn't want for nothin'."

"Well, you should have thought about that before you started on one of your fits again," Glass says to the rearview. He makes a slow left turn. He could take a more direct route to the station, Arden knows, but apparently he's humoring Arden's newfound interest in interrogation.

Rose scoffs. "Henry knows just how to push my buttons is all."

"So what shifts do you normally work?" Arden says, determined to make her focus. "Breakfast?"

"I get the best shifts, since I've been there the longest."

"Which are?"

"What do you care?"

"I'm just trying to make conversation," Arden says, hoping his smile looks authentic. "You've had a rough night and I wanted to get your mind off things." *And I want to fill your position pronto.*

This softens her up a bit. "That's awfully sweet of you, Arden. Isn't that sweet of him, Deputy Glass?"

Glass casts him an ironic look. "It is, Ms. Walker. Arden here's a sweet boy when he wants to be." And by the sound of his tone, Glass doesn't believe that's what Arden's being right now.

"You get a lot of snowbird action at the café?" Arden presses. It's still hot outside, but school's already started in most states, and the tourist traffic has died down a lot in Destin. Snowbirds usually keep the place up and running, especially some of the more popular hangouts like Uppity Rooster.

"Oh yeah. I work breakfast shift Monday, Wednesday, Friday, and the weekends. Saturday and Sunday are my bread and butter though. I make more on Saturday morning than I do all week." Rose is particularly proud of this. Then her countenance falls as if weighted with a concrete block. "I *did,* anyway. I'm pretty sure May's going to let me go over this. I already got wrote up last week for taking too many smoke breaks."

Perfect.

Thirteen

I hear Arden's truck and feel the rumble on the dirt road. I know it's Arden because this has become his ritual the past two days: follow me home from school and beg me to speak to him, driving alongside me as I pedal my bike faster and faster before coming to a complete stop when he doesn't expect it, then dart through the woods while he's trying to back up.

It's an exhausting but necessary ritual. And slightly entertaining.

Today shall be no different from the last two. I already have my sights set on which part of the woods I'm going to launch off into. He'll never see it coming.

Unfortunately I don't see something else coming: a soft spot in the dirt road. My front wheel pirouettes almost backward, bringing me to a violent, immediate standstill, which nearly sends me flying over the handlebars. As it is, I turn at an unnatural angle, and my right ankle scrapes against the pedal and I'm forced to forfeit the bike into the red clay and my pride along with it. Also, I trip, fail to catch myself, and land squarely on my rear.

My hurt ankle and mutilated ego make it difficult to want to get back up.

Arden's truck skids to a halt beside me as I begrudgingly pull myself to a standing position, patting a red dust cloud off my butt. I continue to ignore him as I attempt to arrange the handlebars in rideable order. There's no getting around the fact that he saw everything. If our roles had been reversed, I would find this funny for the rest of my days. The kind of funny that, out of nowhere, cracks you up in the middle of a library or someone's funeral or an important conversation.

But Arden isn't laughing. I know this, because I steal a glance at him—his eyes are all determination and his mouth is set in a straight line. Laughing is the furthest thing from his mind. Because for the second time in our brief history, Arden Moss steals my bike again. With superhero ease, he snatches it from my hands and puts it in the back of his truck, sliding it to the middle of the bed.

I can't decide where I'm going to hide his body after I murder him.

Before I can say that, or anything, his hand is covering my mouth and he's turning me around in his arms so that my back is to his stomach and it dawns on me that maybe I'm the one being kidnapped and that nobody will find my body and that even if they do he'll get off scot-free because he's the sheriff's son.

A scream wells up inside me.

"For God's sake, will you just listen to me without opening your mouth?" he says in my ear. His voice is gruff, like he has a cold.

I try to bite the soft part of his hand, but he cups it just in time.

He tightens his grip on me and presses his cheek against mine. I stomp on his foot and he grunts, but doesn't let go.

"I'm sorry, Carly," he says. "So sorry. I'm a pathetic particle of dust that doesn't deserve to land on your feet. What I said at lunch was the stupidest thing that's ever come out of my mouth. But I'm trying to make it up to you. Will you just listen to me?"

Trying to make it up to me? By stealing my bike? Holding me hostage?

"I have good news," he continues, as if I'm not squirming like a hooked worm. Arden is rock solid. It feels like struggling against the inside of a stack of tires. "I got you a job. A better one than the Breeze Mart. You can start this Saturday if you want. It's good money, less hours." With this, he turns me loose and shoves me away from him.

He wipes his wet hand on his T-shirt; he didn't release me in time to avoid me spitting into his palm. It was the least I could do.

I want to push him against the truck and kick his nuts up his throat. But his words are sinking in. And I want to hear more of them. It's then that I realize I'm about to hyperventilate.

Arden seems to realize it at the same time. "Whoa, you don't have asthma or anything, do you? Calm down. Breathe in, breathe out. Put your hands on your head. I hear that helps with asthma attacks."

"I don't have asthma, moron," I screech. "It's not asthma attacking me, it's you!"

He wipes both hands down his face, then interlaces them behind his neck as if trying to appear harmless. "I wasn't attacking you. I was . . . subduing you."

"For real? That's what you're going with?"

"Ohmigod, I can't talk to you! You're impossible to deal with!"

"I'm impossible? You took my bike—again! Then you . . . you . . ."

"I'll give your bike back. I'm sorry I sub—took actions to neutralize your anger. I knew you wouldn't listen to me."

I cross my arms and start to walk in a circle. A tight circle that traumatized people walk in when they're trying to get a grip. "He's stalking me," I say more to myself than to him. "Why is he stalking me?" I stop and face him. "Why would you stalk me?"

He looks mortified at the thought. "That's reaching a bit, don't you think?"

"Look up the definition of stalker, then get back to me on that one."

He shakes his head, cussing under his breath. Then he reaches into his jeans pocket and pulls out a folded-up piece of paper. Slowly, he hands it to me. "This is the restaurant. They need a waitress for Saturday and Sunday mornings. You'll need to talk to Miss May. She's the manager. Tell her I sent you and you've got the job."

I open up the paper and examine it:

Uppity Rooster Café
Miss May
Saturday + Sunday from 6 am to 1 pm

I've never seen Arden's handwriting before, but I'm betting it's his. It's definitely boy-scrawl, anyway. It doesn't have all the frilly loops and neatness of a woman's penmanship. "I don't understand" is all I can say.

He sniffs. "Look, I know I've pissed you off worse than an

alligator in a bathtub. But I'm trying to make it up to you. This is a good-paying job. These two shifts are the best, and I guarantee you'll make more money there than the Breeze Mart. I talked to one of the servers who used to work there. She said she can make up to three hundred dollars a shift. Cash."

Three hundred bucks a shift. That's nearly six hundred dollars a week. That's more than double what I make at the Breeze Mart. "I've never waitressed before," I admit, awestruck at the revelation. Julio would melt in my hands if I brought home that kind of money.

"How hard can it be? You learn the menu, take people's orders, then bring it to their table. Believe me, if Rose can be a waitress, you can."

I don't know who Rose is, but Arden's argument seems valid. I'm not helpless. I'm a hard worker—that is, if there was actually hard work to do at the Breeze Mart. "But then I'd be working seven days a week." I say this more to myself than to Arden.

Standing at the Breeze Mart cash register isn't exactly strenuous, but never getting a day off? Could I really do that? In the back of my mind, I think about my grades. I know it's wrong to think about myself at a time like this, to think about what if. What if I can keep my grades up and get a scholarship after my family gets back to the States? What if I can make something of myself? But I have to let go of selfish thoughts like that. I have to keep focused on the most important thing. As Julio says, family first.

But the disappointment frothing in my stomach betrays me.

"Why would you need to work at both places?" Arden says. "Think how much more time you'll have during the week if you just work weekends."

I shake my head. "I don't need time. I need money."

Arden bites his lip. "Can I just interject something here without getting you all pissed off again?"

Knowing Arden, probably not. "Sure."

"Well, it just seems that you're uptight all the time. I know you and your brother need money, and I don't blame you for wanting to take on both jobs. It's just . . . what about you? This is supposed to be the best time of your life. Geez, we're in high school. We're supposed to look back on this time in our life and remember how fun it was. How can you do that if you work yourself to death?"

"When I look back, I'll have something to be proud of. That I helped my family." I don't expect Arden to understand. Really and truly I don't. But I don't want to have to explain it to him, either. Especially when doubt has become a congealed puddle in my gut.

"You said that if you didn't have to work so much you'd spend time with me. That you wouldn't mind having a little fun. Was that a bunch of BS?"

I look down at the paper in my hands. He's gone to a lot of trouble on my behalf. This boy who has pulled a gun on me, scared my friend half to death, stolen my bike (twice), insulted me in front of practically the entire school (accounting for gossip), and held me hostage for one-point-five minutes.

This boy who stood up for me in the hall, gave me a ride home, let me dump a carton of milk on him without retribution, checked on me at the store in the middle of the night, and has now procured me a good-paying job if I so want it.

God, but Arden Moss is confusing. Confusing, and persistent.

I meet his eyes. "I'll check into this restaurant thing. And we'll go from there. No promises."

His eyes light up. "Awesome. You'll need to see Miss May this Saturday at two p.m. That's when things slow down at the café."

"Wait. Isn't this place in Destin? That's too far for me to ride my bike."

"I'll give you a ride."

"Every Saturday and Sunday? I don't see that working out." It's not just that Arden isn't what I would call dependable. Even if he keeps his word and picks me up, I'm afraid of what Julio may think of it. And especially what Julio will think of it when he finds out whose son Arden is.

That's when I decide that Julio will never find out. Problem solved, right?

Arden shrugs, unconcerned. "I guess you'll just have to trust me."

"Do I even dare ask what you expect in return?" It's a valid question and we both know it. Our little lunchtime squabble replays in my head. *I'll pay you for your company.* Oh. My. God.

Arden grimaces. "Consider it penance for my sins."

"How about gas money instead?"

"Deal."

⁓ ⸱ ⁓

I wait for Miss May on the bench seat in front of the hostess stand. There are still a few tables with guests in the dining room and I wonder if I've come too early. "She'll be right with you," the hostess says.

The restaurant is fancier than I expected and I'm immediately intimidated. The last time I sat at a table with an actual tablecloth on it was never. Orange juice is served in what looks like wineglasses. There are decorative roosters everywhere, some made of cast iron, some made of porcelain, some small, some large, some almost hidden among the others. It's the mascot of the place, apparently. It's definitely uppity. And rooster-y.

I take a menu from the stand to study, in case Miss May is in the quizzing mood and I'm disgruntled to find that even the menu is made with fancy paper and ornate font, and the prices are listed as whole numbers without the cents or a dollar sign or anything. It lists things like Blackberry Grits and Baked Brie Delight.

Definitely intimidating.

While I'm trying to memorize the names of the scrambles—so far I've got The Floridian, The Hey Lucy! and the Bacquezo down—an older woman with wise eyes tips down the menu to peer at me. Her reading glasses almost slip off the tip of her nose.

"Carly, I presume?" she says. Great. She says things like "presume." I'm screwed.

"Yes," I say. "Miss May, I presume?" Yep, didn't pull it off. The older lady smirks, but not unkindly.

"Yes. Would you like to come sit with me? I have an open table in the corner where we can chat."

The table is set for four with real cloth napkins wrapped around the silverware and fancy wineglass thingies and a lovely bouquet of hydrangeas in the center that might actually be real. And did I mention there's a white tablecloth?

I pull up one of the plush comfortable chairs and wait for Miss May to speak. I'm suddenly less intimated by the tablecloth and more grateful for it because it hides my hands fidgeting like mad in my lap.

"So, you know Arden from school?" I can tell by the look in her eyes she thinks I'm dating him.

"He's in a few of my classes," I say. I don't want her to think we're dating, but what if she's only considering giving me this job *because* she thinks we're dating?

"He's a sweet boy." She's baiting me.

"Is he?"

She laughs. Out of the corner of my eye I see a waitress tucked into a corner table on the opposite side of the room. She's counting a giant wad of cash, bill by bill, and I can tell they're not all ones. I'm hoping Miss May doesn't ask me directly if I'm dating Arden, because now I'm tempted to lie just to get this job.

I need a job that offers wads of cash that aren't all ones.

"He is when he wants to be," she says. "So. Down to business. When can you start?"

Okay, good. No lying involved. "Today. Right now."

She smiles, nodding. "That's a good answer, Carly. But I won't put you to work on the spot like that. Can you come in tomorrow morning? And I'm talking early, about six o'clock. I need you to replace one of my openers. Is waking up early an issue for you? That's the one problem I always have when I hire a teenager."

"I'm a morning person," I say, and it's actually the truth, but by now I would tell her anything to get this job. I visualize in my head how many shifts and wads of cash it would take to get my parents back to the States. I imagine a huge box that I keep stuffing money into and then presenting it to Julio with a big bow on the top.

"Good. We'll do all the paperwork today so you can start training first thing in the morning. I'll supply you with a couple of our logo T-shirts and an apron, but you'll be responsible for wearing nonslip shoes and nice black pants to work."

I nod, relieved that I already have those things from working at the Breeze Mart. "So that's it? I'm hired?"

"You're hired. Any friend of Arden Moss is a friend of mine. I just hope you're a good friend *and* a good waitress." She chuckles. "But there's a secret to making money here, Carly. Would you like me to share that secret with you?"

I nod.

"Secret is 'yes.' That's your answer to everything our guests ask of you. If they ask if they can have an extra plate with butter on the left side, you say yes. If they want their coffee mug heated in the microwave before you even pour the first cup, you say yes. If they want you to take a picture of their family sitting at the table—even if you're up to your eyeballs in work and don't have time for it—you say yes. Yes makes money for all of us. Think you can manage that?"

"Absolutely yes."

⌒•⌒

Arden puts the truck in park on the side of the road. The headlights of an oncoming car light up the cabin, illuminating his disdain. "The least you could do is act happy even if you're withering on the inside," he says. Then he mumbles something that sounds like "grouchiest person on the planet."

I sigh, watching him take out a pocketknife and open the small cardboard box in his lap. He pulls out what looks like a bunch of crayons all attached together. "I'm not withering on the inside, I'm just tired and I have to get up early in the morning, remember? What is that?"

"Fireworks, of course. I told you, we're celebrating."

When the next car passes by, I see on the label of the box that the "fireworks" are actually Black Cats. Who celebrates with Black Cats? They're just loud and annoying—nothing pretty or celebratory about them. "There's nothing to celebrate. I got the job because of you, not anything extraordinary that I did to earn it."

"Who cares how you got it? I swear you're determined to be miserable."

I yawn. "Six o'clock comes early for the both of us. It's almost eleven. You're not getting out of giving me a ride." It bugs me to have to depend on Arden for a ride, but I don't want to take any chances on being late in the morning so riding my bike is out of the question, in case I misjudge how long it will take me to get there. It's way farther than the Breeze Mart, and I'll probably drop ten pounds just from the commute, but I'm still practically salivating over the thought of being flush with cash. Riding my trusty old bike a few extra miles one way is so worth it.

A tiny pang of guilt washes over me; I haven't told Julio about the restaurant gig yet. In fact, he would probably (possibly) be wondering where I am right now, except I told him I picked up an extra shift at the Breeze. He doesn't expect me home until I'll be leaving again—at which point I guess I'll break down and tell him that I have another job. I didn't want to tell him yet though. I don't want to get his hopes up about bringing in extra income in case the job doesn't work out for whatever reason.

It's just that Julio holds tightly to his hopes. They are fragile, delicate things and he clings to them with a desperation I pray I'll never know. Sometimes I don't think it's even that he misses our parents. I think it's that he's terrified of being responsible for me all by himself.

I think Julio feels like he's alone.

He's never said that, of course, but how can he not feel that way? Maybe when I start bringing in more money, he won't feel so burdened with me. Maybe he'll start to look at me as a true helper instead of an obligation.

"Seriously, can we skip the celebration tonight? I've got to get some sleep." I don't want to screw this up. *So* much depends on it. I glance down at my study menu wishing it were still daylight so I could see the ingredients of the Fountainbleau omelette. The more I can memorize now, the less time I'll have to spend training, the sooner I can make my own money and not split it with the trainer.

Arden's face falls and I almost regret my tone. But I can't afford feeling sorry for Arden Moss. Not if he's going to jeopardize the job he just got me. "Just one hour?" he pleads. "I'll get you to your house by midnight, I swear."

"Fine, but you have to keep ordering stuff from me."

He purses his lips. "Let me see the menu."

I hand it to him and turn on the overhead light. His eyes scan up and down. "I'll have the Veggie Delight, no bell peppers."

"It doesn't come with bell peppers, sir. Just mushrooms, tomatoes, and spinach."

He grins. "Good job."

I grin, too. "Okay, one more order and then we'll celebrate."

"I want the, uh . . . Black Bean Benedict, please. With the sauce on the side." I can tell by his expression that he would never in a million years order this, which is hard not to find charming.

His order stumps me, though. I have no idea what sauce he's talking about. "Uh, okay."

"You're faking it, I can tell. What'd you forget?"

"The sauce."

"It's chipotle hollandaise sauce, whatever that is."

I sigh. Hollandaise sauce? Might as well be blueberry ketchup for all I know. It makes me feel better that Arden doesn't know what it is either. "I'm going to screw this up."

"No, you're not. It's not even your first day. Geez, calm down. It's probably just a fancy word for ranch or something."

"It's not just that," I say, aware that my voice has now grown whiny. "How can I recommend any of the menu items if I've never had it before? And I can't afford to have it, even with my employee discount."

"You're overthinking this. And you're sitting on my slingshot."

"What?" I feel around under me and sure enough, there is a small metal slingshot with rubber tubing. "Why do you have a sling-shot?"

"For these," he points down to the pile of Black Cats in his lap. "We're going hunting."

"We definitely are not going hunting," I say with finality. I only eat animals out of the package.

"Well, we're going terrorizing then. To the skate park first, then we'll swing by Mayor Busch's house to see if he's home. Here, let me show you how to do it."

I'm terrified to find out what "it" is exactly. Especially when it sounds like Mayor Busch is one of our "targets." And I'm pretty sure targeting a public official is a felony. I lick lips shriveled dry. "Remind me what we have against the mayor?"

"He's a friend of my dad."

"Nope. Not a good enough reason." Not by a long shot. I get it; Arden has no love for his dad. But me? I've learned enough about him through Julio to have a hearty respect for him, even if I've never met him. Julio says he's to be feared—so I definitely fear him.

Arden smirks. "So we need a reason to terrorize people?"

"If we don't, then we're just jerks like that guy at Destin Commons."

He laughs. "Well, it just so happens that Mayor Busch is nothing less than a douche."

"You're just saying that to make me feel better about whatever it is you've concocted tonight."

"No, I'm serious. When I went in to talk to Miss May, he was eating breakfast there. She says he comes in every single day, runs the waitresses ragged, then leaves two quarters on the table as the tip."

It sounds legit, but I scrutinize his face in the moonlight. He seems sincere. Slowly, I nod. "You're right. He sounds douche-y."

"So here's what we're gonna do."

I watch in horror as this lunatic rolls down his window, places a Black Cat in the slingshot, lights the firecracker, waits a second for the fuse to burn, then shoots it out the window and into the woods. It explodes before it hits the ground, the glow of which illuminates a nearby fern. It dies out on the ground in an unimpressive string of orange ash.

"Oh, no way, I'm not doing that," I say, taking the slingshot from him and testing the weight of it in my hand. I roll down my window without realizing it. Then I pull back on the slingshot and pretend to aim at something in my side of the woods.

Arden hands me a Black Cat. "After you light it, count to three, then shoot it."

"What if I wait too long?"

"Just going out on a limb here, Carly, but I think it will actually explode in your hand."

I take in a deep breath. I don't want to do this at all, but at the same time, I want to do it so much that my hands are almost shaking. "Give me the lighter."

I watch the flame dance for a second, then let it go out.

"Just do it," Arden says, as if auditioning for a peer pressure commercial.

I strike the lighter again and, without letting myself think about it, hold the fuse to the flame until it ignites.

One.

Two.

Three.

The slingshot snaps in my hand, startling me. The Black Cat hits the inside of the door and bounces down, glowing on the floorboard between my legs. It makes a sizzling sound that resonates all the way down to my stomach. "Oh no!" I scream, throwing myself across the truck cabin into Arden's ready-but-surprised arms.

Crack!

I squeeze my eyes shut, expecting pain on my legs or my ankle, a burning sensation bleeding through my jeans. But it doesn't come. Slowly, I open my eyes and they bring into focus Arden's amused face—about an inch away from mine.

"So, next time," he drawls, "you'll want to aim outside of the truck."

It's the first time I've ever noticed how Arden smells, and I don't know why I'm disappointed to find that he smells excessively good. Excessively male. Mortified with my new line of thought, I disentangle myself from him and reclaim my seat, trying to keep my feet lifted up in case the Black Cat has any spark left. The smell of smoke wafts up at me from the floor board, tickling my nose.

And that's when I laugh. So hard that my stomach aches and my breath comes in wheezy gulps. Soon Arden is bent over the steering wheel gasping for breath himself. Even when it isn't funny anymore, it's still funny.

I pick up the slingshot again. "Let's go to town. But not to the skate park. Only Mayor Douche's house."

Arden puts the truck into drive.

Fourteen

Arden pulls into his uncle's driveway, knowing he won't be awake at the ungodly hour of seven o'clock in the morning. He probably won't even remember that Arden promised to come over today to help out with the hedges and the driveway. Arden doubts Cletus will wake up before it's time to pick up Carly from her first day of work.

He takes a big swig of the to-go coffee Miss May made him when he dropped off Carly just an hour before. Miss May had put him on the spot, asking if he liked it black, and he'd felt obligated to say yes, because black sounds more manly than the concoction of cream and sugar he prefers, and she'd asked in front of Carly.

And for some reason he still can't explain, he'd felt the need to appear manly at that moment in his life.

His cell phone rings then, and he's satisfied that the ring tone is sufficiently masculine. "Hey, Mom, what's up?"

There's a pause on the other end, and Arden wonders if it's a faulty signal or if his mom's meds are slowing down her response time. "Arden, sweetie, are you going into town today?"

"I can. If you need something."

Another lapse. She sniffs. "Do you mind running to the drug-store and picking up my prescriptions?" She must be having a bad day. She's probably calling him from Amber's room. She always goes in there when she runs out of pills; it's like she starts thawing into a live human being again, capable of emotion and memory and even genuine affection. But mostly just grief.

"Sure, Mom. You need anything else? You can ride with me to town, if you want. Get in a little sunshine?" He doesn't offer this option often enough, he knows. She needs to get out of the house. Out of her pajamas and into some real clothes.

"Well, that sounds nice, honey, but today is laundry day."

Laundry day. Arden does his own laundry, and his dad's uni-forms are washed, starched, and pressed for him by the county. She might have a load of towels to tend to, at most. "You sure? We could have lunch at Doris's. I'll buy you a slice of pie." He regrets it as soon as he says it. Amber used to love the coconut cream pie at Doris's. He knows that's what's going through his mother's head right now.

He listens for her reaction, but is met with several long seconds of vacant silence. Then he hears her sniffle. "No thanks, honey. I think I'll stay in today." She hangs up.

Dammit.

He considers ditching Cletus and going to get the meds now, so she can slip back into her emotionless chasm. It's the right thing to do, he tells himself. But his hands won't start the truck. Because Amber deserves to be grieved by her mother, even if it is in bits and pieces here and there, small moments of memories that can't be stolen away by some powerful drug. And his mother deserves the healing power of grief.

He gets out of the truck, leaving his cell phone on the seat.

Arden lets himself in the back door to his uncle's house, careful not to make too much noise while still doubting that any amount of clamor would wake a slumbering, hungover Cletus. Even from the Florida room in the back, he can hear his uncle's snores resonate from the ballroom.

Arden finds the keys to the massive shed in the backyard and sets out to find a pair of trimmers. Of course, he finds them in the very back of the huge wood building, and has to dig them out of a pile of yard tools probably not used since the 1980s. The dust he stirs up reminds him of the smoke in his truck cabin last night after Carly took aim at the passenger door with the slingshot.

The corners of his mouth draw up in an involuntary smile. He remembers the sheer delight on her face when her first attempt at Mayor Busch's house resulted in a dead-on shot of what Arden knows to be his bedroom window. The crack of the explosion was so loud that Carly let out a little surprised scream and Arden had to pull over to keep from wrecking them, he was laughing so hard.

"Crazy girl," Arden says under his breath. He throws the trimmers over his shoulder and makes his way toward the front driveway. He'll never get all of them done before he has to go back and get Carly, but he figures he can come here on the weekend while she's at work and . . . He stops in his tracks.

Am I working around a girl's *schedule?*

No, he decides adamantly. He's working around a *friend's* schedule. That's completely different. Carly is a girl, sure, but she's not that kind of girl. She's not, like, date-able or anything. (Of course, he felt the exact opposite when he found her in his lap last night and her lips were *this close* to touching his.) *No no no.* She's his accomplice. And he can tell he's already got her hooked on raising Cain.

Hours come and go and Arden's shirt is soaked through with sweat and dirt and whatever kind of powdery fungus is growing on the azalea bushes in the driveway. He was able to get the right side done; next weekend he'll come back and do the left. Right now though, he has to run home and get a shower before he picks up Carly.

He scowls. *What do I care if she sees me all gross and grimy?* He wouldn't care if Luke saw him like this. *Hell, I'd probably pull him into a headlock so he could get the full sense of my noxious pits.*

"I figured out it was you," a voice comes from behind him as he's lowering the trimmers.

Arden turns to face Cletus. The old man is wearing house slippers, faded jeans, and a wrinkled T-shirt; all look clean. His white hair is wet and combed back, as if he'd just showered. Arden tries to calculate the odds of that scenario. "Well, it's not like I was hiding out here. What are you doing awake, anyway?"

Cletus scowls. "I'm talking about the store, boy. It was you. Wasn't it?"

Arden wastes no time on regret. His uncle might be humiliated, but at least he's not in the morgue—and at least no one else is as a result of that night, either. "It was me."

Cletus nods, tucking his thumbs into his jeans pocket. "That rifle was your dad's from three Christmases ago. He never uses it."

This is true. Arden thought it a pretty good idea to use his dad's own rifle in case any shots were fired—not that there were going to be shots fired, it wouldn't have come to that—then the casings would match a gun registered to the one and only Sheriff Moss. "It was his."

This confirms what Cletus already knows. He seems relieved to have gotten a confession so easily. "I got up today to come pay you a visit. To have a little chat about . . . about what happened."

Arden understands perfectly. His uncle is embarrassed. Wants to keep it between them. He shrugs. "Nothing happened."

Cletus nods again, rocking back on his slippered heels. He clears his throat. "Well. Now that we got that all settled . . . You want some breakfast? I can cook up some eggs and bacon real fast."

Arden positions the trimmers between his legs to keep them steady, then peels off his drenched T-shirt. Wringing it out in the sand beside him, he says, "I would, but I've got to pick up Carly from work."

Cletus's eyes light up. "Carly from the Breeze Mart?" Then his eyes narrow to near slits. "Why are you picking her up from work? Boy, you'd better return that bicycle to her—"

"I already did. She needs a ride because it's too far to ride her bike."

"What do you mean?"

Arden wipes the sweat and dirt from his arms. "I mean I got her a job at Uppity Rooster as a waitress. She's working the morning shift today. I've got to go shower before I pick her up."

Cletus is all mean mugging and evil eye. "What business is it of yours where that girl works? Now, boy, you'd better not be trying to—"

"We're friends," Arden says quickly. When Cletus gets too

excited, his hands start to shake. Right now they shudder like a washing machine on spin cycle. It's the beginnings of a massive tantrum, Arden can tell. "I'm just trying to make up for scaring her to death is all."

"Like you're doing to me?"

"I'm just trying to help you out."

"Did I ask for your help, boy?"

Arden gives a hard laugh. "You didn't have to. Anyone with eyeballs can see how badly you needed these trimmed. I brought the dragger from the baseball field too, to flatten out the driveway. I'll drive up and down it a couple times."

Cletus thinks on this, pushing out his stubborn bottom lip, his gaze resting over Arden's shoulder, on the dirt road stretched before him. "I suppose that'd be okay." Then he snaps back to attention and pushes his index finger into Arden's chest. His breath smells like mint instead of the deep end of a whiskey bottle. This whole coming-to-Jesus meeting with Arden he'd intended this morning must have been important to him. "But let's get something straight right here right now, boy. You're to stay away from Carly Vega. She ain't got nothing you're interested in."

"And how would you know what interests me?" Sure, she's not his "type" or whatever. He usually goes for blondes with legs that stretch across centuries. Not petite Latina chicks whose hobby seems to be putting him in his place.

Arden is disgusted with himself for categorizing Carly as a type at all. *She's not a type, she's my wingman.* However cheesy that may sound.

"I talk to your mama, son," Cletus drawls. "She tells me what you do—and what you don't do. Carly's a good girl. Hard worker.

She's not interested in wasting her time with clowns and their shenanigans."

Arden wants to correct him. To tell him that until midnight last night, she acted a clown herself, shooting firecrackers out of the passenger seat of his truck. At the mayor's house, no less. Of course, her aim left something to be desired, so usually stop signs and bushes and sidewalks were her main victims, but the point is, she loved every second of it.

In fact, Arden would venture to say that Carly Vega—underneath all that do-gooder exterior and overachiever shell—is a closet fan of nonsense.

But Arden doesn't say anything. It's not his place to correct Cletus, and what's more, it's not worth arguing with the old man. He'd just accuse Arden of tainting Carly or something else along those frayed, eccentric lines.

"You sure didn't mind this *clown* coming to help you with your hedges today," Arden says, picking up pace with his uncle on their way back to the house.

"And I wouldn't mind if you brought your whole circus of friends back to help, either. This place could use some attention, you know."

Arden scowls. This place could use more than attention. It could use an overhaul. But instead of trying to persuade his friends to come over and work, Arden has a better idea. "How about I come by on the weekends and pick up some projects around here? Your fence in the back wouldn't stop a toddler from getting in and your barn needs to be organized something fierce. And when's the last time you had the house cleaned? It's starting to smell like you, old man."

Cletus wrinkles his nose. "You ain't too old to take a belt to, boy."

Arden grins. "I'll be back Saturday morning to finish those hedges. Then I'll start on the fence in the backyard." It all works out perfectly. He'll drop Carly off at work on Saturdays and Sundays and then come help Cletus with things around the house. That will keep his mind off his new accomplice.

Wait, what?

"I don't need your charity," Cletus is saying unconvincingly.

"No, but your fence does."

Cletus hesitates a moment, scrutinizing Arden. Then he spits on the ground. "She's already rubbing off on you, boy. Since when were you ever interested in hard work?"

"Since it's become obvious you're actually going to let my aunt Dorothy's house fall into shambles."

This shuts up the old man, as it should. It's not just his house; it never has been. This estate was the pride and joy of Aunt Dorothy. There was never a minute of the day that she wasn't doing something to improve it or beautify it, and never a weekend went by without guests at her dinner table. Cletus knows it. Arden knows it.

"Fine. You come by on the weekends. But I don't want your charity. I'll pay you for your work."

"I didn't ask to get paid." As it is, Arden's ashamed of himself for letting it get this bad in the first place. He can only imagine the look of disappointment he'd get from his aunt. She'd always thought the world of him. She'd never say anything, she just wasn't like that, but he'd see it in her eyes that he'd let her down. She was really good at the pretty-Southern-belle-disenchantment pout.

Plus Arden knows his uncle isn't capable of keeping up with these sorts of things anymore. He'd never say it out loud, because stubborn makes up part of his bloodstream—the part that isn't alcohol.

"You didn't ask, so that's why I'm paying you. And anyway, it would tickle your pa's temper to see you making money instead of asking him for it all the time. You wouldn't have to go to him for anything. Especially if I'm the one paying you. That's worth it all by itself." This is true. The great Sheriff Moss has always been opposed to Arden picking up a job. He'd always assumed it was because his father wanted him to play sports, make good grades, get into FSU. But Cletus just made him realize it's more than just that. It's exactly what Arden has been trying so hard not to relinquish to anyone.

His freedom.

If I had a job, I wouldn't have to go to him for anything.

Arden hasn't played sports or made good grades since Amber died. He hasn't resembled a good son since then. Yet, his father still leaves money on the kitchen counter for him every Sunday night. Before, he was glad to relieve his old man of some cash and blow it on whatever he wants. He thought that was hurting his father somehow, to waste his money on frivolous things. Now he realizes what it really is. Taking his dad's money doesn't hurt his dad, it hurts himself. *It's a way of controlling me. Of making sure I'm dependent on him. So he can say he did all he could for me. Just like he did with Amber.*

Materially, Amber had it all. A new car that she never got to drive, new clothes, new laptop whenever she asked. But Amber never had her father. Not after he found out she was schizophrenic. Not after he realized she didn't fit in with the "normal family" image he was trying to maintain because God forbid the county sheriff should have mental illness running in his blood, sleeping in his own house. Election years were the worst. He kept Amber on a short leash, sometimes locking her in her room for days at a time. Never letting her go out in public, lest potential voters get a chance to see her talking to herself. From the minute their father found out she was ill, she was homeschooled. Cut off from her friends. Cut off from the world except through television and the Internet and whatever news Arden could tell her from school. He even stopped letting her come to Arden's football games—something she loved dearly.

Amber was alive but not living.

Arden's mother didn't like it, thought it was a bit extreme, but she never disagreed. Never stood up for her daughter. Nope. What Dwayne Moss said was law. Period.

After Amber died, his mother was torn to pieces. At first, Arden was glad. He thought his mom deserved the torment. To be a rag doll with few signs of life except for lung capacity and a beating heart. But then he realized she was a victim too. She wouldn't eat, wouldn't sleep, would hardly talk. She needed help, Arden knew, just like Amber did, but Dwayne Moss was too prideful to let his wife actually see a therapist. So she got pills from the family doctor—a good ol' boy who would refill the prescriptions without requiring something so inconvenient as regular visits. With Sheriff Moss, it's all about appearances. Which is why his father went on with his life without much outward remorse, or really any kind of reaction, about his daughter's death. In fact, he actually blamed *Amber* for what she did in the end.

That's what happens when you're not content with your lot in life, he'd said. *We did all we could for her.*

Arden had wanted to kill him.

"You're right," Arden says, unballing fists he didn't realize he'd clenched. "It would make him mad if I got a job."

Cletus scratches his belly, nodding. "It would gall the hell outta him, I'd say. Getting paid cash under the table, not paying your taxes on it. How could he explain that to his precious voters?"

Arden laughs. "He'd say I was working for free. That you didn't pay anything. That he always paid for everything I needed."

"Guess I'd better write you a check then." The mischievous glint in his uncle's eyes says it's a done deal. Arden would work here on the weekends while Carly worked at the café. Uncle Cletus would pay him under the table. Arden would no longer accept money from his dad. He and Carly could turn the county upside down with their reverie.

Life just got perfect.

Fifteen

Life sucks.

At least, it sucks when your feet feel like anvils in your nonslip work shoes. And the swelling. Oh my God, the swelling.

As soon as I'm done closing down my tables—filling up the salt, pepper, sweeteners, and jellies—I sit down at the last one and hoist my feet onto the closest chair. I wanted to untie my shoes and rub my feet, but I hold back for a couple of reasons. For one, I know they stink like hot dog water, and two, my trainer is making her way over to me. My only hope at this moment is that I don't have anything else to do before I leave, because I don't think my new blisters can take it. Plus, I know Arden is in the parking lot waiting for me; he revved his engine as soon as he got here. Must be some weird sort of redneck communication.

Darcy, my trainer, sits beside me at the table and pulls out a bundle of neatly folded cash from her apron pocket. She starts counting aloud and stacking the bills by denomination. When she gets to two hundred dollars I start getting really excited. Then she counts the ones. Together we earned two hundred seventy-five dollars in six hours.

I think I might pass out. She gives me my half. "You earned it," she says. "I've never seen someone move so fast in my life. When you're fully trained, you'll be pulling this all by yourself. I don't know what I would have done with that family from Spain. Thank God you can speak Spanish."

But all I'm thinking is that I could score almost three hundred dollars in six hours selling fancy breakfast to fancy people. "When do you think I'll be ready to be on my own?"

Darcy tilts her head at me. "Tell you what. Learn the menu this week, and when your Saturday shift rolls around, I'll let you have a few tables on your own. But I'll be here if you need me. Trust me, I want you to stay. You're way better a worker than Rose was. We'll get you trained as fast as we can."

Apparently I've replaced this Rose person, who is currently in jail—but for what, nobody knows. She had a lot of regulars though, so I have a lot of kissing up to do in order to turn her regulars into my regulars.

"Pretty soon you and I will be working on ups and making a killing," Darcy says.

"Ups?"

"Yeah, where we just take turns taking tables. Me, you, me, then you again. It's way better than having a section of tables. And with the way you work, Miss May won't have to hire anyone else to take up our slack. Just don't quit on me. I know it's hard."

It is hard. Today was the hardest I've ever worked in my life. The Breeze Mart is just exactly that—a breeze. But I don't mind working for my money. My feet though? They freaking hate it.

"I won't quit," I tell her. "But if I'm finished here, my ride is waiting for me. Unless you have something else for me to do?"

Darcy slides my pile of cash toward me on the table. "Nope. You're done. See you next week."

When I get in the truck, I try not to act as giddy as I feel. Arden can tell I'm holding out though. "So it went well, I take it?" he says. I'm surprised, and disappointed, that I notice how he smells again. Like he just showered with man-soap or something. And maybe he did. His hair is a little damp.

"Very." I don't want to tell him how much I made though, in case he's not impressed. He probably gets that much for his allowance. "All I need to do is memorize the menu before Saturday and I can work my own tables. Darcy—she's the waitress who trained me—said I'm a natural people person."

Arden laughs. "That's what we Southerners call sarcasm."

I lift my chin. "I am a Southerner, idiot. And just because I'm not an Arden person doesn't mean I'm not a people person."

"Touché. But for the record, most people are Arden people. So it could be considered a flaw that you're not."

"I don't fall for the mob mentality."

"Believe me, I've noticed." He shrugs. "I went to Cletus's house to help him out with a few things. Nothing much."

"How is he?" I haven't seen Mr. Shackleford since the faux robbery. Maybe he'll come in tonight and give me another Question of the Day. *Ugh. I have to work tonight.* On these same throbbing feet. At least I have a stool to sit on at the Breeze.

"He's fine," Arden says generically.

"You told him, didn't you?"

"He figured it out on his own, actually." Arden grimaces, as if he'd eaten something bitter. "He took it well, though."

"By making you work it off?"

"He's paying me. I figure if you're working on the weekends, then I should too."

Huh? What, are we married? "What does my working have to do with you working?"

He shrugs, uncomfortable with the turn in conversation. He jerks the steering wheel hard right, as if he was about to miss his turn. That's when it occurs to me that we're not heading in the direction of my house.

"Where are we going? I have to work at the Breeze tonight."

"How much money did you make today, if you don't mind me asking?"

When I raise a brow, he amends, "I mean, did you make more than you do at the Breeze Mart? Oh, don't give me that look. I'm just asking if you think you could quit the Breeze Mart and only work at the Uppity Rooster. Then you'd have your weeknights off. You know, to do homework or, uh, fun stuff."

Fun stuff. He's still going after this whole accomplice thing. Not that last night wasn't a complete riot. I can't remember laughing so hard in my life, not even when that kid dug his hand around in our shitty purse. But fun is not the important thing here. Getting my parents home is.

"I need both jobs," I say with more harshness than I intend.

Arden is undeterred. "I thought you might say that. But you're going to work yourself to death with two jobs and school and then I'd feel rotten for putting it into your head. Couldn't you just cut down on your hours at the convenience store instead of quitting cold turkey? Maybe just work two nights a week or something?"

For once in his life, Arden has a point. Working two jobs and school will be exhausting. My grades might start to slip. And I just can't let myself be okay with that. Besides, with all the money I'll be making at Uppity Rooster, why shouldn't I give myself a break? *Because our parents are counting on us*, I can hear Julio say in his sternest voice. *Don't you want your parents back?*

Of course I do.

"We need the money," I say decisively. "Cutting my hours is not an option."

Arden squeezes the steering wheel tighter. I can tell he's trying to be diplomatic with me. "But what about you? What about what you need? I see how hard you work at school. That's going to suffer, you know."

"You just want me to give up my shifts at the Breeze so I can spend those nights with you." I fold up my apron and nestle it between my legs so the precious money doesn't spill out and so Arden might focus on my hands instead of the blush I feel burning my face.

So I can spend those nights with you.

Idiota.

He grins as if he knows I just freaked out my own self. "There's more to life than working and school."

Life. What an abstract concept that's become. Life is something I've put off until my parents get back. Life is something other kids have the luxury to worry about. It's not something I should give a second thought to, not until my parents are on US soil again.

Right?

"Look, I'm sorry. I don't mean to pressure you. I'll take you home. You need some rest if you're really going to work tonight."

Then I remember that tonight we're getting in a big shipment, which translates to endless boxes that will need stocking, and suddenly the thought of working at the Breeze is less appealing than walking across a floor made of cactus. I'm not even sure my feet could handle it. Heavy lifting. Standing on my tiptoes. Ew. "Maybe I'll call in," I'm saying out loud. "I could use a good foot soak." A foot soak? When have I ever needed a foot soak? I don't even have anything to soak my feet in, except maybe a bathtub full of shampoo bubbles or something.

"You know, the creek is the perfect place to soak your feet."

"And to do what else?"

"Fish, of course. I happen to need some fish. You know. For something."

I can't help but smile. What will he think of next? The truth is, I like spending time with Arden. It's fun. Liberating, to an extent. I feel like a different person around him—in a good way. I feel a rush of freedom. Which sucks, because that means that normally, I must not feel free.

Arden seems to read my mind. "It's just that you act like Julio's slave or something. Like you're not allowed to enjoy life. It seems unfair."

It is unfair, I want to tell him. But not because I'm Julio's slave. No, because I slave for my parents. Here in the States, it's the other way around. Parents sweat and grind for their children. They labor for their education, for them to have nice things, for them to be protected from the world's darker side, like hunger and violence and disease. Here in the States, kids are spoiled.

My parents? They slave to come over here, in order to slave for . . . I'm not exactly sure. A better life for my siblings, probably. Not me, I know. I'm already sixteen. A junior in high school, probably a senior by the time they get back. They expect me to take care of myself when they get here. Mama has made that clear. That she has two younger children to raise and that she needs my help more than I need hers. And that's okay with me, really it is. I'm proud to make such a contribution to my family. I want my younger brother and sister to be raised in America, even though Americans can be such snobs. I mean, if Canada offered better living conditions and more money and opportunity, wouldn't Americans be sneaking their family across the Canadian border? I'd bet money they would.

But people just don't understand, especially in these parts. They complain that Mexicans take their jobs and their money and their government benefits.

But I'm not about to lay this on Arden. All Arden knows is freedom. The American way.

And I'd be a liar if I said I wasn't jealous.

"Julio does the best he can," I tell him. It's all I can say. Giving him a speech about poverty and responsibility and family ties would spoil the mood of me making killer money today.

"Can I at least offer some advice?"

Oh here we go. "Sure."

"Give it two weeks. I'll bet after two weeks, you'll be ready to quit the Breeze Mart."

"I'm sure I will. But I can't."

"Oh, come on, Carly. You can't carry the world on your shoulders. If, after two weeks, you're too tired, then promise me you'll quit the Breeze Mart. What have you got to lose? Minimum wage? Just ask to open and close on Saturday and Sunday at Uppity Rooster. You'll make up for your puny minimum wage easy."

"You're just saying these things because you want me to go with you on little mini–crime sprees."

"So?"

"So, what am I gaining by quitting one job only to go around stirring up trouble with you?"

He pulls over on the side of the road. Puts the truck in park. Puts his arm on the back of my seat. It's not intimate, the way he does it. But somehow I find it endearing. Oh geez.

"Life, Carly. You're gaining life."

What can I say to that?

❧·❧

Julio is like Mama; he only speaks to me in Spanish. "How did your day go?" he says, flipping the chicken and cheese quesadilla he's making in the skillet. I sit at the counter on a bar stool, hovering over a jar of homemade salsa Julio made, trying not to actually drool.

"It was great." This is the part I've been waiting for. This is the kind of cash I hand Julio after a week of work. Not one day. "Look what I've brought you." When I've got his full attention, I pull the clump of cash from my apron pocket and let it splay out on the sideboard in front of me. "This is all for the jar." Okay, so I kept five bucks for myself, but Julio will never know the difference.

His eyes grow as round as the quesadillas he's cooking. "What is this?" He says this as he gathers it up and starts arranging it by denomination. Licking his finger, he counts through it. *"Ay, Dios mio,"* he says. "I can't believe it. Where did you get this?"

I can't help but beam. Finally, Julio is happy with what I've given him. I know my paychecks from the Breeze probably look dreary compared to what he makes at his construction job. But not this. This is comparable, if anything. This is impressive. It's all over his face.

"I started working at the Uppity Rooster. Breakfast shifts on the weekends. I didn't want to say anything until I knew it would work out," I tell him proudly. "Plus I'll get a paycheck in two weeks for the hourly wage. This is just tips."

"Either you're a good waitress, sister, or those rich people feel sorry for you." So he's heard of the Uppity Rooster. And he knows what kind of place it is. There are tears welling up in his eyes. He's relieved. Relieved that I'm finally pulling my own weight.

Which makes me feel like a molecule.

"Imagine how much you can make with both jobs," he says. "You'll be up there with me, no?"

And that's when the guilt settles in and becomes a part of me.

I am smaller than a molecule. A molecule is twice my size.

Because I'm toying with the idea of cutting my shifts at the Breeze. The truth is, I'm tired. In the six hours I worked today I think I must have walked twenty miles. And how tired will I be after working six nights a week and two twenty-mile morning shifts on the weekends plus school?

Then I think of how tired Julio must be. And how he never mentions it.

Julio sees my hesitation and scowls. "You know Papi and Mama are counting on us. They need our help, Carlotta. This new job is great. But we need the income from the Breeze Mart too."

"I know that. Did I say anything?"

"Your face does not hide things very well, little sister."

"I just thought that with the cash I can bring in at the restaurant, maybe I can cut some shifts at the Breeze Mart."

With deliberation, Julio pulls down two plates from the cabinet and sets one in front of him and one in front of me. He eases half the contents of the skillet onto each plate, then makes work of unscrewing the salsa jar. Julio is gearing up to be political with me.

He picks up a red pepper—probably from Señora Perez's miniscule garden—and a cutting board. Methodically, he begins to slice it into columns, then squares. "You're growing into a beautiful young woman. You are making money." He eyes the cash on the counter. "Good money." With the knife, he corrals the massacred pepper into a pile on the cutting board. "With money comes a certain amount of independence. I understand that." He divides the peppers between us, even though he knows I don't like them. "You're a good girl, Carlotta. A smart girl. I know it seems like we're asking much from you right now. Mama and Papi will be so proud of you."

It stings, the words "will be." Because it means that right now, they aren't. Despite everything. I wonder what the conversations between Julio and Mama are like. I wonder if they talk about me, how lazy I am. What an underachiever I am. I wonder what Julio truly thinks of me. He never put much stock in school—only work. He's worked full-time hours since the age of fifteen, and taken care of me since our parents got deported three years ago. He was only seventeen at the time, and taking care of someone else.

I wonder if Julio is jealous that I only have myself to worry about. That he didn't have anyone to look after him when he was my age.

Julio is the oldest twenty-year-old on the planet.

And looks at me with chastising eyes. "Think, Carlotta. Think if the tables were turned. Don't you think Mama and Papi would do everything they could to get us over here? Do you think they'd be talking about cutting their shifts at work?"

Of course they wouldn't. They want our family to be together. And don't I want that? Or do I? Guilt pillages through my insides. It's not whether or not I want us to be together. I do. It's at what cost, that's the thing. "They wouldn't cut shifts," I concede. But I'm angry. I want to rebel against his reasoning, no matter how sound it is. "Maybe it would help if I knew how far off we were. How much do we owe *El Libertador*? How much longer do I need to work like this?" I don't expect him to answer. I don't. But his body language, the way he moves with deliberate ease? It makes me realize he's going to give me an explanation. And I'm not sure I'm ready for it.

The only thing I'm sure of is that I want my parents back. I want them here, with us.

Julio walks to the sink and turns the faucet on, holding the knife under the running water for a long time. He opens the drawer in front of him and pulls out a coffee filter—we use them for everything, since they're cheaper than paper towels—and wipes the knife dry. After setting the knife down, he turns to face me, palms on the sink behind him. Slowly, he nods. "Mama says we shouldn't tell you how much. That it would only stress you. But I think differently. I think that if we are asking these things of you, then, yes, Carlotta, I think you have the right to ask how much. And I think you can handle much more than Mama realizes."

I hold my breath. Maybe I can't handle more. What if this number, this ransom we owe *El Libertador* to bring my parents back, is so huge that it's unattainable? It would mean that I'm trapped. It would mean that this small morsel of freedom I've had with Arden these past few days has just been a cruel tease. It would mean that living life, actually *living* it, is a pastime enjoyed only by those whose lives are not indentured by the need for money.

I am an American. And yet I am a slave.

"How much?" I choke out.

"*El Libertador* requires fifteen thousand US dollars for each person he smuggles across the border." Julio says this as if he's talking about the number of cracks in the ceiling or the variety of scuffs on our linoleum floor. He even shrugs a little, as if the blast radius of the bomb he just dropped wasn't catastrophic.

Mama. Papi. My brother and sister.

Sixty thousand dollars.

I swallow. Once. Twice. But the bile slides up and down my throat like an enraged serpent. I try to translate sixty thousand dollars into shifts worked at the Uppity Rooster and Breeze Mart but my brain won't do the math.

"Was I wrong?" Julio says softly. "Was I wrong to tell you? That price includes getting them across the desert, you know."

I shake my head and brace my forearms on the counter in front of me. I wonder whether this sideboard can hold me up, what with this new weight of the world on my shoulders. "How . . . How much do we already have saved?"

At this, Julio perks up. "We have nearly fifty thousand saved, *bonita*. You see how much progress we've already made?" There is a flash of pride in his eyes, and why shouldn't there be? He's the reason we've got even that saved up. I'm impressed. My Breeze Mart checks hardly buy groceries each week. And that's stretching each deflated dollar to its death.

Plus, we send money home every week. So all of that savings came from Julio. He is the true slave.

Julio seems relieved to have shared this with me. As if by sharing the information, the actual accounting of it, he's also sharing the burden of responsibility. This should feel like a privilege and I know it. Julio has deemed me fit to speak about adult things with him. He's truly making us a team, instead of just saying it all the time. He's bringing me into the proverbial loop. I should see it as an opportunity to prove myself.

But all I see is how much work it will be, how much work it's already been.

And I don't know how much longer I can do this.

But my family is worth the sacrifice.

Sixteen

Arden slips into his seat in social studies and tries not to look at Carly, who is already doing a fantastic job of pretending that he doesn't exist. He's come to accept this weird relationship of theirs, that they aren't to acknowledge each other in school. She claims to not want the attention, and he can't help but feel relieved at that. The more questions people ask him about their relationship, the more questions he would have to ask himself.

Because the truth of the matter is, he's not sure what it all means yet. Or if it means anything more than the sum of the parts: They hang out. They cause trouble. They laugh while doing it.

Still, he can't ignore that these past few weeks he's felt like he's been having an affair with life. He thought he'd been truly living before Carly Vega. He thought Amber's death had scared life into him, had stirred up the need to do more than just exist. But he's coming to realize that life can be lived in fractions and he has been portioning some of it out to merely existing after all, despite his best intentions.

All those nights riding around in the police car with Deputy Glass, when the conversation fell quiet and so did the incoming calls. Staring out the window as Glass drove round after round throughout town. He would have called that living; it was rare, something only an insomniac had the pleasure of seeing, the world at rest. At peace with itself.

Even when he'd devised his own entertainment, the fun was lacking by exactly half. He just didn't know it at the time. But now he does. And he can't stop thinking about why.

And he can't stop thinking about why it even matters, but the answer whispers back at him almost immediately: *Because what if you lose this too?*

He pushes the thought aside, all thoughts in fact, until class is over and he can finally align himself with Carly in the hallway and pretend not to be talking to her. She stops at her locker to shift books and folders around, which is her version of appearing too busy to notice him.

She opens her locker and proceeds to shuffle the contents in an almost predictable way. He leans against the locker to her left. "Is this even necessary anymore?" he says, keeping his voice low. "Everyone thinks we're a couple. Maybe we should act like one. Then all the mystery and curiosity is gone and they'll eventually stop talking about it. *Poof.* No more attention. Isn't that what you want?"

Carly raises a well-defined brow at him, briefly giving him the pleasure of looking directly into her mischievous eyes. "If they thought we were actually a couple, they'd feel obligated to talk to me and invite me to their stupid parties and sit at their secret society table at lunch. *Poof.* Ten times the attention. You'd put me through that?"

Yes, in a heartbeat, if it meant his friends would stop wondering if Carly Vega is taken or not. *Is this what a crush feels like?* "I don't even go to their parties anymore. And I don't eat lunch here, remember?" He still drives to Taco City, even though he'd stay and eat the palatably challenged cafeteria food if she asked him to.

But she never does.

"How can I forget that you waste five bucks a day on lunch?"

"Three ninety-nine. The special is three dollars and ninety-nine cents. Geez."

"Speaking of three ninety-nine," she says, slamming the locker shut. A brilliant smile shimmers across her face. "Are we still on for this afternoon?" Arden can't help but smile himself. He promised to take her to Best Buy in Destin. She'd finally skimmed enough cream off the top of her tips to buy a laptop—without Julio ever questioning where the money had gone. Now she won't need to borrow the school's laptop anymore—something Arden knows means a lot to her.

"Are we ever off?"

She scowls. "Maybe I shouldn't do this. I shouldn't hide things from Julio."

Arden rolls his eyes. Little hypocrite. She's already hiding the fact that she cut her shifts at the Breeze Mart. "Really? You think now's the time to grow a conscience? Besides, you've given him enough freaking money to buy a Lamborghini. Oh, I know," he says, waving his hand at her. "You don't want to talk about what he's doing with it." He covers her mouth with his hand, to prevent the usual *well-it's-not-your-business* remark, which she says with a stinging effortlessness. It's true, it's not his business, but who likes hearing that? And especially in the way she says it? All hoity-toity.

His reflexive action earns them some knowing glances in the hall, and another scowl from Carly. He steps away from her then, shoving the offending hand in his jeans pocket. "Oh God, I'd better go. I think someone's pulling a party invitation out of their pocket and we can't have that now, can we?"

He nearly breaks into a run to get away from her, and behind him he can hear her giggling in his wake. And he decides it's one of his favorite sounds.

∽·∽

Arden pulls the truck around to the front of Best Buy to pick up a beaming Carly. The box she's holding barely fits in her arms, but when she passes it to him across the seat of his truck so she can get in, he decides it's full of cotton balls instead of the latest and greatest technology. "Um, is the laptop in here?"

Her eyes actually sparkle. "I know, right? It's supposed to be the lightest model. It will fit almost anywhere in my room, and Julio won't have to know. He can keep using the old junky school computer and I can have this all to myself."

She slams the door, something Arden has asked her not to do time and again. But this time she's all apologetic. "Sorry," she says. "I'm just excited is all." And he believes her.

But before he becomes enchanted for the rest of the darkening afternoon, he has a phone call to make. He pulls into a parking spot and gives Carly a humor-me look as he dials his cell phone.

"Gulf Coast Florals" is the answer he receives.

"Hello, this is Clarence Barnes. I'd like to send a dozen roses to my sweetheart, Sherry Moss."

There's a long pause on the other end. Then, "The last time she received these from you, sir, she said she didn't know who you were. Said she couldn't accept them ever again, as she's a married woman."

Arden winks at Carly, who's giving him an inquisitive look. "She might not accept them, but you'll still be paid for delivering them, is that right?"

Another pause. "Well. Yessir."

"So then it's good business for you to deliver flowers without questions and get paid for doing it. I'm sure this sort of situation has come up before, hasn't it? Where it was a friendly admirer who wanted to show their appreciation anonymously? What the lady wants to do with the flowers is her business. Good God, man, if you can't do this, then how do you ever survive Valentine's Day?"

Arden can tell his mind game is working. He hears scribbling on the other end. Beside him, Carly is covering her mouth in case of a giggle. "I suppose we've done it before. From an anonymous gentleman, I mean. Mr. Barnes, last time I see we delivered the roses to Forty-Two Longfellow Lane, is that correct?"

Arden is delighted to hear his own address. "That's still correct, yes."

"And we delivered two dozen roses. Is that the standing order?" Arden checks his wallet. Since he's been working for Uncle Cletus, he has a little more cash to go around. "That's right. What's that come to, about fifty bucks?"

"Delivered? Oh no, sir, that's more like eighty dollars. Plus tax."

Arden grins into the phone. "Anything for my sweetheart, you understand?"

A sigh resonates through the receiver. "I understand, Mr. Barnes. How would you like to pay today?"

Arden pulls out his gift card that he'd loaded money on. Gift cards can't be traced; there's no name on them, just good old-fashioned money. "Today will be Mastercard . . . er, what did you say your name was?"

"This is William, sir."

But Arden already knows it's William, the store owner, taking the order. He's done it countless times with William. William is more concerned with making a sale than delivering roses to a married woman from a mysterious man. Arden reads him the card number and expiration date, and William reads back the information to him verbatim.

"Will that be all today, Mr. Barnes?"

"I think that's quite enough, don't you, William?"

"Indeed sir. Indeed." William hangs up then, probably clinging to his last shred of morality.

Carly's eyes are almost bulging out of her head. "You sent flowers to your own mother? Who is Clarence Barnes?"

Arden shrugs. "That's for my mother to fret over, and my father to lose sleep over." Though he doubts the great Sheriff Moss loses sleeps over anything. And his mother only called the florist at his father's insistence because of how it looked. Secretly, he hopes she likes getting roses, even if they are from a perfect stranger.

Carly is quiet for a few minutes as he turns the truck onto Highway 98 and heads in the general direction of Roaring Brooke. "Are you trying to break up your parents?"

If he thought it could be done, then he would get his mother away from Dwayne Moss in the space of two heartbeats. But she's become too dependent on him. "Maybe he'll appreciate her more. He takes her for granted you know. It doesn't hurt him one bit to think someone else might be interested in her."

Carly laughs. "How often do you do it?"

"Every few months or so. Keeps them on their toes and whatnot."

She gives him a sideways glance, clearly impressed. "And what is on the agenda for this evening, Moss?"

He likes it when she calls him Moss, because ever since she told him that Arden reminded her of "garden" with pink flowers, he's been feeling slightly emasculated. Moss though? Moss sounds manly enough, he's decided.

"Tonight we work in real estate." He motions to the back of his truck and Carly peers through the window separating the cabin from the bed.

"For Rent signs?" she squeaks. Then she laughs. "Oh, this ought to be good."

"I was thinking of putting them up around a few houses in Hammock Harbor." Hammock Harbor is Arden's own neighborhood. They'd know instantly who'd done it, but they wouldn't have the proof.

No one would ever have the proof.

"Then I was thinking we could put City Hall up for auction. Tape a final notice on their door and everything."

Carly shakes her head. "Lame. But no matter what we do, we wear gloves this time. And we buy fresh tape from one town over. No trail left behind. And I need something to cover up my nose. It's a noticeable nose."

To Arden, everything about her is noticeable. He just didn't notice it until the night they actually met at the Breeze Mart. "You act like we're robbing a bank or something."

"I'm just covering our—my—bases. If Julio found out about—"

"I cannot even describe how tired I am of hearing about what Julio thinks about this and that." But he knows the conversation is over before it starts. He knows not to press the issue further too. Carly will insist he take her home and then where will he be? Sleepless and bereft of her company. It's in his best interest to keep her pleased. "We'll drive over to De Leon Springs and get some latex gloves and tape. Does that make you feel better?"

"What about the signs? Did you already touch the signs without gloves?"

"You must be joking." No evidence that gets planted will ever carry his fingerprints on them.

"It's just that you don't have a healthy fear of getting caught. Your daddy's the mighty sheriff. You have too many get-out-of-jail-free cards. I don't. I get caught, I'm screwed."

She's already explained to him what getting caught means. She's busted with Julio, she now has a record, and a record gets her disqualified for all the scholarships she's nurturing her GPA for. He gets it, he does. But they're not going to get caught.

They pull into the Dollar Tree in De Leon Springs and purchase a few essentials for tonight's escapades, plus some candy and soda to keep them wired. As the cashier rings up their purchases, Arden makes a mental list in his head with each item. Tape, check. Gloves, check. Flimsy toy hockey mask, check. Fake mustaches, check. Sharpie marker, check. The whole store is like one big birthday party central with every theme imaginable for the bargain price of one dollar. They split the cost—which always bothers Arden since Carly is so serious about money, or the lack thereof. But these days she seems more flush with cash than he does.

When they're safely in the truck, Arden pulls out a file folder from the driver's side door. In it are generically typed foreclosure forms he whipped up in the library at school. He shows them to Carly. She shakes her head. "We're going to hell for this."

"You believe in hell? Really, truly?"

"Don't you?"

Arden grunts. "Isn't God supposed to be all lovable and stuff? I mean, how fair is hell really? Say you're a sinner—and we're all sinners, right?—but say you're a really bad sinner like a murderer or something and you live for ninety-nine years then you die. You sin for ninety-nine years, but you're supposed to burn in hell for the rest of eternity for it? What kind of weird justice is that? The punishment doesn't fit the crime."

"Well then, where do bad people go?"

"You're not a bad person, Carly. We're juking people, not murdering them in their beds."

"But, for argument's sake. Where do they go?"

Arden considers. "They just die."

"And good people?"

He thinks of his sister, Amber. These Southern preachers want him to believe that she's in hell right now because she committed suicide. Because her life belonged to God and it wasn't hers to take and all that mess. But Amber was the type of person who wouldn't kill even the most vicious-looking spider. She'd simply scoop it up with a magazine or newspaper and set it outside. It's just that Amber was sick. She had real-life chemical imbalances in her head. Imbalances that made her do and say weird things. Would a loving, caring God really put her in hell because she wanted to end that?

Arden doesn't think so. "But are there really good people? Good people, through and through? Or are we all just varying versions of bad people, some trying harder to be good? In which case, we would all just die. Everyone dies. That's all I know."

Carly seems to realize where his thoughts have strayed. They haven't had the talk about Amber, and Carly seems curious about it, but in the end she changes the subject. Maybe she thinks it's too painful a memory for him to discuss. And maybe it would be too painful, but he feels he can tell Carly anything. She won't coddle him. She'll be honest, whether he likes it or not. She always is.

And it's nice. After Amber, everyone tiptoed around the subject. Gave him sympathetic looks and treated him like a porcelain version of himself. Fragile and breakable and dainty. Probably afraid he'd do what Amber did. He wished he'd had Carly back then. So she could punch him in the arm and say things like "Well, it's not like you killed her."

Even now, true to form, she maneuvers the conversation elsewhere. She doesn't offer to talk about it with him. She doesn't offer any excessive ridiculous condolences. She's just Carly. "I'm not worried about heaven or hell really. I am worried about jail though. Jail doesn't delight me."

"We're not going to jail. I mean, if we get caught, we might take a tour of the department and answer some questions and get cereal in a Styrofoam bowl and a cup of old coffee or whatever, but we're not getting booked or charged or anything. Never happen in a million years."

"How many times have you been caught?"

"Really caught? Like, red-handed? Once. And it was my friend's fault. I mean, these local cops, they're not stupid. But there's this cop code remember? Especially when it comes to family members of other cops. Everything gets brushed under the rug."

"Nice. So you're going to get Lucky Charms in a Styrofoam bowl and I'm going to get a cell mate named Brutus."

"Don't be ridiculous. They wouldn't put you in with a guy. You'd be in the cell block with all the prostitutes."

She grins. "So whose house are we going to put up for rent tonight? Not all Hammock Harbor residents, I hope?"

"I was thinking the mayor's house should go up on the market. Unless you have something more scandalous in mind?"

"The mayor it is. Let's list it on Craigslist too."

"Excellent idea."

☙·❧

Carly dons the hockey mask. Then she separates the fake yellow mustache into two pieces and sticks them to the outside of the mask where her eyebrows would normally be. "How do I look?"

Utterly adorable. "Fierce. And creepy."

"Good."

She opens the truck door, pulling the For Rent sign out with her. They decided to list the mayor's plantation house for the exorbitant price of $500/month including utilities. The house is a veritable palace, with a pristinely manicured lawn and a man-made pond in the middle with a fancy water spout and giant goldfish guarding the perimeter.

Well worth the $500, in Arden's humble opinion.

He watches as Carly steals across the street to the curb of the yard. She steadies the metal rods of the sign into the ground and tries to push down, but when it doesn't budge, she's forced to put her whole weight into it. The sign sinks into place and Carly is back in the truck within thirty seconds, giggling like a lunatic. It's a nasally sound with the mask on.

They move on to Hammock Harbor, where Arden handpicks his first victim. "He brought it on himself," he explains. "We have a landscape company that takes care of the public areas in here and Mr. Honaker treats them like his personal butler."

"You little Robin Hood, you."

He grins. "Does that make you Maid Marian?"

"I think I qualify more as Will Scarlet, don't you?"

It was worth a shot. "A cute, high-strung Will Scarlet?"

"You mean like your mom?"

"Really? You told a mom joke?"

She pulls her hair around to one side and purses her lips. "Get on with this, Robin."

When he gets back in the truck, he's scrounged up enough courage to ask the unthinkable. "Since we're already in the neighborhood, you want to come to my house?"

She gives him a suspicious look. "Why?"

"For one, I have to piss. For two, why not? And for three? I make the best sweet tea in the South."

Seventeen

Sitting on Arden's bed is not as intimate as I thought it would be given his reputation. I'm not sure what I thought I'd find, but a crisply made bed sporting a simple blue comforter with tightly tucked corners wasn't in the mental picture. I guess I imagined a tousled king-size bed, with sheets twisted after a passionate one-night stand, possibly lipstick stains on a pillow or two. I just knew there would be walls lined with posters of half-naked women; any real estate left would of course be devoted to shelves of football trophies and other boyish things like model sports cars or something. I even expected to feel dirty here, knowing how many girls had to have been seduced in this very room, on this very bed by those green eyes and sensual lips.

But Arden's bedroom is . . . boring. It's sparsely furnished—a (twin) bed, a single nightstand with a wrought-iron lamp, an outdated wood desk, a worn red recliner facing out of the one window next to a telescope on a tripod. And it's way neater than I'd figured. For some reason, I had pegged Arden for a slob, I guess because he seems unmotivated in every other aspect of life. But his room is clean, almost unlived in, with fresh vacuum tracks on the carpet by the bed and netted hamper with just a few articles of clothing in it. There are no posters or trophies or shelves on the walls, only a flat-screen TV hung out of the way.

Aside from Arden himself, there is nothing in the neighborhood of sexy here. I try not to acknowledge the relief I feel about this fact. What Arden does or doesn't do in the privacy of his room—or for that matter, anywhere—is not my concern.

So why do I feel concerned about it?

I'm enfolded in these thoughts when Arden gets back from the restroom. He gives me a quizzical look. "Does it stink in here or something?"

I hope my laugh is not as revealing as it sounds. I would die a slow death if he knew I'd been thinking about him . . . doing things . . . in here . . . *Dios mio*. "No. I was just . . . admiring how clean it is."

He wrinkles his nose. "Why wouldn't it be? I'm never here."

"Good point. Does that mean your parents are never here either?" Because from what I've seen so far, the rest of the house is just as spotless.

"Mom stays in her room mostly. Dad's always gone."

I wait for him to talk about his mom some more, but he doesn't, so I nod toward the telescope. "Astronomy or pervert?"

He shrugs. "I like the idea of feeling small. Sometimes life can seem bigger than you, you know? But knowing you're less than a speck in the whole scheme of things takes the pressure off, sort of." The words hang in the air between us. So much for small talk.

But in a way, I wanted to have this conversation. There are so many things I want to know about Arden. He's already blown my first impressions out of the water. And at the same time, I don't want to know what's inside him. I don't want to delve into the raw Arden Moss.

Because I don't want to fall for him.

"Life?" I say, against my better judgment. "Or death?" I nod toward the black-and-white picture on his desk. It's of a girl about our age smiling in classic school-picture style. I know it's Amber. She has his dimples. His smirk.

He sits down on the bed beside me. He doesn't bother to give me space. Our legs touch. Our arms. His scent devours me. "Not so much life or death," he says quietly. "More like emptiness."

I know emptiness. I felt it when my parents got deported and it was just me and Julio. We clung to each other in those first few months. Needed each other. I felt hollow, misplaced, at the time. But I know my misery then doesn't come close to the gaping chasm Amber's death left behind in Arden. I can see it still, in the fresh anguish in his eyes.

"I shouldn't have brought it up," I say, swallowing hard. "I just . . . It's just that we've never talked about it. Not that we should have. I mean, if you want to, we can."

"She was sick," he blurts. "Toward the end she cried every day. Our bastard of a father wouldn't acknowledge it. Wouldn't get her the help she needed."

I want him to stop talking about it now, to stop hurting himself with it. Regret is a tornado in my stomach. But there's no way I'm cutting him off now. As hard as it is to hear, as bad as it burns, it must be like a thousand flames licking at his insides. He actually looks like an uninhabited version of himself. His eyes are pools of unspilt tears. And he doesn't take his gaze off me.

"As cliché as it sounds, she was everything to me. We were two years apart, but she was like an extension of me. Well, I guess since she was older, I was an extension of her." He interlaces his fingers in front of him, then leans his elbows on his knees. I can tell he's sifting through memories in his mind. "She was my accomplice. My *first* accomplice," he corrects, giving me a small smile. "I don't think there was a single moment after I turned ten that we weren't jointly grounded for something."

"She overdosed on Mom's pain pills," he says. "I'm the one who found her. At first I thought she was sleeping. But something wasn't right. She'd gotten fully dressed. Put on makeup—something that she hadn't done in months. That was the first thing that threw me. Her eye makeup was a little smeared too. But more than anything I noticed how still she was. She looked like a doll lying there with her eyes closed. That's when I saw the bottle on her nightstand. The lipstick mark on the empty glass sitting next to it." He looks at me then. "After her funeral, I didn't sleep. My mom even broke down and took me to the doctor for it behind Dad's back. The doctor pre-scribed me pills, which I flushed for the sake of irony." His corre-sponding laugh is humorless. "Night after freaking night I stared at my bedroom ceiling. Then one night I got up and went for a walk. And I've been up ever since."

"Are you . . . you're saying you still haven't slept yet? How is that possible?"

Did he just lean toward me? "That's the funny thing," he says, his eyes on my lips.

"What's funny?" I whisper.

"All this time, I couldn't sleep. Until about three weeks ago. After a certain incident involving a purse and a cow patty and a girl with the longest eyelashes in the county."

My breath catches. I can't help it.

"Carly, you're my cure. The opposite of emptiness. When I come home after I've been with you all night I sleep like a rock." He snaps his fingers. "Just like that. It's amazing. I'm not saying you've replaced Amber or anything creepy like that. No one could ever replace her. And trust me, I don't think of you like a sister." He clears his throat. Awkwardly.

"What are you saying?"

He sighs, running a hand through his hair. A war wages in his eyes. "I'm not sure if I should. Say it, I mean. It might change things. And I don't want to scare you off."

Will it scare me off? Will it change things? Yes. No. Yes. I don't know. It *will* change things on the outside, I realize. It will change how we act around each other.

But it's going to change things on the inside. Things on the inside are too far gone already. I've fallen for him and I know it. And I want to hear it. I want validation, that this isn't some sort of weird platonic relationship, that I'm not imagining it. Or worse, that the feelings are one-sided, and I have to keep them cooped up forever because he just doesn't look at me that way. What does that mean, exactly? He also said I have the longest eyelashes in the county. He sees me, notices things about me.

And what don't I notice about Arden Moss? Aside from his physical perfection, I know that he likes a little coffee with his cream and sugar. That he drives with his right hand and leans on his door with his left arm. That he only uses the rearview when backing up.

That he doesn't seem to have a favorite food, but will eat anything you put in front of him. That he orders water when he really wants sweet tea. That he's a philosopher like Mr. Shackleford.

That he winks at me before every class we have together. That his face is what I think about at night before I go to sleep. That every time I see his truck pull into the parking lot of the Uppity Rooster to pick me up my stomach does an honest-to-goodness flip. And the nights he doesn't visit me at the Breeze Mart feel ruined and useless.

Yes, I want to hear it. I want to hear it very much, whatever it is he's trying to tell me. "Say it."

He leans impossibly closer, so close I can feel the warmth of him emanating off his body. I've been this close to him before. I've been in his lap before, what with the whole firecracker incident. But it wasn't like this. This is different. I suck in a breath when his fingers trace the line of my jaw and his thumb caresses my bottom lip.

"Do I have you, Carly?" he says softly. "Do I have you like you have me?"

Like you have me.

In the second it takes for me to nod, his lips are on mine. Gentle at first, as if tasting me, as if determining whether or not this is the right thing to do. It doesn't take him long to decide. I feel the second our friendship ends and something else starts. His hand comes to rest at the nape of my neck, his fingers entwined in my hair, and he pulls me closer against him. His lips are soft, so soft and swollen, and the way he uses them against me is surreal.

He leans until his chest touches mine, his free hand sliding down my arm, leaving behind a molten trail in the wake of his caress. And that's when my hands start working. They have a mind of their own, my hands. They're on his shoulders, then his biceps, wrapping his arms around my waist in, pulling him to me until our clothes are just thin dividers between flesh.

He moans against my lips and my mouth opens up to him and—

The door to his bedroom opens. We break apart like ground separated by an earthquake. And I'm nearly rattled out of my mind.

My cheeks become pools of lava.

Arden's jaw tightens. "Knocking is a common courtesy," he says to the silhouette of a man filling up the doorway of the bedroom. But Sheriff Moss isn't looking at Arden. He's looking at me. And he doesn't appear to like what he sees.

I cringe inwardly at what this looks like. At what he thinks I am. Just another of Arden's conquests. What bothers me the most is that I'm wondering if that *is* what I am. I'm wondering if I've been had. How does he woo other girls? Have I been a project from the beginning? Was it all leading up to this?

"Common courtesy is following the open-door policy I have in this household," Arden's father says. "Both of you in the kitchen. Now."

I jump up, but Arden reaches out and grabs my wrist. His intention is to walk in front of me. I don't like the fact that he obviously feels he has to shield me from his father. A bit of terror steals through me.

What would Julio say if he knew I just got caught kissing the infamous sheriff's son?

Arden holds my hand and leads me down the hall behind his father. We take the stairs down into one of the living rooms that leads to the kitchen. Sheriff Moss separates himself from us with the island in the center of the room. His badge seems to shine like a flashlight in my eyes.

Arden doesn't let go of my hand. I can't decide if this is good or bad. Good, if it's meant to show that I mean something to him and that he's going to bat for me. Bad, if it's meant to prepare me for something disastrous that he thinks is about to happen.

"What is your name, young lady?" Sheriff Moss asks.

"Carly," I croak. Yay for remembering my name.

"Carly what?"

"Carly Vega."

"Carly Vega, *what*?" Is this happening for real? "Carly Vega, *sir*."

"Jesus, Dad," Arden says. "She's our guest. We were just—"

"Oh, I saw what you were 'just' doing. And I don't remember you ever making a mortgage payment on this house, boy, not once. That being the case, I decide who is and who is not *my* guest. And if you're not my guest, then you're an intruder." With this, he rests his hand on the gun strapped to his side.

A little something stirs inside me, and it's not healthy fear. It's my temper.

Arden must sense me stiffen because he squeezes my hand again. "Carly is my girlfriend. You should get used to seeing her around."

Well, that just happened. And I'm kind of excited about it. And scared.

"Really? Your girlfriend? The same girlfriend who put the For Rent sign in the mayor's yard tonight? Oh, don't look so surprised, Carly. Mayor Busch may be on vacation, but he still has a live-in housekeeper. And guess whose truck she recognized? Maybe you know her, Carly. Her name is Carmen. She's one of your own."

The housekeeper recognized Arden's truck! Oh holy crap.

Wait, one of my own? What is that supposed to mean?

"Knock it off, Dad." The tension radiating off Arden is almost palpable. His jaw clenches and unclenches. He squeezes my hand so tight it hurts.

"Watch your tone, boy. So you think you've got a girlfriend? She knocked up?"

"I swear to God if you don't respect—"

"Careful, son." Sheriff Moss is a tall man built like a pro wrestler with a receding hairline tinged with gray and a large vein leading from the beginning of said recession to the tip of his left eyebrow. That vein is threatening to bulge out of his face. "Answer the question."

Arden slowly releases my hand and puts both of his palms on the marble countertop in front of us. I can tell he's trying to maintain composure. I've never seen him this rigid before. This tense. I feel so waylaid by this conversation. Pregnant? Is Sheriff Moss related to Julio? Has Arden gotten someone pregnant before? "You're not going to disrespect Carly like that. You're not going to insult her heritage. And you're going to watch *your* tone."

Wait . . . Insult my *heritage*?

Mr. Moss crosses his arms. "Is that right?"

"That's right." Only, it's not Arden who says that.

It's me.

Eighteen

Arden usually admires Carly's fearlessness. But right now is not the time.

He can see that his prayers for her to back down will not be answered today. Pride mixed with frustration race through him. The recipe for a fight is all over her face. Her nostrils are flaring like the wings of a moth. Her eyes practically glow with ferocity.

Oh geez.

His father seems impressed, for about a half a second. Then his face is all cruel amusement. "Your English is commendable," he says. "I'll bet your parents appreciate that when it comes time to ask for a price check on rice and beans at the grocery store."

Arden nearly springs across the counter, but Carly throws her arm in front of him with the strength of an ox. "Arden, don't!" But her focus never leaves the sheriff. Her brow arches in defiance, but she says nothing.

Arden slides back. He has no idea what to expect. Is Carly trying to handle this on her own? She's way out of her league. His dad is ruthless. But then again, Carly is strong. How can you predict what will happen when a tsunami collides with a hurricane?

His gaze shifts from Carly to his father. His weight shifts from one leg to the other. His insides shift with indecision. *Should I let them do this?*

The sheriff narrows his eyes. "Let me guess." He taps his chin with his index finger. "You were born here, right? Is that why you think it's a good idea to mess around with my son? What about your parents? Do they know where you are? Should we give them a call? Tell them what you were doing? Or maybe they'd prefer you were given a ride home in the back of my work vehicle?"

Work vehicle? "Her parents are dead, Dad." Arden folds his hands atop his head. It's the only way he can keep from jumping across the counter and wrapping them around his father's thick neck. That kind of reaction would make the situation ten times worse. It would clue his father in to just how much he cares about Carly—which Arden knows he would use to his advantage. And his father might actually pull his gun out of its holster this time—which would put Carly in danger, because it might misfire while Arden beats his father to the ground.

This is all my fault. He knows how prejudiced his dad is. He knew it was a bad idea to bring Carly here, to the lion's den. Not just tonight, but any night. Still, he wanted her here for reasons he can't explain. He's never brought a girl home before. Never brought anyone into his sanctuary. This house only had room for one girl: Amber. Except that's all changed. Carly is allowed here. More than that, he wants her here. The house feels less empty with her in it.

But these are the wrong circumstances. He never wanted it to be like this. He wanted their first kiss—because, by God, there was going to be at least one kiss between them if it killed him—to be extraordinary. And it was . . . until the mighty Sheriff Moss had interrupted it. He thought his dad was supposed to be two towns over, giving a speech at the American Legion.

What must Carly be thinking right now?

And why didn't I trust my instincts? He knew to keep her away from his father for as long as possible—for forever, if he could pull it off. To hide her—no, *protect* her—from exactly this. And now he's blown it.

"That's a shame," the sheriff says, his tone full of false sympathy. "Of course, I'm sorry for your loss. I was hoping to have them over for dinner. You know my wife, Sherry—have you met Sherry yet?—she makes the best enchiladas this side of the border. And what's not to celebrate? It's not every day my son brings home a girl. He usually reserves this sort of thing for his truck or, more appropriately in your case, an abandoned barn somewhere."

"You son of a bit—" This time even Carly can't hold him back. Arden flings himself over the counter. His father moves out of the way just as Arden slams into the fridge. Smooth as butter, Arden is pressed against the fridge, his father's hand tight around his throat.

"How many times do we have to do this, Arden?" his father growls in his ear. "Why the back-and-forth? Why the battle?"

"I'm not Amber," Arden chokes out. "I won't give up." His father could control Amber with words, and if not words, then actions like these. He can't control Arden, and it eats at him, Arden knows.

Arden hears the sound of metal scraping against . . . what? Then *clink clink clink.*

"Let him go," Carly says. He peers around his dad's shoulder and his stomach drops. Carly has the granddaddy of all kitchen knives in her hand. *Clink clink clink.* She taps it against the counter. Then she points it at a bemused Sheriff Moss.

"Carly, don't," Arden pleads. Even with the knife, he knows his father can overtake Carly. And because she's pulled the knife, he can hurt her and get away with it. His father knows all the gray-shaded boundaries of the law. He'll cry self-defense. He'll cry breaking and entering. He'll cry anything he needs to cry to win.

The same way he cried at Amber's funeral without feeling a thing.

"Are you attempting to assault an officer, young lady?" His father laughs. "You're making it too easy for me."

"I'm Mexican, remember? We're experts at butchering pigs, Sheriff." Still, she takes a step backward—much to Arden's relief. The knife trembles in her hand. If Arden sees it, his father sees it. His father sees everything.

The sheriff tilts his head at her, but doesn't loosen his grip on Arden. "You'd better be ready to use that."

Carly's jaw clenches and unclenches. Her eyes glisten but she doesn't yield to the tears threatening to spill out. She blinks once, twice. Lowers the knife slightly. "Let him go. Please."

Arden feels as deep as a shot glass. She's *trying to protect* me. This is all backward. "He won't hurt me," Arden tells her. "Just put the knife down." *Please God, make her put the knife down.*

The sheriff snorts. "This is getting exciting, isn't it, Carly? Tell you what. For showing a little spine, I'll let you walk out of here. Go on. Don't let the door hit you where the Good Lord split you."

She takes another step back, giving Arden an apologetic look. "I can't . . . I'm *not* leaving without Arden."

Arden struggles against his father, but the sheriff tightens his grip to the point of cutting off air. "Just let her go," Arden gets out between gasps.

"I tried to, son. Seems she's too ignorant to recognize an opportunity when it presents itself."

"Aren't you an elected official?" Carly says, her voice barely above a whisper. "You don't need a scandal like this on your hands. Think about everything I'll say to the press."

His father stiffens then. It's the best possible thing Carly could have said. Even though her body language screams that she's bluffing. "It's your word against mine, now, isn't it? You think anyone with a brain will believe you over me?"

His father is right. No one would believe Carly, even if Arden backed up the story. Even if they did, his father has connections everywhere, at every level of government. Relationships he's built over decades of time served. But Carly has him by the balls right now. Because no matter what happens to her, this incident would be plastered all over the news. Carly has a bagful of seeds in her hands. Seeds of doubt. And it's something the sheriff won't—and has never—risked. The smallest chance that this could tarnish his reputation has Sheriff Moss backed into a corner.

The conundrum is all over the sheriff's face. Arden takes advantage of his father's now-relaxed grasp. "We'd be willing to find out, wouldn't we, Carly?" Arden says, breathless. "All she has to do is snap a pic of us right now with her phone, right? A nice little Moss family photo."

Arden and Carly both know she doesn't have a phone. But his dad doesn't. To his father, words are bad enough. But pictures? Those are *much* more difficult to explain away. With a disgusted snarl, the sheriff abruptly releases Arden and shoves him toward Carly. "Get out of my house. Don't you ever bring that tramp here again, you understand?"

Carly begins to back toward the exit to the kitchen, keeping the knife in position. Arden rushes to her, putting himself between her and his father. Together, they edge toward the front door, never turning their backs on the threshold of the kitchen. Carly is shaking badly; the knife wobbles in her hand now. She doesn't need it anymore, Arden knows. His father will let them leave. This situation is over.

Maybe she's going to use it on me when we get in the truck.

Nineteen

"Well, that was traumatizing," I say, slamming the truck door behind me. I buckle up as quickly as possible, laying the knife carefully on the seat between us. My heart thumps in a wild rhythm. I hope Arden doesn't notice that I'm about to shake out of my own clothes. "We're dumping this. Tonight." I can't believe the words coming out of my mouth. Not now, not thirty seconds ago in the Moss residence kitchen.

Ohmigod ohmigod ohmigod. I just pulled a knife on the sheriff of Houghlin County—the extremely prejudiced sheriff of Houghlin County. How could Arden have grown up in this kind of environment and not be at least a little racist himself? Or is he?

But that's not fair and I know it. I've never picked up a single prejudiced vibe from him. He can be dense sometimes, and self-involved, but he's never so much as hinted at being racist. In that regard, he's more like his uncle, Mr. Shackleford, I guess—or at least, I hope.

Because now I'm all in with Arden. And I know it.

Arden's face is expressionless as he puts the truck in drive. We speed out of the cobblestone driveway and make a hard right, hopefully toward the closest exit of this godforsaken neighborhood.

"You think he'll press charges? Will he tell Julio what I did?" *Dios mio,* but my heart palpitates with the thought of it. Adrenaline courses through my body, making me replete with unspent energy. I pop every knuckle I can. My knee bounces uncontrollably.

"No," Arden says finally. He answers as if I've asked him if he wants mayo on his sandwich. Emotionless. Final.

He takes a left, then a right at the next stop sign. He slows to a crawl. This isn't the way we came in. "Where are we going?" My hands are fidgeting fidgeting fidgeting. I wonder if this is what being on crack feels like.

"Somewhere. Anywhere. Home. I'm taking you home."

"Do you think he'll come after us?"

Distracted, he glances at me. "No. No, he won't. It's all a mind game, what he just did. He wouldn't want a public confrontation. It wouldn't suit his image."

"Are . . . are you mad?"

Maybe his dad's words got to him. Maybe he regrets spending time with me after all. Maybe I'm going to go insane if he doesn't start talking.

I'm startled out of that line of thought when he slams on the brakes, pulls over on the curb. We're halfway on the sidewalk. I'm pretty sure the homeowners association here would have a fit.

Arden faces me suddenly. I'm too stunned to stop my mouth from hanging open. His behavior has never been this erratic before. He's always so self-assured, like he's found equilibrium in the universe or something. "Mad? At you? You've got to be kidding. You think I'm mad at *you*?"

"Well, I mean, I'm not sure if you noticed, but I pulled a knife on your dad." I'm ready to defend my actions though. They're at the tip of my tongue in case this escalates into an argument. In case Arden is losing his mind like I feel I am.

"I have a deranged father and you're the one apologizing. That's classic." He beats his hands against the steering wheel. "It's me who's sorry, Carly. I should never have brought you there. He wasn't supposed to be home."

I think I might be sick. "Did you . . . did you bring me there to—" I can't even say it. Because what if he did bring me there for . . . for . . .

"No! I knew you would think that. After all those things he said. God, I'm so sorry, Carly. So, so sorry."

"I'm just trying to figure out what you're apologizing for," I say. No, I yell it. Because I'm a little excitable at the moment. And if he didn't bring me there for the intimate setting, then what could he possibly have to apologize for?

"Those things he said. The way he insulted you. I knew how he felt about . . . about . . ."

"You're apologizing for your dad," I say as if I'm coaching a witness at court. "Because he was mean to me. Because of where I come from."

"Yes."

"But not because you kissed me?" *And then introduced me as your girlfriend? I didn't imagine that part, did I?* I know I'm being vain here, absolutely know it. It's not that I'm not angry at all. I am. I'm super-offended. I mean, Arden's father dissed my ethnicity, and therefore my family. Therefore Julio, who is the hardest-working person I know. I should be foaming at the mouth, telling Arden to turn the truck around and let me have another shot at his arrogant dad.

I think of Mama and Papi and the struggles they go through to put food on the table back in Mexico. They basically live in a shed—our trailer is luxurious compared to their little shack. We all work so hard for one another, to make something better for ourselves, for our family. We are people, and Sheriff Moss looks at us like we're rats. I saw his face. The disgust there when he looked at me. Like his son had just kissed roadkill. How can such a hateful man have persuaded so many people to give him this much power?

I should have attacked him like a rabid dog, on principle. I shouldn't have been afraid, I should have been ferocious. But then again, wouldn't that have proven that his opinion of me is true? That I'm a wild animal, incapable of complex human feelings and thoughts and emotions? He would have pointed that out to Arden right away, I know it. No, attacking him is not the way. Losing my temper is not the way. Losing Arden is not the way.

But neither is losing who I am. I'm going to figure this out, I will. The sheriff won't catch me helpless again.

And I can't imagine there won't be an "again," because Arden and I just kissed. So maybe that's what I'm asking. If Arden and I are going to be a thing, I'm going to have to learn to deal with his dad a little better than pulling a knife on him every time he opens his mouth.

But that kiss. I can't forget that kiss. My lips still swelter from that kiss. They're still swollen with eagerness to do it again. And I'm pretty sure that makes me a bad person. Because I'm full of all this rage about what the sheriff did—what he said—and yet I'm thinking about Arden kissing me.

I'm a straight-up psycho.

Arden leans back against the door, giving me a long hard look. His eyes focus on me as if he were seeing me for the first time. "Not because I kissed you? I'm not sure what you're asking."

I throw my hands up in the air, mainly because I still don't know what I'm asking. "Did you *mean* to kiss me, Arden? Or are you apologizing for that too?" My instincts tell me to open the door and run before I embarrass myself further.

His mouth falls open, and he gives a dazed look. "You're serious?"

I nod, aware that I'm holding my breath.

He closes his eyes and exhales. "Oh, I definitely meant to. I'll never be sorry for kissing you." And just like that, he's on my side of the truck, pulling me into the crook of his arm. He rests his chin on the top of my head. "I'm just sorry it happened like that. That it will always be tainted with my dad going ape shit right afterward."

"And the part about being your girlfriend?"

"I was getting around to asking."

"Liar."

He laughs into my hair. "Haven't you figured out that I'm afraid of you? I've been alluding to this for days now. You either suck at taking hints or you've been avoiding it. And I need to know which one."

"I thought you just wanted it for show. Not, you know, for real." Which is the truth. I thought he just wanted to give in to the rumors and let everyone think that they were right about us so we had a valid reason to hang out with each other. Now that they were actually *right* about us . . . How do I feel about it?

"Well, it is partly for show. To show everyone that you're not freaking available." He pulls away completely then. "Wait a minute. Is this your way of rejecting me? You're not going to be my girlfriend?"

My hand has a mind of its own as it pulls his face closer to mine. I indulge myself by taking in a deep breath of his masculine scent. "I am so your girlfriend." And then I kiss him. Arden Moss. But he's no longer *the* Arden Moss. He's *my* Arden Moss.

His response is hungry but not feral. He doesn't do anything I'd imagined Previous Arden would do to his oh-so-willing victims. He doesn't try to cop a feel. He doesn't put his hands up my shirt or down my jeans. He just holds me. Holds me, and kisses me like I'm the thing he's been craving since life began.

❧•❧

School becomes exciting in a weird sort of way. We thought by acting like a couple, everyone would just stop staring. But they don't. We turn heads, Arden and I, as we make our way from class to class holding hands. Arden makes it a point to kiss me as he drops me off at calculus—a class we don't have together. I make it a point to stand on my tiptoes and accept his lips. Screw the Public Eye. What harm am I doing? If anything, I'm acting more normal than I was when it looked like I was rejecting my Arden Moss.

He walks me to all my classes. We enjoy scandalizing our classmates as much as we enjoy the kissing. After the day is done, we go to the media center to drop off my borrowed laptop. It feels good to hand it over to Mrs. Goodwin and say, "I'm turning this in. I don't need it anymore." I've decided to tell Julio that the school upgraded—that way he won't question where the new one came from.

Mrs. Goodwin is shocked. Maybe she's shocked that I'm turning it in. Maybe she's shocked that Arden Moss is holding my backpack open in order to do so. Maybe she's shocked that I'm wearing a laced-up bodice shirt and wedges instead of a T-shirt and tennis shoes.

Maybe she should get over it.

"Uh, thank you, Carly," she says.

"I have a new laptop," I can't help but tell her.

Arden grins at me. I grin back. Life is good.

❧ ·❧

"So, the point of mudding is to get your truck stuck?"

Arden rejects my proposal with a scoff. He changes gears and mashes the gas again. The tires spin and spin but we don't move forward. Mud shoots everywhere. The woods around us are no longer visible through the red clay caked onto all the windows and windshield. "We're not stuck. And point? There's no *point* to mudding. It's just fun."

But by the tone of his voice, it doesn't sound like he's having fun. It sounds like he might be a bit frustrated. Which is why I shouldn't say, "It's like the road took a crap on us." But I do.

He flashes me a disgruntled look. "A little dirt never hurt anyone. Matter of fact, I'm pretty sure dried mud is what keeps this truck in one piece."

Switching us into reverse, he braces his arm on the back of my seat and turns around, I guess to get a better view of us not going anywhere. "How often do you get stuck?"

"We're not stuck. This is just a puddle for ol' Betty."

"My. God. You named your truck?"

Again with the gear changing. I love the natural bulge of his biceps when he's grasping the steering wheel. But not as much as I love the natural bulge of his biceps when they're wrapped around me.

"She's not just a truck."

"Oh, but she is."

"And we're not stuck."

"But say we are. Then what—"

"We absolutely, positively are not stuck, are we, Betty?" He pets the dashboard before revving the gas again but to no avail. Then his butt rings. He pulls himself up enough to dig in his back pocket for his phone. "Yeah, man?" he answers.

A male voice greets him on the other end, but I can't tell who it is or what he's saying. "We're on our way," Arden says. "About fifteen minutes out." Then, "We hit a hole right past the old creek sign . . . Yeah . . . No, we're not stuck . . . Everyone's there already?" He scowls at me. "Well, maybe you'd better come get us then."

I waste no time in confronting him when he hangs up. "Someone's coming to get us? So we're definitely, absolutely stuck."

He rolls his eyes. "The word 'stuck' implies that our situation is permanent. That's not the case. Betty would have gotten us out of it eventually, but since we're the only ones not at the party, I thought you'd want me to get us there quicker."

Oh, right. I'd want to get to a party full of his obnoxious friends quicker. I'm not even sure why I'm coming—except that he's been doing his part of the bargain. He's actually been studying and doing his homework every day. In exchange, I'm trying to make an effort to get to know his friends. I mean, we sit with them at lunch sometimes. That's enough for me, frankly. But a tailgate party in the middle of the muddy woods with a bunch of rich kids? No thanks. Still, Arden thought it was a good idea to let our friends—his friends, since I don't have any—"acclimate" to our new relationship.

I can't tell if this is a test for me or a test for them. Maybe both. Or maybe Arden is testing out whether or not *he* can adjust to having a girlfriend. Either way, I'm stuck going. He actually got an A on his last social studies test—I owe him this much.

"That's very considerate of you."

He smirks at me. "Do I get a reward for being considerate?"

I inch across the bench seat, until there's no space left between his lips and mine. He pulls me into his lap to get a better hold on me. That's how his friend Braden finds us a few minutes later—or how he would have found us if not for the dirty windows. Maybe mudding has its benefits after all.

Arden waits for me to move back to my seat before opening the driver's side door and greeting his friend. I think Braden is on the football team—he's certainly big enough to be—but I'm not sure. Braden stands at the edge of the "puddle" we're not stuck in. He's got a big chain in his hand, which ends in a big hook.

Arden balances himself between the door and the truck and pulls himself up onto the roof. Getting dirty is inevitable at this point, but I guess it's better than actually walking around in what looks like several feet deep of red clay. When he maneuvers onto the hood of Betty, Braden carefully tosses him the chain, which

Arden catches with the grace of an old pro. Arden crawls to the front and leans forward with the chain. After a few grunts and shifts, he's crawling back into the truck cabin.

"Braden's going to pull us out," he says cheerfully.

I wipe some of the orange mud off his arm, then rub my hand on the seat between us. "Braden is nice?" I say without looking at him. He must be somewhat civilized if he's willing to leave a party to come tow his friend out of a mudhole.

Arden puts his hand over mine. "They're all nice, Carly. Once you get to know them."

When we finally get to the party—which turns out to be a clearing in the woods with a bunch of trucks backed up to what looks like an actual pond of mud—I'm mortified to find that I should have worn a bathing suit. All the girls, every single one, are wearing bikinis. Small bikinis. Microscopic bikinis.

"You didn't say anything about swimming," I accuse Arden.

"There's nowhere to swim here."

"Please tell me they're not mud-wrestling. I swear I'll bludgeon you, right here and now."

He presses his lips together. "August ended like, yesterday, Carly. It's still hot out. They like to wear their bathing suits. It's not a big deal."

But it is a big deal. I'm in a T-shirt and shorts. I'm already different from them in so many ways. Couldn't he have just prepared me for this one thing? "I could have worn my swimsuit."

"I've seen you in your swimsuit, Carly. And there's no way you're wearing it around this bunch of perverts."

I grin. Also, I blush. "You did it on *purpose*? To, like, protect my honor or something?"

"I'm protecting their noses from my fist." He sounds gruff and agitated, and it's adorable.

"I've never seen a jealous Arden Moss."

"Take a good look," he says, giving in to the slightest of smiles. He lifts me out of the truck then, pressing me into him before letting my feet touch the ground, so that I slide down the length of him.

It's definitely hot out.

"Hey, Arden," a girl calls out. "It's about time you showed up. Where have you been lately?"

He nods to the voice behind me. "Hey, Jen," he says with too much familiarity. Or is it just me being jealous now? "I've been around."

Does he have a past with this Jen? Does he have a past with every girl here? How am I supposed to *not* think about that now? I know his reputation. I know the rumors. But I haven't directly asked him about any of it. Clearly I was in denial. Because now I want to know all of the things.

"Let's go to Chris's truck and get some food. He usually brings a grill, and I'm starving," Arden says, taking my hand and hauling me behind him. "You like hot dogs and chips and other gourmet items, right?"

"I eat school lunches," I tell him. "I got this."

We find an empty tailgate and manage to hoist ourselves up on it without spilling the contents of our Styrofoam plates. Everyone who walks by greets Arden—a few people even know my name, at which I'm impressed.

"The new will wear off soon," Arden says quietly. "Just give them some time."

"How many of these girls have you been with?" Yep, I just said that out loud.

He pauses before taking a bite of his second hot dog. He gives me a quizzical look. "Not everything you hear about me is true."

I nod. "How many?"

"Not as many as you think."

We're quiet for a while, and I try to decipher his answer into actual numbers. I watch the girls in the bikinis watch Arden, and the general consensus seems to be *Why is he here with her?* That, or I'm letting my imagination run rampant and free.

Either way, I'm in a pretty terrible mood by the time we're done eating.

"You want to go watch the trucks climb out of the pit?" He motions toward a hill ahead of us, behind which all sorts of trucks come and go. We'll have to walk halfway around the "pond" to get there.

"Sure."

He hops off the back of the truck, and his hands are at my waist, ready to lift me down, when Braden walks up, a pretty blond girl wrapped around him piggyback style. He sets her on the ground. "Hi," she says to me. "Carly, right? I'm Eve." She holds out her hand and we have an awkward shake.

Eve looks at Arden. "We should all get together sometime. How about a movie on Friday?"

He looks at me. I can't tell what it is he wants me to say. His expression is expectant though, so he definitely thinks I should say something. "I actually have to work Friday," I tell her.

"Oh," she says. "Well, how about we go to the beach Saturday?"

"I work Saturday too." I try to sound apologetic. I don't think

Eve has to work to get the money for her highlights or her perfect French manicure.

"Sunday?" she asks inevitably.

"Actually, Carly works a lot," Arden says. "I'm lucky I could steal her away for today."

He is lucky. I took the night off at the Breeze to come with him this afternoon. I can't do that every time his friends want to get together though. And I especially can't miss my weekend shifts at the Uppity Rooster.

Not to mention I don't *want* to spend my time with these people. Eve seems nice enough, but there's the whole problem with getting to know someone too well. They'll eventually ask questions about why I work so much. They'll ask questions about my parents, like Arden did at first. But unlike Arden, they might not drop the subject when I want them to.

Coming here was not a good idea.

"I'm sure we can make it work some other time," Braden says, giving me an encouraging smile. I could probably learn to like Braden. To like Eve. But that's a dangerous thing to contemplate.

"Hopefully," I say a little too late. I feel Arden staring at me. But this is partly his fault. I told him I wasn't good in social situations.

"Alright, man," Braden says, looking back at Arden. "We'll catch you later."

After they're gone, Arden pulls me behind one of the trucks. "How's it going?" he says, brushing the back of his hand along my cheek. "Everything okay?"

I push it away, feeling like a brat as I do it. "I don't think this is going to work out, Arden."

He visibly stiffens in front of me. "What do you mean?" There's a bit of raw panic in his voice.

"I mean us. Together. It will never work."

"It already *is* working."

"Arden." I cross my arms and move away from him when he reaches for me again. "Arden, I've already cut all the shifts I can cut. How can you have a girlfriend who isn't around to actually *be* your girlfriend? I can't go to the movies every Friday night and to the beach every weekend."

"I think you're getting things confused," he says. "You're *my* girlfriend. Not *their* girlfriend. What do I care if you can't hang out with *them*?" He takes a cautious step toward me and I let him.

"But don't you want to be a normal couple? Do normal couple things?"

"Carly, you pulled a gun on me the first time I met you. I don't think 'normal' is in the cards for us." This time I let him pull me to him. He tucks my head under his chin. I can't help but notice the contented sigh he lets out.

"What did you do with your other girlfriends? I mean, besides, you know . . ."

He laughs into my hair. "I haven't called anyone my girlfriend since, like, the third grade. And even then, it was sketchy."

I giggle into his chest. "I just don't want you to have any regrets with me. I don't want to hold you back."

He lifts my chin with the crook of his finger. "You've filled a hole I didn't know I had in me, Carly. What is there to regret?"

His mouth covers mine.

Twenty

Arden pulls up to the front steps of Uncle Cletus's house and honks the horn. Cletus opens the door immediately, as if he's been watching for Arden's truck. He probably has been.

The morning is beautiful and fresh, with tendrils of sunlight shining down through the oak trees in the front lawn. When Cletus gets in the truck, he comments on as much. "Good day to go out," he grumbles, as if he'd said the opposite.

But Arden knows he's excited to be going to breakfast with him. Because he's excited to be seeing Carly. "You already know what you're going to order?"

Cletus scoffs. "I haven't been to the Uppity Rooster in decades, boy. Probably changed the menu twenty times since then."

"They have coffee. Looks like you could use a pot of that."

"You know what that place is full of?"

"What?"

"Cocks."

Arden swerves slightly in the driveway. "Come again?"

Pure glee shines in Cletus's eyes. "Cocks, boy. Roosters. Miss May was obsessed with 'em, if you know what I mean."

"Nice, old man. Nice."

The drive is a short, talkative one. Cletus remarks again on how nice the weather is, how much moonshine he just purchased, and how horrible but potent it is.

"Tastes like sweaty butt crack," Cletus insists. "But it gets the job done."

They pull into the Uppity Rooster Café and Arden revs the truck engine to let Carly know they've arrived. This earns a disapproving look from Uncle Cletus. "Is that supposed to be some sort of mating call, boy?"

The hostess seats them in Carly's section. She waves to them from behind the drink station, and signals that she'll be with them in a minute. Arden acknowledges with what he knows is a cheesy grin.

"Oh no," Cletus says. "You're dating her, aren't you, boy."

Arden didn't plan on having this conversation with his uncle just yet. That is to say, he had planned on having it in a different way—a way in which he started and finished it. "So what if I am?" *Nice way to begin maturely.*

"Just in case you're unaware, son, she's too good for you."

"She doesn't seem to think so."

Cletus waves his hand in dismissal. "Psh. They never realize it."

"You're the one who's always talking about how smart she is. Can't be that smart if she's dating me." *Wait, what?*

"Smart people make stupid mistakes."

Carly arrives then. Her hair is swept back in a messy bun and her cheeks are an alluring pink. Arden's not sure she could be unattractive if she tried. "Sorry about that. I have a party table in the back. What can I get y'all to drink?"

Arden loves it when she says "y'all." It means he's rubbing off on her. "I'll have my usual."

"Sweet tea it is. Uncle Cletus?"

Cletus seems enchanted that she's calling him Uncle Cletus instead of Mr. Shackleford now. "I'll have a Bloody Mary. More Mary than Bloody, if you know what I mean."

"Gross. But okay."

She disappears again, and Cletus wastes no time in resuming the conversation. "End it, Arden. For God's sake. What would your father say?"

"You know I don't care what he thinks."

"You know I don't care what that S-O-B thinks either. You know what I'm talking about. Does he know?" There has never been any love lost between Cletus and Sheriff Moss. Cletus was against his niece marrying Arden's father from day one; even back then, he knew Dwayne Moss was a punk.

And Cletus knows the depths of the sheriff's racism. That's why he retired from the county when he did. Arden's father was already developing his platform to run for sheriff. And Cletus would be damned if he sat by and watched it happen on his shift.

"Unfortunately, he does," Arden says. He feels his jaw locking, remembering what happened that night. "He's already expressed his disapproval."

Cletus balls his fists. "What did he say? No, don't tell me. That nitwit. Does Carly know how he feels?"

Arden feels the blood draining from his face. "She was there when he expressed his sentiments."

"You took her to your house, didn't you? Are you stupid, boy?"

"Yes."

Cletus nods, satisfied. "Maybe you're not a lost cause after all. If he would have hurt her—"

"I wouldn't have let that happen."

"But if he had? I would put my fist through his skull. That's what I would do. And I trust you to do the same."

"He won't lay a hand on her."

"And what about you? You thinking about putting your grubby hands on her like you do all the rest of them senseless girls?"

"I'm in love with her." Now the blood rushes back into his cheeks. It's the first time he's said it out loud. He feels relieved and burdened at the same time.

A slow grin crawls over Cletus's face. "You are, aren't you."

"Bad. Really bad."

Carly comes back then, and sets the drinks down in front of them. "Do you guys know what you want? If you hurry, I can get your order in before the big party. It's a bridal shower, so they're sipping on mimosas right now." She leans down then and whispers to Arden, "Huge money, hopefully."

Cletus has a gleam in his eye as he says, "I don't know what the fancy name for it is, but I'll have scrambled eggs and bacon and some biscuits and gravy."

This takes Arden off guard. He didn't expect Cletus to be ready to order yet. Or to be so . . . alert. "I'll have pancakes."

"Bananas Foster?" Carly says.

"Sure." *Whatever that means.*

"You have no idea what that is, do you."

"Nope."

"Plain pancakes then?"

"Yep."

She smiles. "Will do." She grabs the menus and saunters away, as if she knows what he's just admitted to.

"Please. Don't," Arden says quietly.

Cletus chuckles. "You don't think she's got you figured out?"

"No. You think?"

"Well, look at you. Giving her a ride to work on the weekends. I'll bet you check on her every night at that dumpy convenience store, don't you?"

"Nothing that you didn't used to do." And, if it weren't for Arden scaring the life out of him, he would still be doing it.

Cletus ignores the jab. "Spending every waking minute with her. And when you're not, you're at my house keeping busy, until you can spend your next waking minutes with her."

It's obvious. So obvious. But does she really know? And what if she does? "Should I just come out and tell her?" *And what's with asking an old man for love advice?*

Cletus moves the giant celery stalk out of the way before taking a big swallow of his Bloody Mary. He contemplates. "I don't think so. I think you should just show her. That's always the best route."

"But don't girls like it when you say it?" He wouldn't know. He's never told a girl he loved her before. He's never had to. He's never wanted to. Girls have always been easy creatures to decipher, up until this point. Compliment them on their hair or lip gloss, spend a little money on them—and when all else fails, kiss them senseless.

But Carly is a whole different species of girl. She's the bloodhound of false compliments, she hates wasting money, and the only thing he's sure of is that *she's* the one who kisses *him* senseless.

As far as being a guy goes, he's completely failing.

Cletus must perceive his desperation. "Boy, get it together. I may not know much about what a woman of today's world wants or needs. But I do know women in general don't like a groveling mess, that's for dang sure."

Arden sits up straighter. "I'm not a mess."

"You need a mirror then?"

"You started this conversation."

"Shut up, son. Here she comes."

Carly motions for Arden to scoot over so she can sit next to him in the booth. After the conversation he just had with his uncle, it feels like he's sitting next to an open flame. "I got your order in before our lovely bridesmaids," she brags. "Their bill is easily going to be five hundred bucks. You think I should auto-gratuity them, or take my chances?"

"With a smile like that?" Cletus says. "I think you've got a clean thirty percent off 'em. I say take your chances."

Graciousness radiates from her. "I think I will."

Arden clears his throat. "You having a good day?"

She nods. "Great one. I had a family in earlier who was vacationing from Argentina. We spoke Spanish the whole time. It was nice." She gives him a wistful look. Like someone homesick.

He wants her to look like that when she thinks of him.

"Well, I've got to check on my tables," she says, sliding back out of the booth. "I'm sorry. I didn't expect to be this busy when you came."

"Don't apologize," Arden says hurriedly. "It's a good thing."

"Yeah," Carly agrees.

After they eat, Arden and Cletus wait around for Carly to clean up her tables. Cletus proved right about the bridal shower; they ended up leaving her forty percent of the bill after everything was said and done. Carly practically glowed while she vacuumed her section of the restaurant; she made more today than she ever had.

After rolling her silverware, Carly is ready to go. She walks out with Cletus and Arden.

"I think I'm going to take a cab," Cletus announces.

"What?" Carly says. "No. We're going to the pier, remember?"

Cletus gives Arden a knowing look. "It's been a while since I've been out of the house. And I've got some errands to run and a lot on my mind. You two go ahead without me."

It's as good a blessing as Arden is going to get from his uncle.

And he'll take it.

Twenty-One

I'm more than a little startled to find Julio sitting on the couch wait-ing for me when I get home. I'm pretty sure he should be at work tonight. And I'm pretty sure I'm busted. "Where have you been?" he asks, a frown tugging at his mouth. Julio would be handsome, I think, if he wasn't so serious all the time. He's got a strong jawline and big brown eyes. He's clean shaven. He's everything he should be. Including angry that I'm late getting home.

My stomach drops. Did he hear Arden's truck when he dropped me off? "I was at work?"

"All day?"

I shake my head. "No. I walked around Destin Commons for a little while to clear my head." Complete and total lie. I spent the day fishing with Arden off Okaloosa Pier. We caught a baby shark and set it free. Then I buried him in the sand underneath the pier.

Julio purses his lips. "You shouldn't walk around alone. It's dan-gerous."

Nice. He has no problem letting me ride my bike back and forth from the Breeze Mart in the dead of night, yet, to walk around a populated-by-mostly-rich-people area like Destin Commons is unacceptable. "I know" is all I say. To lighten the mood, I open up my apron and hand him my earnings from the café, rolled up with a rubber band for his jar-stuffing convenience. "It's three hundred forty dollars," I explain, not un-proudly.

His eyes light up instantly. "Seriously?"

"Yep. And it's all yours." Well, except for twenty dollars. That goes in my secret stash for whatever-the-heck-I-want. "We got killed today. My feet are about to fall off." Complete and total truth.

He accepts the mass of bills in his hand gingerly, as if it were a baby bird. He looks at it for a long time. I lie next to him on the couch and hoist my feet up onto his knees. He makes room for me.

Julio smiles down at me, ignoring what I know is a pungent smell coming from my work shoes. Then he tosses the bundle of cash onto my belly. Three hundred forty dollars in ones, fives, and tens is heavy. "You can keep your earnings now, *bonita*."

I sit up. "What?" A thrill runs through me. "What do you mean?" The thought of keeping the cash in my lap is mind-blowing. If I can start keeping what I earn, then that means I could save up for a car. Whoa. "What is going on?"

Julio scratches at a beard that isn't there. I honestly don't know if he can't grow one or if he keeps it shaved. I've never seen him shave. "You have grown up, little sister. I'm very proud of you. You've helped me so much these past months. I'm grateful for that."

"I don't understand."

"Because of your help, we've saved enough money to bring Mama and Papi back, Carlotta. We have an appointment with *El*

Libertador tonight. Go take a shower and change. I want you to be with me. You earned it."

My shower is quick and unappreciated. I dress for comfort instead of style. I don't know what to expect. My stomach is one big tangle of emotions. Relief, that I don't have to work as much, unless I want to. Anxiety, about what *El Libertador* will have to say. Sadness, that this part of my life—the part where Julio and I eke out a living on our own together, united—is over. Happiness, that this part of my life—the part where Julio and I struggle to make ends meet and send money to my parents and suffer—is over. Guilt, because I still haven't told Arden the truth about my parents, and now I'll all of a sudden have immigrant parents who happen to be document challenged and his dad is practically the founder of People Against Undocumented Immigrants. If that were an actual thing.

Julio knocks on my bedroom door, bringing me back to the reality: This is happening despite what I feel about it. "Are you ready, Carlotta? We have to go. I've called a taxi for us."

It's out of character for my brother to waste money on things like taxis, so either we're traveling a longer distance than we can feasibly walk, he doesn't want to be hot and sweaty when we arrive, or we're running that late—or all of the above. "I'm ready," I breathe.

The taxi is old and smells of body odor and fake cherries and cheap aftershave—all of which I assume belong to the driver in some form or the other. Julio sits quietly beside me, hands folded in his lap, so I do the same, even though I feel like spazzing out.

We leave city limits, and drive and drive and drive. We keep making turns here and there away from Highway 20, until I would no longer be able to find my way back to it. Which makes me feel unsafe—something I never thought I'd feel with Julio.

The cab pulls into an old abandoned office complex, the kind with glass front windows that probably used to house things like nail salons and Chinese buffet restaurants. Grass grows in all the cracks of the parking lot.

We get out of the taxi and Julio pays the driver in cash, and asks him in Spanish to stay and wait for us. The driver complies and lights a cigarette. We make our way to suite D, which I only know is suite D because the grimy outline of the missing lettering is still present on the glass door.

There is an old wooden desk with a dim lamp set upon it and two chairs in front of it. A brawny man sits behind it, and though the lamp creates more shadow in the room than actual light, I can tell he's wearing a mask. Of course he is. He's *El Libertador*.

We sit down in the chairs and Julio folds his hands on the desk in front of him. I don't know where he's gotten this new hand-folding habit, but I keep mine to myself in my lap. *El Libertador*'s mask is creepier upon closer inspection. It's a clown face, and it looks like it might be made of porcelain. I wonder if he picked it to be that much scarier to his victims. I say victims, because he's practically bludgeoning us with his fees.

And I say scarier, because really, the man is terrifying. Even the black clothing he wears cannot hide the fact that he dwarfs both me and Julio put together.

"You're late," *El Libertador* says in Spanish. His voice is muffled behind the mask.

"We apologize," Julio says submissively. "Please forgive us."

"Who is this you've brought with you?"

"This is my younger sister, Carlotta. She knows the importance of the situation. She helped earn the cash for our parents." There is a tinge of pride in his voice. I imagine it sounds pathetic to *El Libertador*.

"Has the cash been dropped off?"

Julio nods. "It has."

This surprises me. Julio has already made arrangements with this man. He has already taken our savings and dropped it off somewhere. The thought makes me nauseous. And so does the clown face. I concentrate my attention on *El Libertador*'s massive hands. Even in the dim lighting, I notice an angry scar between his left thumb and index finger. I imagine all sorts of gruesome ways he could have gotten it.

Was he tortured? Did he get it in a fight? Did he get it while he was murdering someone? Something about the scar is evil, I decide.

"We will wait for the phone call after the cash has been verified," *El Libertador* announces.

The next ten minutes are the longest in my life. Julio says nothing. *El Libertador* says nothing. I say nothing. Yet, the air is full of unspoken words. Julio, with reverence for *El Libertador*. *El Libertador,* with obvious disdain for the both of us. Me, with fear of *El Libertador*.

Relief from everyone when the phone rings. *El Libertador* says nothing when he picks it up, just listens. He hangs up without a word. Then he focuses his attention back on Julio. "Your parents will be given safe passage across the border. Customs won't bother them. My men will meet them in the desert and bring them as far as Austin. It's up to you to transport them the rest of the way."

"And the passports?"

The clown face nods. "The passports will be provided to them as soon as they cross the border."

"What if they get caught?"

The question isn't from Julio. It's from me. And Julio is just as horrified as I am. Still, I press on. "Well," I say defensively, "we're paying this man a lot of money. What if he fails? Then what?"

"Carlotta!" Julio whispers.

"Your sister is foolish," *El Libertador* says, "to question me."

"Yes, she is," Julio seethes.

"I think it's foolish to hand over all that money and not have any collateral," I say. I feel Julio tense up beside me. He shifts his feet beneath the desk.

El Libertador stands and leans over the desk. The clown face is inches from mine. I think I might be sick. "Shut. Up." He looks at Julio. "Get her out of here."

I don't ask any more questions. I don't wait for Julio to tell me to leave. I just get up and walk out.

As I wait in the cab for Julio, I decide two things:

One. I'm going to have to tell Arden the truth about my parents. Soon.

Two. If *El Libertador* turns out to be a fraud, and he can't get my parents back to the United States, I'm not trusting Julio with my money again.

Twenty-Two

Arden laces the string through the tab of the first empty soda can and Carly sucks in a breath. "I don't know about this," she says. He knew he would need to really put up a good argument for this one. But it will be so worth it. She'll just have to trust him on it.

"It's Deputy Pardue. He won't do anything about it." Mostly because he's lazy, but partly because Arden is the son of the esteemed Sheriff Moss.

"I seriously doubt that."

"I've done it before. I swear, he just gets all mad and blustery. He won't talk to me for about a month. That's pretty much the extent of it."

"Won't he get in trouble?"

"The beauty of it is, he doesn't tell because he doesn't want to get in trouble. I don't tell because *I* don't want to get in trouble. See how that works?"

She massages her temples with her fingertips and inhales again.

"What's with you?" She's been acting weird the past couple of days. Quiet. Distracted. Woefully inattentive, if Arden does say so himself.

"It's just . . . I've had a lot on my mind."

"Such as?" He pulls the string through the second soda can tab and ties a knot. Then he ties the two cans together and picks up the third one. "Talk it out with me."

"It's about Julio. I'm not sure I agree with the way he's spending our money."

"You think?"

"It's more complicated than that, Arden. There are things you don't know about."

"Such as?"

She shakes her head. "Forget I said anything."

"You need some serious practice with communicating." He smiles to himself, because he knows he's pounded on a sensitive button of hers. But what she says next surprises him—and makes him feel guilty for goading her.

"I'll tell you one of these days. I promise. When I'm ready."

Arden wavers in his crafting. "Sounds heavy. Should I be worried? Because if you think Julio's spending your money on me—"

She punches him in the arm, but the mirth in her smile doesn't quite reach her eyes, which almost alarms him. And true to Carly Vega form, she drops the subject altogether, in favor of the one at hand. "This plan of yours is insane. Tell me how Pardue deserves this."

Arden decides to take the bait. Carly can be an ornery bit of goods, and if she's done talking about it, she's done. "I happen to know that he lets the bad guys go."

"What do you mean?"

"I mean, Glass told me that he thinks Pardue is a dirty cop. That he takes money in exchange for not arresting drug dealers."

She bites her lip. Staunch disapproval is all over her face. "But you can't prove that. Besides, why doesn't Glass turn him in?"

"Because of the cop code. You don't turn in other cops. You'll catch hell if you do."

Carly considers. But she doesn't seem entirely convinced. "Cops are beginning to sound like some weird cult. And I don't want to get on their bad side. Your dad already hates me."

Arden shrugs. He doesn't want to rehash all the things his dad said that night, and he's sure Carly doesn't either. He'd love to say that his dad doesn't hate her, but he's positive his dad would have despised her no matter how that situation played out. So he skims over the subject. "I'm telling you, this will be harmless. You'll see."

"I don't see this Pardue guy falling for it again though."

"Same crime, different execution. It's brilliant, really. I've been searching the interwebs. Everyone falls prey to it. Everyone."

She waves a hand in the air. "You think everything you do is brilliant."

Arden pauses again. Now all three cans are tied to a string, and tied to each other. He gives it a good shake and marvels at the ruckus it makes. "It's true, I'm of above-average intelligence. But I can't take the credit for this one."

"It's just that I can't get caught for this."

He lifts her chin with the crook of his finger. "We absolutely will not get caught."

❧·❧

They ditch their bikes in the woods about a quarter mile down from where Arden knows Deputy Pardue takes his 2:00 a.m. naps. The moon gives them plenty of light as they walk along Highway 20, stepping around the occasional dead possum and away from the road when the sporadic car passes by. The humid late-September air clings to them like invisible netting. Arden feels his hair sticking to the back of his neck and wonders if Carly is getting eaten alive by mosquitos like he is.

It's hard to imagine that he didn't even know her six weeks ago, when school started. It's hard to imagine a life where there was no Carly. He wonders whether she and Amber would have gotten along. *Probably would have teamed up against me.*

Arden gives the signal to slow their pace as they approach the small gravel inlet where the deputy pretends to be monitoring for speeders, but where he's actually got the windows of his patrol car fogged up in his deep slumber. Carly gives him a quizzical glance.

"You think he's got company in there?" she says.

"Nope. He gets those results all by himself."

"Gross."

"Yep. Your mind should pay the gutter rent."

She laughs. "He's sleeping? Really?"

"Like a baby hedgehog."

She slides the backpack off his shoulders as they near the car, handing it to him with the stealth of a ninja. "The cans won't wake him up?" Then she cringes as she snaps a twig beneath her feet. "How about that?"

Arden shakes his head. "Nope. That's why we brought the air horn."

They creep along, and Arden slowly unzips the backpack and eases the cans out of it. He crouches down by the trunk and ties the string connecting all the cans to the exhaust pipe. Motioning for Carly to get in position in the woods behind him, he fixates his thumb on the go button of the air horn.

And presses hard.

In the moonlight, he sees the silhouette of Deputy Pardue jump to life in the front seat. Arden takes off for the woods behind him. "Carly?" he whispers.

"Over here," she returns. She's just a few feet away. They squat in the light brush, watching their prey. The engine to the patrol car roars to life. Arden can hardly contain himself. A deep laugh swells up inside him.

"Be ready," he says. "It will be fast."

And it is. Deputy Pardue puts the car in gear and doesn't even get onto the highway before the sound of the cans stops him. He opens the car door, putting one leg, then both outside the vehicle. He stands, then, shining his flashlight toward the back of the car, walks toward the trunk at a steady pace.

"Go!" Arden whispers, and they both take off, Arden to the driver's side, Carly to the passenger's side. He puts the vehicle in gear before ever shutting the car door.

"Arden, you son of a bi—" he hears Pardue roar.

But they are already gone.

"Ohmigod, ohmigod, ohmigod," Carly squeals beside him. "I can't believe we just did that!"

Arden rolls down the window and shouts his adrenaline rush into the night. Feeling unstoppable, he grabs Carly's hand and gives it a big sloppy kiss. "Darlin', believe it!" He starts flipping buttons on the dash until the woods around them are illuminated with electric blue.

She snatches her hand away from him and covers her mouth with it. "Ohmigod. Pull over. We have to give it back. Now. Arden, please. I'm freaking out here."

She really is freaking out. She's got her knees pulled tight to her chest. Back and forth she rocks, the seat belt the only things restraining her from dumping herself into the floorboard. This is the first time Carly Vega has ever looked small and frightened. He turns the lights off. "Geez, Carly, you should have told me if you had any reservations like this."

"I did! I specifically said—"

"But you went through with it!" He runs a hand through his hair. "You always say no and then you're the first one out of the corral!" God, what has he done?

"I know! I'm so sorry. You've got to pull over. I can't do this. I can't. I have so much to risk. I should have told you sooner."

"Told me what sooner? What have you got to risk?"

"It's my parents. They're not dead."

"*What?*" And what does that have to do with stealing a sleeping deputy's patrol car?

"Arden, how fast are you going? You need to slow down."

But it's too late. The blue lights are already flashing behind them.

Twenty-Three

The room has no windows, no creepy two-way mirrors. Just a single camera in one of the ceiling corners. A card table with a fold-up chair on each side, no cushion. It's not meant to be comfortable here. The institutional décor, the cold temperature, the hard metal chairs. It's all meant to be intimidating.

And it's doing a great job, by my standards.

They're leaving me here on purpose, to contemplate what I've done. What I've lost. What I've thrown away with two otherwise capable hands. They're leaving me here to stew in my guilt.

I knew though. Deep down. Didn't I know? Yes, of course I did. As soon as Arden proposed the idea, I knew we would get caught. In my very being, I knew. We have been too cocky. Too risky.

And this was the end-all of risky pranks.

I wonder where Arden is right now. Is he in a room like this, waiting to be interrogated? Or is he already in the comfort of his own bedroom, sitting in his tattered recliner, thinking about how close he came to juvie tonight? But that's not fair of me. I know that wherever he is, he's worrying about me.

The same way I should be worrying about him.

It's just that *he's* not trying to smuggle his parents across the border. He hasn't entrusted his blood, sweat, and almost-tears to a man who gets off on wearing a clown mask and wields a power complex like a machete. Arden will never see the inside of juvie, because of who his father is. Me? I'm a shoo-in. A shudder runs through me.

I am the stupidest person on the planet.

Just as I'm on the verge of a panic attack, the worst of all my imaginings happens: The door opens and Sheriff Dwayne Moss strides in. Slowly, he pulls out the other metal chair from the table and takes a seat. "Carly," he says, leaning back. "Imagine my surprise at seeing you here."

I swallow. Hard. I want to cry so badly. What do I have to prove to this man? Who cares if I cry in front of him? It's what any sane person would do. But I just can't. Not now. Not ever. "Sheriff Moss." My voice is shaky. I've got to get a grip.

"You seem upset. Want to talk about it?"

"Nope. I want an attorney." That's what they ask for on TV. Plus, the state trooper who arrested me mentioned something about me having the right to one.

"Nope."

Can he do that? "I . . . I have the right to an attorney." Now I'm just reciting what the state trooper told me.

"Oh, you'll get an attorney. When I'm good and ready for you to have one."

"You can't do that." I point up to the camera. "That thing working?"

His smile is unfiltered evil. "Unfortunately, a work order has been put in for it. About ten minutes ago."

Rage. It sifts through my body like ravenous magma. I stifle the urge to jump across the table. After all, the camera is under repair. It would be his word against mine.

The sheriff twists his wedding ring around and around his finger, watching it like it's evidence being processed in the investigation of a murder. "Arden has always been a spontaneous person," he says, amused. "Even when he was knee high to a grasshopper, he'd come up with the craziest of ideas and act upon them without thought to the future. I reckon you could say he's always viewed life as one big joyride." Sheriff Moss tucks his thumbs in his pockets and studies me from across the table. "Bet you can't guess where my son is right now."

When I say nothing, he laughs. "No? Well then, let me help you out. He's on his way home. Charges all dropped. Have you ever heard the phrase 'high cotton,' Carly? I didn't think so. To explain it accurately, let me illustrate. Arden is high cotton. You? You're burlap. Are you reading me?"

Against my will, a tear slips down my cheek. I've never felt so helpless in my entire life. I'm at the sheriff's mercy. And the sheriff is fresh out of mercy.

"You're going to jail for a very long time, you little tripe. I'm going to personally see to it. By the time you get out, Arden will have moved on to about twenty new flavors of the week, though let's just hope he doesn't take an interest in your particular flavor again, eh?"

"You racist bastard," I say, through clenched teeth. What have I got to lose now? He already said I'm going to jail for-basically-ever. I might as well say my peace. But before I open my mouth again, I see it. How could I have missed it before?

A scar.

On his hand.

Between his thumb and his index finger.

A scar of evil.

"You," I say, withering on the inside. "*El Libertador.*"

Sheriff Dwayne Moss stiffens in his chair.

All of it, the whole picture, falls together in my head like a puzzle. "You're double-dipping," I half yell. "With one hand you take our money to bring over our families, and with the other you deport them, playing the county hero."

"Carly—"

"You might send me to jail for the rest of my life, but you? I'll make sure every reporter in the entire nation knows about what you do. Anyone who will listen. The word privacy will be a pipe dream to you. Maybe you won't spend a day in jail for what you've done, but your days preying on desperate, decent people are over, I swear it. You wait until you *decide* to let me have an attorney, you piece of—"

"If you talk, I'll have your family killed. Including Julio." He leans across the table so quickly I think he's going to grab me. "Only you? I'll let you live. Just so you can get the full sense of suffering out of the ordeal."

My mouth snaps shut.

"Good. Now that I have your attention, I assume your rant is over, Miss Vega?"

I nod. Chewing off my own tongue seems appropriate right now. How could I have done that? Knowing who I was dealing with? Not only the sheriff, but *El Libertador*? Who do I think I am?

"Of course, I don't want to kill your family. I'd much rather negotiate. It might surprise you, Carly, but I'm a nonviolent sort of man."

"Naturally." My head is spinning. Negotiate. What is there to negotiate? What do I have that he wants? He already has all of my money. Every dime. He has my family. He knows where Julio lives; he can get the address from my driver's license, even if he doesn't already know. I have nothing left to interest the man.

Then the answer pops into my head. The answer's face. The answer's lips. The answer's smile.

Arden.

My blood drains down to my feet. To the very tips of my toes.

The sheriff nods. "You'll stay away from my boy. You'll never see him again. You'll do whatever it takes to make sure he stays away from you. Break his heart, whatever. What's more, you'll never speak a word of this to anyone. Ever. In exchange, I'll pretend this never happened. Any of it. You'll walk out of here a free young lady. The charges disappear. Your family will arrive as expected. They'll never be deported again."

He makes it all sound so simple. It's just that I'm in love with his son.

"And Julio?" I can barely whisper.

"Julio? Are you asking if Julio gets to live? I told you, I'm non-violent—"

"Save us both time and answer me." I feel like the life has been sucked out of my body and all that's left is a hull of something that used to float around Arden.

The sheriff seems to sense his victory. He leans back, folding his hands behind his head. "Julio will be none the wiser."

The tears flow freely now. I don't care about this man's expectations of me. I've lost a limb. A lifeline. My heartbeat. "You have a deal."

Twenty-Four

Arden paces the six-by-four-foot interrogation room two strides at a time, waiting for his father, waiting for word on Carly, waiting for anything besides this vexing silence. The only noise in the room is his own cussing, and that's toward himself.

If he had an iota of common sense, he wouldn't have pressured Carly to go. He'd already noticed that she wasn't herself; he should have taken that as a sign to back down. He should have made her talk about it, even though she can be more ill-tempered than a stump full of fire ants when pushed.

But what gets to Arden the most is that Carly has been right about him from the start. She's the one going down for this, not him. She's the one waiting minute after torturous minute to see how badly she's screwed up her life by listening to him. All he's waiting for is to find out when he'll be sent home, how long it will be before his father wipes the slate clean for him. All while Carly catches charges. Real charges that could change her life.

He presses his forehead against the cold cinder-block wall. This whole time, she's the one who shouldered all the risk. He had nothing to lose. She had everything. Her grades. Her relationship with her brother. Her two jobs that she absolutely needs. She risked it all. And he let her.

I'm such a selfish jackass.

Arden checks his watch. It's been two long hours since they were hauled to the station. Two hours he's been separated from Carly. Two hours his father has had to break her down.

He's ready to pull his hair out when the door opens.

His father closes the door behind him wearing a grim expression.

"What did you do to her?" Arden says immediately. "If I find out—"

"Sit down, son," his father says quietly. This is worse than screaming. This calm and controlled speech is how he used to talk about Amber after she died. "Carly is fine, for now. We have a lot to discuss, you and I."

Arden sits. Something is off. Way off.

His dad sighs, as if the weight of the universe lies on his massive shoulders. Arden wants to strangle him, but at the same time shake him and make him talk. "I'm afraid your little girlfriend has been keeping some secrets from you."

"What do you mean?"

"Don't I recall her one visit to the house wherein you told me her parents were dead?"

"She was about to tell me about that. Before we got pulled over."

"I doubt she was about to tell you all of it."

Arden hates the self-satisfied grin on his father's face. "You don't know anything about it."

The sheriff chuckles. "Here's what I know, son. Carly's charges don't end with your little escapade tonight. She's being charged with trying to smuggle her illegal immigrant parents over the border. Her brother, Julio? He's in on it too. They're both in a lot of trouble, Arden."

Arden buries his face in his hands. *Oh no. This is what she was going to tell me. This is what she was risking.*

And I've ruined it all for her.

"Dad, please. Don't do this."

"Don't do what, exactly?"

"I know you can make this go away. I know you've got your connections. Make this go away for Carly."

Slowly, the sheriff nods. "I suppose I could, couldn't I?" He leans forward, folding his hands on the table. Arden wonders if this is how he interrogates other suspects. Eerily poised, like a rattler about to strike. Do they cave? *Will I?*

He thinks of Carly then, of all the balls she has in the air right now dropping to the ground and scattering. Her parents. Julio. Her job at the café, at the Breeze. School, her scholarships. She was right. She was risking everything. Arden swallows. "What do you want from me?"

"It's an election year, boy. You've caused me nothing but trouble, all these fun little screwups I've had to cover up for you. And now you're running with a girl trying to smuggle her illegal parents over. What do you reckon would happen if the news media got wind of that? What do you think the good people of Houghlin County will think of it?"

"You want me to stop seeing her." It's not a question. It doesn't have to be.

Arden feels gut-punched. Carly is his salvation. She pulled him from a trench he didn't even know he was in. She made him take a good hard look at himself and he found himself wanting. Wanting more for himself, for his life. Wanting to be more.

And wanting her.

But how can I hold on to her when she stands to lose so much?

The sheriff laughs. Sneers, really. "That's a good start, boy."

A good start? What else could he possibly want? Arden lays his forehead on the cold hard table in front of him. "Dad, I just . . . I don't know what you're asking. What else do you want?"

"Let's just say 'stop seeing her' is an understatement. You're to cut off all communication with her. I mean that if she says hi to you in the halls at school, you look the other way. If I so much as catch you smiling at her, I'll bring down the rain."

Fury clenches inside Arden like a wound-up vise. Slowly he brings his head up off the table. "You bastard."

"That's not all, boy, so keep your enthusiasm to a minimum until I've finished. I'll be needing a few other things from you as well."

"Like what?"

"Did I mention it's election year? Your grades are piss poor. You dress like common trash. All that changes. You're going to talk to Coach Nelson about getting back on the team. Enough football and you'll sleep well enough at night. Which reminds me, curfew is at eleven p.m."

"Why? Why do you have to be such a prick?"

His father shrugs. "Giving my son a curfew, encouraging him to join a school team, and telling him to dress nice means I'm a prick? I'll take it."

"You're blackmailing me. What does any of this matter?"

"I'm negotiating with you. It's all about appearance, son. And I'd advise you to think very carefully on it."

But there's nothing to think about, not really. There are a million reasons why he doesn't want to let his father get away with this and only one—the biggest one—why he's going to take this deal and run with it. That reason happens to have the longest eyelashes in the county and the idea of those lashes being soaked with tears makes Arden want to punch through this cinder-block wall.

The sheriff must mistake Arden's silence for hesitation. "You do all of this for me, Arden, and I'll drop the charges against Carly and Julio. Clean slate. I'll turn a blind eye when her parents arrive. We've already ascertained they have safe passage here. I won't deport them when they get here. I'll leave them alone, all of them, if you do."

Arden stands, putting both palms on the table and leaning so that he towers over his father still sitting in the metal chair. "I just want one thing to be clear, Sheriff Moss. I'm not doing this for you. I'm doing it for her."

Arden walks to the door and waits to be let out.

Twenty-Five

The rain outside hits the metal roof of the trailer like BB gun pellets. In the hall, even through my closed bedroom door, I hear the gravid drops of water hitting the bucket placed under our ever-present leak. It's been storming like this for the past two days, which I find so appropriate.

Lying on my bed, staring at the ceiling has become my favorite pastime these few days. I'm like a sponge teeming with oil; I can't absorb what happened. I can't accept that Arden and I are never going to speak to each other again.

My tears feel like razor blades running down my face.

I didn't have to tell him, didn't have to break his heart. I think his father already did that for me, saint that he is. No telling what he told Arden I'd done or said while I was being detained. Whatever it was, whatever he said, it makes Arden walk right past me in the halls at school every day, with sunken eyes and an indifferent expression.

And a silent mouth that used to cover mine with such eagerness.

I had this breakup speech all prepared about how I'm going to concentrate on school and accuse Arden of being a distraction and that getting arrested really opened up my eyes, put things in perspective for me. All BS, except for the perspective part.

I got perspective in one big overdose.

It made me realize that I've been slaving for the wrong things. That if I felt truly free, then I wouldn't have to do things to prove that I am. I've been slaving for my parents, for Julio, but never for me. I'm sixteen years old and have yet to experience a childhood. I've been robbed, and I'm pissed about it. And so when Arden came along and offered me an alternative to childhood, I took it and ran. And never came back.

But now it's over.

It's over.

Why is it over?

Could I have done something differently? Couldn't I have negotiated better with Sheriff Anus? How could I have given up Arden so easily?

Or maybe this all worked out for the better. Maybe I'm being selfish about the whole thing. Shouldn't I *want* to labor for my family? Shouldn't I *want* to do everything I can to bring them over? Who cares if I didn't have the greatest childhood? I have the rest of my life to make it up to myself. What's more important is getting my family back together. Right?

And, God, don't I miss my mother? Sure, she's asked a lot of me, but things would be different if she hadn't been deported. I believe that. I shouldn't resent her so much for something she couldn't help.

And where did all these tears come from? What, suddenly I'm a crybaby?

Over the rain I hear Julio talking on the phone in the living room. He's so happy these days, Julio. All his work is done. All his slaving. Or is it, I wonder? Will the esteemed *El Libertador* deliver on his promise? Or will he use my parents, my family, as one last way to stick it to me? Everything about him screams malicious. I think back to all the things I said to him, threatened him with. He'll retaliate somehow, won't he? How could he not?

It would be wrong of me not to tell Julio. Wrong of me not to warn him. After all, he looks at *El Libertador* like some sort of earthly savior. It's disgusting.

I sit up, using my shirt to wipe the tears from my face. I check the mirror on my dresser to make sure I don't look a mess and find out that I do, in fact, look a mess. But there's nothing anyone can do about swollen, puffy, dried-up wells for eyes. I lift my chin, and decide that even though I don't look like I should be taken seriously, it's still my responsibility to do what I'm about to do.

I make my way down the hall and into the living room where Julio is still on the phone with Mama. They're discussing which part of the yard they can use to grow a small garden, and they're talking about bunk beds for Juanita and Hugo.

I can't bring myself to interrupt. Julio gives me a wide, proud smile when he tells Mama that I'm saving up for a car and how a car will make going to the grocery store much easier. I try not to throw up in my mouth.

When Julio hangs up, I give him a few moments before I destroy his high. "How are Mama and Papi?"

"They're excited. Selling things they can't bring with them. Getting Hugo and Juanita used to dry meals."

The situation is so sad, because they actually think these things are going to happen. It makes what I've got to do that much more difficult. But Julio deserves to know the truth. They all do. "I know who *El Libertador* is, Julio. And he's a bad man. You can't trust him." Lovely. Instead of easing him into the conversation as I'd planned, I go straight for the jugular, straight for confrontation, telling Julio what he can and can't do—and this from his younger sister.

But I know what I know.

Julio's nostrils instantly flare. "You know we never did talk about your behavior the other night with *El Libertador*. I was too angry to tell you how disappointed I was in you. Carlotta, you could have ruined it for us."

Did he not hear what I just said? Spanish or English, or even a mix of it when I'm mad, Julio understands it all. "I'm trying to tell you something here and you're still trying to suck up to *El Libertador*."

"Watch your mouth, Carlotta. You will treat me with respect."

I bite back another smart remark because, really, I want to treat Julio with respect. If anyone is the victim here, it's Julio. Slaving for our parents to bring them over while he could be starting his own life, even his own family. And getting stuck raising his baby sister in the mix of it all. Julio does deserve my respect.

But I deserve his too.

I know Sheriff Moss said not to tell anyone. But I have to. I have to get it out, what happened to me. What I lost. Except the person I lost is exactly who I want to burden this with. Talk it out with. My brother? He's a distant second choice by miles and miles. Not because I don't love him and we're not close in ways, but because Julio is too perfect. He has been a better person than I have from the get-go. He never would have even considered doing the things

I've done these past couple of months. I can already see the disapproval dripping from his stoic face. He has always been there for me. We have come to rely on each other, he and I.

But this he will not understand.

Of course, it's not entirely for him to understand. The part that I want to make him understand isn't *why* I've done all the things I've done, it's what I found out while doing them. That the sheriff and *El Libertador* are one and the same. And he's going to royally screw us, I feel it.

And if there is anyone who is the best at keeping secrets, it's Julio Money-Saving Vega. "Julio, I have a lot to tell you. Will you just sit down please and let me explain?"

I can tell he's curious, and also sorry that he just scolded me. His remorse will dissipate shortly, I'm sure of it. He gives me a small smile. I'm sure he's feeling like the savior of the world, being able to talk with Mama about how he's made enough to bring them over, mostly by himself, and finished raising their child for them. I've never seen Julio so relaxed before. So . . . free.

Should I tell him?

But the answer is yes. It must be yes.

"Would you like a cup of coffee before we sit?" he says, walking the two steps it takes to get from the living room to the kitchen. The coffee is almost ready, and it smells good. But I don't want any charity from Julio, however small.

We are silent as the coffeemaker spits and spews and huffs the last of its load into the pot. Slowly and with a kind of majestic grace, Julio pours his coffee, leaving it black of course, because he needs no frills and thrills in life. He takes the smallest of sips, savoring it as if it were the gourmet-est of all espressos.

We buy it in bulk from a bent-and-dent warehouse across town.

Julio makes his way back to the living room and sits on the couch next to me, where I've settled into the corner and into a mild panic attack. "What do you need to tell me, Carlotta? If it's about your laptop, I already noticed it doesn't have the school sticker on it. But I've overlooked that, because you deserve a reward every now and then." Julio wraps both his hands around his mug. "Though I wish you would have asked me. That was a big expense. What if I needed it for groceries?"

"I know. I'm sorry." Wait until he hears what else I've done. But first things first. "*El Libertador* is Sheriff Moss."

Julio blinks. "What? What do you mean?"

"The sheriff of Houghlin County? The one whose office deported our family three years ago? Yeah, he's *El Libertador*."

Julio sets his mug on the flimsy wood coffee table in front of us. Some of the coffee sloshes out, making a ring around the cup. "You can't go around saying things like that, Carlotta. What would even make you say such things? If *El Libertador* finds out—"

"I've struck a deal with *El Libertador*," I say. Ohmigod. This was supposed to be a delicate conversation. I'm handling this delicate thing as if with a hammer. "He'll give Mama and Papi safe passage. If I do what he says."

"No, *I've* struck a deal with *El Libertador*," Julio counters. "And if you've been talking to him since our meeting, then you've been putting my deal in jeopardy." His brows knit together. Julio's freedom—the freedom that comes with everything going as planned—was short-lived. Deep down, I mourn the loss of it. Because this conversation isn't even halfway over. And Julio deserves freedom.

I shut up then, too, because he couldn't be more right.

I've put so much in jeopardy. All for a boy. But Arden's not just a boy. He's a piece of me that's been missing. A vital part of my heart that makes everything else function correctly.

I will never function correctly again.

"I didn't mean to meet with *El Libertador*. It's just that . . . I've been dating someone."

"You've been dating someone, Carlotta? Without telling me? Without asking me?" His hand gestures are all over the place, erratic movements that get speedier the madder he gets. I get somewhat pissed that he's going to go there. He's not my father. Technically I don't have to ask. But our situation is just a little outside the Normal Box. "Who is this boy?"

I swallow. I can't look him in the eyes when I say, "It's Sheriff Moss's son."

Julio goes quiet. So quiet that I can't hear his breathing, even though his chest is heaving up and down like a bull focusing in on its next target. "Tell me. Tell me everything. Right now."

So I do. From the beginning. All of it, no detail spared, except the extent of the kissing. That's mine to keep to myself and remember how I want. I don't want Julio's opinion tainting what were the best moments of my life.

I tell him about the faux robbery, how I met Arden. I tell him about Arden being the one who actually found me the job at Uppity Rooster. I don't know why I even bother to paint Arden in a positive light though.

Julio will hate him in about five minutes anyway—if he doesn't already—just for being the sheriff's son. And my boyfriend.

I tell him about our little prank spree (I say prank, because really, if we were caught for any of them—except for that last one—we'd get slapped with misdemeanors maybe) and that I secretly cut down on my shifts at the Breeze just for this purpose. And then I tell him about our stupid joyride. The one that ultimately led me to the truth about Sheriff Moss.

And I tell him about the deal I struck with the sheriff in the interrogation room of the county jail with the only camera in the room under repair.

And Julio says nothing. He says nothing for a long time. I stay quiet too. I'm giving his temper space to breathe. I feel the malevolence expand into the room and settle in. The furious energy in here could be picked up on thermal energy radar.

"Julio, we can't trust the sheriff." I say it as gently as possible. Before my eyes, Julio has turned from a free spirit to a chained and shackled vassal again. And I'm the reason for it.

But these are things that need to be said. Sheriff Moss will find some way to screw us over. I know it. I've made a dark enemy out of that man. This won't end well for us. We are the ones who stand the most to lose, and lose we will.

"There is no other way, Carlotta," Julio says finally, defeated.

"Maybe we could just keep sending Mama and Papi money. American dollars buys them a lot in Mexico. They should be living pretty well. Better than us, actually. We could just send them a monthly allowance or—"

Julio's eyes are wide, accusing. "They are our parents, Carlotta Jasmine Vega. They belong with us. We are a family."

"Don't yell at me, Julio. I know you're mad. And I get why, and

I'm sorry. So sorry. But there's got to be another way. We've got to remove *El Libertador* from the equation somehow."

"We've already made the deal with *El Libertador*. We've already paid him. We've already put that trust in him." He sits up straight then, and looks me in the eyes. "Which is a better place for my trust to be than with you, I see."

Wow. That hurt worse than I was anticipating. And I didn't realize how badly this conversation was going to fail. He's not listening to me at all. Just accusing me and blaming me. *El Libertador* is still a saint, whose only misfortune was to have to deal with me. In Julio's eyes, I've shifted from hardworking little sister to the lowest scum on the earth. It's all over his face. I stand up from the couch and take a few steps back, toward my room. This is where the conversation needs to end, I'm sure of it.

"Julio, I can't do this anymore," I say softly. "If *El Libertador*—Sheriff Moss—screws us over . . . I can't . . . I won't . . . I'm not helping out anymore."

Julio's jaw clenches and unclenches. "You think I need *your* help? Look at the kind of 'help' you've given me. Look at what you've done. And now you're saying you won't do what it takes to fix your mistakes?"

A tear slips down my cheek. "I shouldn't have done any of it to begin with. I shouldn't have worked myself to death. Mama and Papi had their chance, Julio, and they got caught. If they wanted to come back to the US, they should have found a way. We should not have been their meal ticket." Everything about the way I was raised screams at me to shut up. Did I really just say these things out loud?

"Meal ticket? Is that what this Arden teaches you?"

No. That's all mine. But he has taught me how to have fun. That it's *important* to have fun. But I won't tell that to Julio. Mostly because he still doesn't see that we are the ones who've turned into the indentured servants. It's not like we can ever get back these years that we've lost working our butts off to get our parents here.

But is fun more important than family? Of course not. Have I been treating it like it is? I'm afraid of the answer. But having fun isn't wrong. Being with Arden isn't wrong. *Is it?*

It's like I don't know who I am now. Like I've lost my identity in the mix of all this.

"It's Mama and Papi's fault they got deported," I tell Julio. "They weren't being careful enough. It is their responsibility to take care of us, not the other way around." These things are all true, but it feels wrong to say it.

Am I betraying my family or have they betrayed me?

Slowly he shakes his head. "You are not my sister. Get out. Get all of your things and get out. You no longer live here."

I didn't see that coming. Not at all.

"Julio, please. Please just listen to me."

"I've heard enough. More than enough. Be out by tonight."

Twenty-Six

Arden adjusts the telescope in his room to look for Orion's belt. The night is clear and the luminaries are crisp, begging to be observed. Orion is one of his favorite constellations because it's the first one he found on his own, without Amber's help. He's almost got the lens in focus when his phone rings. By the ring tone, he knows it's Uncle Cletus.

"I'm coming bright and early in the morning, old man," Arden says, tightening the knob for the lens. "I haven't forgotten about you."

"I swear you came out of your mama's womb talking, didn't you, boy? That's not what I'm calling about. It's Carly."

The name is like a physical blow to Arden's stomach. He'd been trying to forget that name, to somehow lift the mark it made on his heart. But his heart still jumps at the sound of it. "What about Carly? Is she okay?"

"She came clean with Julio about all she's been doing with you and about your little cop-car adventure. He kicked her out. She's staying with me now."

Arden presses his forehead against the telescope. Julio kicked her out. That idiot. She's only sixteen. Still in school. Trying her hardest to do what's right. And he hauls off and kicks her out. *And whose fault is that?* he tells himself. *If it wasn't for me, none of this would have happened.* "If she stays with you, I can't come over anymore. I told you what Dad said. If he sees us even remotely near each other, Carly's family is screwed."

"I know that, boy. That's why I'm calling you and telling you that I no longer need your services on the weekends. Carly's going to help me out around the house while she's here. But you don't step foot on my property, Arden. Not until Carly gets on her feet and finds her own place. You two don't need any unexpected run-ins with your pa. You know that's what's best, don't you?"

Arden nods into the phone. It's what's best, but it's the complete opposite of what he wants. He wants to drop everything and speed over there and enfold her in his arms and apologize for ruining her life and beg her forgiveness and kiss her until she does. Walking past her in the halls at school is like walking past his own happiness in human form.

"Tell her . . . Tell her . . ."

"There's not much to tell her, son," Cletus says gently. "I suspect telling her anything would just torture you both, don't you reckon?"

Arden sighs. "Yeah."

"Listen, she won't want for nothing while she's here. She tried to give me rent money but I wouldn't take it. She's saving up to get her own place, and a car. I'm letting her borrow my truck to take to work. I never did like her riding her bike all alone at night anyways." A pause. "She wants to cook me breakfast in the mornings, and do my laundry and such. Earn her keep. It don't feel right, if you ask me. That little girl's been through so much already."

"Better let her, though," Arden says. "She hates feeling like a charity case."

"That's what I figured. Pride sticks to that girl like a skinny tick."

"You're a good old man, Cletus. No matter what the rumors say."

"And you're still my favorite pain in the neck. I just got a few things going on right now. You'll call me if you need anything, won't you, boy?"

What I need is staying at your house, washing your flannel shirts, and frying you up some eggs and bacon every morning. "Of course."

Arden can hear his dad stomping up the stairs. "I've got to go. The emperor is home."

"Alright, son. Talk at you later."

Arden hangs up just in time for the sheriff to swing open the bedroom door. He paces the room, inspecting the closet, and looking under the bed for potential hiding spots. Not many places for someone to hide in here, but the sheriff is thorough.

"Did you misplace your sense again, Sheriff?" Arden drawls, twisting a knob on his telescope. "You could try the hamper."

His father eases up to where Arden sits in the recliner. "Who were you talking to on the phone just then?"

"Uncle Cletus."

The sheriff extends his hand out. "Give it to me."

Arden gives it to him without a fight. He's got nothing to hide.

His father scrolls through the numbers. "What'd you talk to Cletus about?"

Arden shrugs. "He doesn't need my help tomorrow. Calling to tell me so."

"Good. Because from now on, you have football practice on Saturdays. I talked to Coach Nelson today. You're back on the team. Quarterback. It's like you never left."

Arden stands so fast the recliner rocks violently behind his legs. "I said I would go to him when I was ready."

"I've decided that you're ready. See how easy it is for me to get things done, Arden? One phone call, and you're back on the team. One phone call, and that girl's parents are—"

"Fine," Arden says, crossing his arms. "It's fine. Put me back on the team. Anything else I can do for you, Sheriff?"

His father nods, grins a little. "Yep. We're going shopping this weekend, you and I. Get you some decent, family-oriented clothes for election-year public appearances. Starting with a graveside memorial on the anniversary of Amber's death."

"You—"

The sheriff makes a *tsk*ing sound with his tongue. "People mourn in different ways, son. Always remember that."

"Really? That's your explanation?"

His dad crosses his massive arms. "You think I don't miss Amber?"

"I think you've been relieved since the day she died." Arden's voice is full of venom. He knows it's dangerous, to get his dad riled up about Amber. But poison like this festers inside you for so long, and then foams up until you have no way to contain it sometimes. And this is one of those times. "She was your daughter and her illness was a cancer to your campaign. You grieve more over your team losing a football game than you grieved over Amber's death. It was all about you, never about her. You killed her, same as if you gave her the pills yourself."

Strong fingers lace around Arden's neck. "Shut your mouth, son. Have you forgotten how many times I've saved your ass from juvie? And what about your girlfriend? You want her going to prison for her little stunt while I deport her family? Then. Shut. Your. Mouth."

Arden manages to wriggle out of his father's grasp—it's a move Glass taught him—and stands eye to eye with him. He's as tall as the sheriff, and his shoulders are just as wide. "One of these days you won't have a quick fix," Arden says in a low voice. "One of these days your house of cards will come crashing down on you, and the edges will be razor sharp and they'll make their marks on you. One of these days you'll suffer like you've made everyone else suffer. And I hope to God I'm there to see it."

The sheriff flinches, taking a step back. His face softens even though he's scowling. "Do you remember when I was a deputy like Glass? And every night, I'd come home and turn on the flashing lights for you and Amber. And every night, you told me, you wanted to be just like me when you grew up. Do you remember?"

It was a lifetime ago, but Arden remembers. "I was five years old. Everyone wants to be like their dad when they're five."

The sheriff shakes his head. "Remember in sixth grade—that would have put you at right around eleven or twelve years old—you asked me to come to the school for Bring Your Father to Work Day. You still respected me then." He rocks back on his heels, tucking his thumbs into his pockets. "I'm trying to figure out at what point I lost you, son. Was it Amber? Do you truly blame me for her death? Or was it before that?"

Arden feels his eyes brimming with tears. "Get out. Now."

"If you need someone to blame for Amber's death, I'll be that person for you, Arden. I will. I only ever want what's best for you. Always will."

"I said GET OUT NOW!"

His dad backs away then until he reaches the threshold of the door. "Your sister had a lot of friends who want to remember her, grieve her loss. I can't deny them that on the anniversary of her death."

Amber hardly had any friends, because their father whisked her away from society. From curious glances and busy tongues and aggressive rumor mills. He couldn't risk letting anyone witness a meltdown, not in his house. Not in his county. Not on his term. This graveside memorial is strictly for the sake of sympathetic voters.

And this whole I-grieve-in-my-own-way sermon is just another mind game.

Isn't it?

Twenty-Seven

I take the new cell phone out of its box and marvel at it. Maybe not at *it*, really, because I've seen and used Arden's multiple times, but I marvel that I now have my own.

I have a cell phone number. I have Internet at my fingertips.

Because of me. Because of the two jobs I work.

I want to call Mama and tell her, give her my number, but I'm too ashamed of getting kicked out of the house. I'm sure Julio has already told her what's happened, but calling her myself would force me to present my side of the story, and the more I think about it, the more my side of the story falls infinitely flat when told in things as common and ordinary as words. I wish I could explain with feelings instead, because then I think maybe she'd understand. Maybe.

So I dial the only number I can dial, who also happens to be the only person who doesn't want to talk to me. Julio doesn't pick up.

It's after five o'clock, so he's probably at the restaurant working. He hates when I call the restaurant to tell him anything. He thinks it reflects poorly on his work ethic. My guess is that Julio is the best employee they've got and that if he needs to take a call, they'll be more than willing to let him. So, against my better judgment, I dial the restaurant.

He picks up, after about two minutes of waiting for him. "*Hola,*" I say neutrally.

"*Hola.*"

"I have a new phone number to give you so you can reach me."

"That couldn't have waited until I got home?"

"I just wanted to make sure you have it, is all. It's a cell phone. Do you have a pen and paper?"

"Oh. Now I see. You just wanted to call and gloat about having a cell phone. Well, congratulations, Carly."

I knew he would read something into this call. The problem is, he has every right to. Because I am bragging. I'm proud. But there is another real purpose to my call. "I need a way to get a hold of you. You're still my brother."

"You can't just use that old white man's phone you're staying with? Or the help's not allowed to use the phone?"

"I'm not the help, Julio, I'm his guest. Because, you might remember, my own brother kicked me out of the house." That's a low blow and I know it.

Silence. I know it bothers him, that he kicked me out. No matter how much he thinks I deserved it, it goes against everything he believes in: family, unity, sticking together. I wonder how he explained my absence to our neighbors. To his friends. It must have been hard for him.

"What do you want, Carly? I'm working."

"I just wanted to give you my cell phone. In case you needed to get in touch with me."

I hear shuffling on the other end of the phone. "Okay, what is it?"

I tell him the number. "If you don't reach me, leave a voice message and I'll—"

"Fine. Anything else?"

"No."

"I have to get back to work now, Carlotta. Good-bye."

"Bye."

I hang up and toss my phone on my bed. It feels weird to call it my bed, since my bed is still in the trailer I used to share with Julio. This bed used to belong to Cletus's niece—Arden's mother—and this used to be her room when she visited over the summer months. It's all white frilly lace turned slightly yellow with age and silk comforter and brass bed and furniture complete with a vanity and a book nook in the window. I wonder what it was like to live in such a magical little room, to play dolls in here and take breaks to snack on lemonade and cookies. I imagine the echo of childish laughter that must have once resounded through the mansion.

I make my way down the servants' stairs in the back; it's the quickest way to the kitchen. Cletus refuses to let me pay rent, so I earn my keep by cleaning and cooking. I'm no chef, but as far as I can tell from the stacks and stacks of Hungry Man meals piled in his chest freezer, he's not either. I pull out the fixings for a home-made sauce, skimming the cavernous pantry for all the spices I'll need (Miss May gave me the recipe and I nailed it the first time, thankyouverymuch).

As the sauce simmers, I hear a yawning moan. I can always tell when Cletus is stirring because he sleeps in the ballroom, and it carries his grunts and stretching sighs all the way to the kitchen. I begin to boil the water for the noodles and remove the sauce from the heat. I went to the grocery store after my shift at the Uppity Rooster so I have fresh French bread for him to munch on, to help him absorb some of the alcohol I know will make his trip to the kitchen table a wobbly one. At best, he'll need my help. At worst, I'll have to deliver dinner to the ballroom.

But at least he's not driving anymore. I've persuaded him to let me run his errands for him, and take him with me if he'd like, so that he doesn't have to drive anywhere. He's persuaded me to drive his big truck to all my work shifts, because for some reason me riding my bike everywhere makes him nervous.

Which is nice. Nice to be appreciated, nice to be needed. And it's nice to take care of someone who cares about me. I wonder if Julio had the same sense of accomplishment, knowing he was taking care of me. Maybe I wasn't a burden after all. Maybe I was just family—and to Julio, family could never be a burden.

I want to convince myself that Julio is the exception. That not everyone in my family is as accommodating, as hardworking as Julio. But I have a strong suspicion that they are. I have uncles back in Mexico on my mother's side whom I've never met; they're practically strangers to me. Would they be as good to me as Cletus is?

The answer is probably. You can't unweave generation after generation of a family.

"Uncle Cletus!" I yell across the house. He has this rule where we use absolutely no etiquette because when his wife was alive he was "made to follow etiquette to a damned T" and he "ain't gonna do it anymore." Plus, he says I have soft feet and scare the bejesus out of him when I sneak up on him while he's sleeping. "I forget sometimes that I've got a guest in the house," he said.

I set the table in the kitchen for two, and pour Cletus a big glass of sweet iced tea. I've learned how to make decorative lemon slices at the café, so I do one up for Cletus's glass. He'll pretend like it's too girly for him, but secretly I think he likes to be bothered over. "Uncle Cletus!" I yell again when I hear no shuffling down the hallway. "Dinner's ready!"

I sit in my seat and fold my napkin across my lap. If I were eating alone, I wouldn't do this, but out of respect for the etiquette Cletus claims to no longer respect, I do it. After another five minutes have passed, and the steaming pile of spaghetti on my plate has become a congealed pile of spaghetti, I decide to go check on him. I don my flip-flops and stride down the hall to the ballroom. The door is slightly ajar, which means he'd been expecting a call for dinner from me. I can't help but smile.

We've fallen into a routine, he and I.

I push the door open the rest of the way. I'd just polished the floors in here yesterday and the lavender scent of the cleanser still hovers in the air. From across the room I see Cletus's feet hanging over the end of the couch; it's his usual napping position.

When I reach what I call his man-corner, I lean over the couch to determine how soundly he's sleeping. He's become somewhat of an insomniac himself lately, like Arden is, and I worry that these daily naps won't get him the true rest he needs. If he's in a deep sleep, I won't wake him; I can always reheat his dinner for him before I leave for my shift at the Breeze. If he's awake and just got a case of naptime lethargy, then I'll wake him all the way up and we'll have a proper meal together.

"Uncle Cletus," I whisper, giving him a little shake.

And that's when I realize he's not breathing.

Twenty-Eight

Arden takes a huge swig from the water jug on the wooden bench. It's been a three hour practice—on a Sunday, no less. Coach Nelson wants him in top form for the next game. Arden has to admit, playing ball again is not as bad as he thought it would be. The physical exhaustion alone helps him sleep, even though dreams of Carly haunt him well into the early morning hours. And it gives him something to do with his hands, even though they ache to hold *her*, touch *her* instead of the glistening pigskin of a game ball.

This thing with Carly isn't over. It will never be over, not for him. He might have to put on this gut-twisting performance at school, this sickening act to keep up appearances. To force his eyeballs to focus straight ahead in the hallways instead of watching her smooth silhouette melt into the crowd of kids. To ignore the tantalizing curves of her figure as it takes up the doorway on her way out of social studies. To look the other way when she wears a new outfit, or styles her hair to cascade around her face. To pretend not to notice when a guy is talking to her, trying to coax her out of her stubborn shell—to pretend not to want to break his nose.

He might have to convince the world that he is no longer interested in Carly Vega, that their story has ended. But his heart knows better. His heart knows there are endless unwritten pages left between them.

He can't, he *won't* lose her for good.

Which is why he's been scheming with Cletus. The old man has made good on his promise to keep him informed of all things Carly. And if the old man is right, she's suffering as much as he is. Oh, she keeps her head high. She knows how to play this quiet game too, to the point that it almost drives him mad. She doesn't look at him, doesn't speak to him, doesn't grace him with a secret smile when nobody could possibly be looking. One time she ran into him in the hallway and while *he* was tempted to let the contact linger, *she* pulled away as if she'd been struck by lightning.

But Cletus says she listens in when she thinks he's on the phone with Arden. That any mention of his name sends her into a disturbed, fidgeting silence, one that she doesn't recover from for sometimes hours later. That she turns on the radio to the local station that covers the football game every Friday night before she goes to her shift at the Breeze.

So together, Cletus and Arden have hatched a plain and simple strategy. When Carly's parents arrive, they'll just have to become legal. Period. Take all the steps, classes, swears and oaths and what have you. Cletus will help them file all the paperwork to become US citizens—he was the county sheriff back in the day, after all, with his own connections. That way, the mighty Sheriff Moss will have no sway with them. Nothing to hang over Carly's head. Her family will be legal, and Carly and Arden can finally be together again.

Cletus gets regular updates from Carly on their progress to the States. Just last night, Carly told him her family had started on their journey the day before. They are already on their way.

The plan is already in motion.

The revered Sheriff Moss is already undermined.

Right? How hard could it be to get them legal?

It's such a transparent, naïve little plan, the least conniving and most uncomplicated of all his schemes, but Arden has to believe this will work. He has to believe that the universe is not so unfair as to keep them apart indefinitely. Not when staying away from her tortures him like this.

The only problem left for him to solve is how to get out of going to Amber's memorial tonight. Today is the anniversary of her death and though Arden would normally be the first one to arrive, it's somehow been cheapened by the sheriff's insistence that the visitation to her grave be public. Arden doesn't even want to go now. And he knows Amber would understand.

His thoughts are interrupted by his cell phone ringing in his gym bag on the bench. He doesn't recognize the number displayed on the screen. "Hello?"

"Arden, I'm so sorry, I didn't know who else to call."

Carly. Her voice invades his senses, sending a shiver of sweet familiarity through him. But . . . she sounds rattled. Fear snakes through his veins. *Is she hurt?* Arden is aware of what his father used to threaten Carly to stay away from him; Cletus told him everything. For her to be breaking that oath with the sheriff and calling Arden right now, she's either got some incredible woman balls, or something is very wrong. And Arden is guessing she wouldn't be risking her family like this, woman balls or not. "Is everything okay? What's going on?"

"It's Uncle Cletus. I had to call an ambulance for him. He wasn't breathing. They're taking him to Sacred Heart on Highway Ninety-Eight. I'm following the ambulance now."

He wasn't breathing. Oh God. "I'll be right there."

∽∙᷐

Arden barges through the automatic double doors to the emergency room almost before they give him room enough to do so. The waiting room is packed, but he finds Carly standing in the corner, out of everyone's way.

He grabs her hands as soon as she's within reach. They are cold and slightly shaking, but he revels in the feel of her touch. "Any word?" he asks. Sheer willpower keeps him from pulling her to him.

She shakes her head. "He's been back there awhile. I think they pushed him ahead of all these people."

Arden glances around the waiting room. A kid in a sling, a lady with a swollen eye, a man with what looks like the flu, a screaming baby. All bad off, but breathing. "I'm sure he'll be okay," Arden says, his voice speaking volumes to the opposite, he can tell. He can also tell that Carly's not buying it. "He's a tough old coot." Tough and stubborn. But sometimes tenacity loses its battle with death. He's seen it happen before.

"I don't know what could have happened," she says, wrapping her arms around herself. Her hair is pulled back into a thick braid, and wisps of it frame her face. Her eyes brim with tears. "He was fine last night."

Carly's tears slide down her cheeks now, small rivulets of worry that disintegrate his willpower down to mere memories of good intentions. Arden stops fighting it, the need for her. He grabs her wrist and pulls her to him. She's startled at first, and attempts to resist, drawing herself back. It's something he'll never forget, this subtle but pointed rejection in the emergency room of Sacred Heart Hospital. He meets her eyes then, pleading. "I need you," he whispers. It's not what he meant to say. He meant to say that he's here for her, that she doesn't have to worry alone. "I've needed you for so long now."

Indecision washes over her. That, and anguish. But he can tell the moment she relinquishes her hold on the resolve that made her pull away. This is the beauty of Carly—the ability to let go when it counts. She comes to him then, rests her head against his chest. The feel of her in his arms again almost brings him to his knees. He hates his father even more for keeping this from him. "How are you holding up? Are you . . . are you okay?"

She lifts her face to his. Her lips are so inviting. "I'm worried about him."

He leans down, sighing into her hair. "I am too."

"I . . . I was hoping Cletus told you why I have to stay away from you. I told him, so that maybe he would pass it on. My family . . ." She chokes on the word.

He pulls away then, unable to stop his finger from lightly caressing the back of her cheeks. Catching a tear in the crook of it, he lifts it to his own lips and kisses the saltiness there. "You don't have to explain anything to me."

"I do, though. For my sanity. I shouldn't have kept it from you. And I want you to know that I understand, you know, that you have to move on."

" 'Move on'?" *What?*

"I saw you talking to the new girl. Jessica, I think."

"You saw me talking to someone and you assumed I've moved on? Are you insane? So should I be worried that I saw you talking to Chad Brisbane?" Because now he's stressed. Cletus is in the hospital and Carly is moving on? Surely life isn't that sucky. He curses under his breath. "Did Cletus tell you why I have to keep my eyes off you in the halls?"

She sighs. "Yes. And you're doing a great job of that, by the way."

"I'm going through the motions, Carly. But it means nothing to me. Jessica, seriously? Who the hell is that? Tell me I still have you, Carly. Tell me you haven't given up on us. Because I haven't. I'm yours. All of me. All the time. Every second of every day." He wants to shake an acknowledgment out of her. He wants to hear her say that she's still his, that she's as bad off as he is. He wants to kiss the perpetual logic from her face.

"But you've been acting as if I don't exist. I watch you. You look at other girls."

He runs a hand through his hair. She's backing away from him again. Dammit. "I'm looking at some*thing,* not some*one*. Something, *anything* else but you." He won't let her take another step back, he won't. He hasn't been looking at other girls, not once. If he was staring, it wasn't *at* them, it was *through* them. There *are* no other girls. There is only her. He closes the space between them yet again, pulling her back into his arms. She tries to wriggle free, but he will not—cannot—allow it. Not until she hears what he has to say. She can make a scene if she wants to. He won't back down. Not now. "I'm in love with you, Carly."

His confession shuts down the hissy fit she was about to throw right here in the waiting room. He traces his fingers along her lips as they quiver under the weight of his words. He's glad she realizes how profound they are, coming from him.

"You are?" she says, eyes round and wide.

Arden nods, sucking in a breath. "How can you not know that?"

She nestles against him, wrapping her arms around his waist. It's the best feeling in the world. It's like being embraced by bliss. "If my family wasn't at stake, I wouldn't be able to stay away from you," she says, her voice vulnerable.

"It's the same with me. Did Cletus tell you? Dad threatened me with your parents. He'll send them back."

She presses her cheek into his chest. "I know."

"If not for all that, I'd tell him to go to—"

"I wouldn't finish that sentence, if I were you." They both turn to face Sheriff Moss in all his rage veiled by a thin mask of indifference.

The large room seems to shrink. His father's presence, especially right now, is a smothering force. Arden's lungs feel heavy. What will his father say? What will he do? Surely nothing, in front of all these witnesses. "Kindly unhand Miss Vega, son. Miss Vega, you're free to go."

Carly pulls away as if Arden had burned her. This nearly kills him. "I was just, I'm the one who called the ambulance," Carly says, a tremor visibly running through her. "I wanted to make sure Clet—Mr. Shackleford—was okay."

The sheriff's indifferent expression doesn't change. He doesn't even look at her. He keeps his eyes strictly on Arden as he says, "I said you're free to go, Miss Vega. Now."

She bites her lip. "If it's okay with you, sir, I'd like to stay until we get word on Mr. Shackleford."

Finally, his dad looks at her, steel in his eyes. "Do tell your brother I said hello."

And just like that, Carly's face falls. Hurriedly, she collects her purse and walks out. Every step she takes pounds in Arden's head.

His father fixes his glare back on Arden, closing the distance between them in three loud, militaristic strides. Then he makes it a point to soften his expression. "Son, have you heard any word on your uncle? Your mother called me. I came as soon as I could. She should be here any minute."

Arden knows his mother didn't call. The news had spread over the police scanner. Cletus is the sheriff's uncle, if only by marriage. If an ambulance was called for him, his father would know about it in about ten seconds.

Stupid, stupid, Arden thinks. As soon as he saw Carly he should have told her to leave. He shouldn't have indulged in her company, shouldn't have risked her family's safety like that. He should have known his dad would show up, even though he despises Cletus. It's all about appearances. Especially since tonight is the memorial for Amber's death. Now he's had to make a hospital visit to ill family, in addition to giving a speech about how he misses his daughter later this evening. The crowd will practically be eating out of his hands.

Even now, he's acting like Father of the Year. But Arden will have none of it. He wants to stay and see how Cletus is, but he can't stand the thought of remaining under his father's scrutiny any longer. He thinks his uncle would understand. "She was here for Uncle Cletus," Arden says, keeping his voice low. "Not for me."

His father arranges a pleasant smile on his face, tucking away his fury for a more private setting, Arden is sure. Even his voice is monotone when he says, "You can see how I might have trouble believing you." As far as the spectators are concerned, he just made mention of the weather or the number of patients in the waiting room.

"It's the truth. I swear to you, I'm staying away from her."

"We'll talk about this later."

"You'll see that nothing happened here."

The sheriff offers a slight nod. It's the best he's going to get, Arden realizes. Who knows how long his father intends to keep him in suspense. But at least Arden is showing a cooperative attitude. It's all he can do to fix this, to make it better.

No, that's not true. Instant nausea overcomes him. *I can do more.*

He clasps his father's shoulder and gives it a squeeze. "I'm so glad you're here, Dad," he says loudly. Then he brings a very surprised sheriff in for a hug. "I expected you to be making the last few arrangements for Amber's memorial."

The waiting-room audience might as well be passing around a tissue box. The sympathy is almost palpable here. Arden wants to yell at them, to scream at them for being such naïve little fools.

His father pats him on the back before separating himself from the embrace. "Everything's going to be okay, son," Sheriff Moss says, his voice resonating throughout the room. He can't quite hide the astonishment in his eyes though. This is the most Arden has ever given him, since way before Amber's funeral, and they both know it. "You're probably worn out from football practice, aren't you? Listen, why don't you run on home and get showered for tonight? I'll stay here until we get word on your uncle."

Arden nods obediently, trying not to press his lips together, doing his best to look anxious instead of disgusted. "Thanks, Dad. I don't know what I'd do without you." The words taste bitter, acidic on his tongue. Bile competes with expletives to be next out of his mouth. But neither wins. He pushes himself further than he thought he could. "Can I grab you some dinner from the cafeteria? You must be starving, what with all the extra shifts you're working. I don't know how you do it."

His father smiles, and this time it's authentic. *And why wouldn't he be genuinely pleased with his son's newfound enthusiasm for public family unity?* "Thanks, son, but you need to rest up. I'll see you at the house."

Fighting regurgitation, Arden makes his way around the sick and injured people, and out the automatic glass doors of the waiting room. Behind him a chatter builds, and he hears his father greeting someone with a false, emphatic camaraderie. The sheriff is playing the part, and the crowd is gobbling it up, like he's some sort of celebrity.

A bit of doubt claws at Arden's insides as he hoists himself into his truck. *Did I do enough? Will the sheriff have mercy on us this time?*

He tries to reconcile the word "mercy" to his father. And he can't.

Twenty-Nine

I unpack a box of clothes and set it on the bed to fold and put away. The next box has books in it; I can shelve those later.

Miss May's house is not as grand and spacious as Cletus's mansion, of course, but it's pretty nice. Modern. Clean smelling, which is more than can be said about some parts of the old plantation house I just moved out of, I guess. And the best part is, she has an honest-to-goodness spare bedroom, which she doesn't use to store other things in, like most people do.

But there's something missing here at Miss May's. I have a key, free run of the pantry, and my own bathroom. Rent is cheap. It's even closer to the Uppity Rooster than the mansion was.

What's missing is Cletus. Our philosophical conversations. Our breakfast banter after I get off work at the Breeze. Our mutual, slightly psychotic craving for caramel cheesecake at four in the morning.

At least he's not dead. Which, after the stroke he's had, the doctors say, is a miracle.

But there is not room for me in Cletus's house anymore. For the next few months, he requires round-the-clock care, so the nurse had to take over my room there—it was the only space not used for storing old books, magazines, or deer heads and other miscellaneous, unfortunate taxidermy.

Plus, I saw the look on Sheriff Moss's face when he caught me in Arden's arms at the hospital last week. It was this look of finality. If I stayed at Uncle Cletus's house any longer, the sheriff might misinterpret my intentions toward Arden. I've tried calling the sheriff every day since the hospital incident, to explain myself. That it's not what it looked like. That Arden and I were both there for Cletus and nothing more. But Sheriff Moss is too busy to return my calls.

Too busy. Too holy.

Whatever.

I finish unpacking another box and decide that the smell of frying bacon in the kitchen downstairs is just too tempting to pass up. I follow the alluring scent until I'm practically drooling over a plate of it cooling on the counter. A napkin absorbs its greasy goodness. Miss May pours me a glass of orange juice.

Then she picks up a crispy piece and bites at the corner of it. "Almost unpacked?"

"Yep," I say. That's the great thing about not having many material possessions. It takes very little effort to play musical houses with them. Uncle Cletus would add that having fewer possessions gives you less to lose too.

But so far, I feel I've lost everything already and it has nothing to do with my clothes or my earphones or my books. No box could ever feel the emptiness I feel right now. Arden and I still have to ignore each other at school, which is actually way more difficult now that I know he loves me. I didn't get a chance to say it back to him—well, I didn't collect enough courage in time to do it. And now he might not ever know.

The only comfort I have is that my family will be here soon. I'm hoping Mama will take pity on me and have me back at the house. I don't want to miss out on the twins, and more importantly, I have to start pushing my parents to get documented this time. To apply for citizenship. It will be much easier to stay on them about it if I live in their house.

"Have you heard from Cletus lately?" Miss May asks, extracting me from my line of thought.

"Talked to him yesterday. He doesn't like the heart-healthy diet he's on. And he thinks he's hallucinating without the moonshine." He also said the nurse was curved like a mountain highway in Argentina, but that seems too vulgar for Miss May's proper ears.

"Sounds like Cletus."

My pocket vibrates then, and I know it could only be Julio. He's been calling and giving me updates on my parents as they make progress toward us. At first, the calls were short, just a sentence or two. Then, as he got more excited about their arrival, we would talk at length about what we'll all do together when they get here. I suppose he's forgiven me in his own way. But he hasn't invited me back home yet, so maybe not. Ultimately, it will be Mama and Papi's decision though.

Sure enough, Julio's number lights up my screen. "Hello?"

"Carly?" Julio sounds stuffy, like he's got a cold. "Carly, what have you done?"

"Huh? What do you mean?" I take a seat at Miss May's kitchen table, bracing my forearm on the cold surface of it.

"Carly." Julio's voice sounds so full of heartache now. "What have you done to make *El Libertador* break his promise to us?" He takes a moment to sniffle. I've never heard my brother cry before. "When Mama and Papi got to Austin, immigration was at the bus station checking everyone who came through. They were taken into custody, Carlotta. Mama said she had to beg the officer to call me."

"Ohmigod." This earns me a worried look from Miss May. I'm envisioning a raid. Guns being pointed at my parents, and my brother and sister. The unimaginable terror they must have felt. Maybe it wasn't like that. Maybe they just boarded the buses and asked for documentation. "Are . . . were they hurt?"

I assume they weren't, because Julio ignores my question altogether. "Some kind of protection he offered us, eh? But he took our money. All that money. And now what? We're just supposed to start from scratch?"

Cold steals through me. I've never seen Julio panic over anything.

He sniffles again. "So I want to know, Carlotta Jasmine Vega, what you have done."

The hospital, is all I can think. "I didn't do anything." I offer Miss May a fragile smile and motion to excuse myself from the room. She nods.

"Calm down," I say casually in Spanish, walking down the hallway to my bedroom. I shut the door behind me and sit on the bed, bringing my voice down to a whisper. "He saw me at the hospital, and Arden was there. But I wasn't there with him. I'm serious, Julio. I stayed away from Arden. I did what I was supposed to do." Except for the part where I ended up in his arms. But I'm not about to tell Julio that. Guilt settles on me like weighted dust.

"All I know is that Mama and Papi are on their way back to Mexico, Carlotta. How can I trust you? How do I know you tell the truth anymore?"

"That's not fair. I came to you about the sheriff." I lower my voice further, as if the word "sheriff" were cursed with the promise of unspeakable death. Nervously, I glance at the door. Would I be able to hear Miss May approach? "I told you what he said to me. I tried to tell you this might happen, that this is the kind of man he is. You didn't want to listen to me." Oh, but Julio is having none of it.

"You fix this, you hear me? You fix this!"

I close my eyes against the raw torment in his voice. Out of everyone, Julio had the most to lose. And it's technically my fault, all of it. "I . . . I don't know how to fix it." The feeling of helplessness feeds the hysteria fermenting deep within me.

"Not good enough, Carlotta."

"Julio, please." But I don't know what I'm asking for. Forgiveness? Support? A comforting word? I deserve none of those things.

"What about your boyfriend?" Julio's voice gains about two octaves. I knew he felt more betrayed than he let on about Arden. Not only that I was dating someone without his knowledge; that would be bad enough in its own right. But it's *who* I was dating that's the real clincher for him. And why shouldn't it be?

"What about this Arden?" he says, his voice more subdued. "He can talk to his father." There is the sound of small hope in his words, and it sickens me.

I shake my head, but the action is lost over the phone. "He's

not close with his dad, Julio. They don't like each other." Understatement of a handful of millennium.

"You better talk sweet to him then," he snaps.

Of all the things I would predict about my future, my older
brother encouraging me to talk sweet to a boy wasn't one of them.
Julio is truly desperate. "I'm not supposed to talk to him at all, remember?"

"What does that matter now? *El Libertador* has already gone
back on his word."

Oh. Well. That's a good point. All deals with the sheriff are officially off. I hate myself for feeling a tinge of relief. I can see Arden
now—at the cost of my family. "Arden isn't the answer."

"What about this Shackleford man? The one you were staying
with? Can he help us?"

The seed of an idea sprouts inside my head, germinating as
I talk it out. "Cletus? Hmmm. Maybe he can . . ." Probably not
in the way Julio wants, though. I doubt even wise, all-knowing
Cletus could rescue our parents from the jaws of deportation, even
with his connections. Saving my family is a lost cause and I know
it. But retribution isn't. "Let me call you back, okay? You work
tonight?"

"Of course I do."

"Call in sick." Then I hang up and dial Arden.

Thirty

Arden perseveres down Cletus's driveway, so awash with anger that if the moonlight was bright enough, his knuckles would show tighty whitey on the steering wheel. He's thankful though that the moonlight is held at bay by low-hovering clouds; this meeting needs all the secrecy it can get.

Instead of pulling under the carport, he drives straight beside the house, around to the back. Putting the truck into park, he notices two bicycles leaning against the house by the back screen door. His anger fades slightly to nervousness.

Julio is here.

Julio, Carly's older brother, but more importantly—and admittedly more scary—is that Julio is as close to a father figure for Carly as Arden is going to meet any time soon. He's never met a girl's father before, but he always thought he would handle it well if the time ever came. He would be charming and suave and somehow appear completely innocent under the scrutiny of a fatherly radar.

Self-doubt rises in his stomach like a helium balloon, pressing against his diaphragm and making it hard for him to breathe.

It's not like these are normal circumstances either, he tells himself, grasping at self-pity. *This meeting is anything but normal.*

Arden lets himself in the back door, letting the screen ease shut slowly, as opposed to letting it slap the house if left unchecked—and possibly alerting Cletus's nurse to the fact that he has visitors.

He strides down the short empty hallway and comes to a halt when he enters the kitchen. Everyone heard his entrance. Everyone is waiting for him, seated on barstools at the long kitchen island engulfing the middle of the room. From all the faces it looks like a poker game gone sour. One face stands out more than the others, and for once it's not Carly's.

Julio is shorter than Arden imagined he would be—though to Arden, his presence takes up the room—standing only a bit taller than Carly. He looks like her too, but with a wider face and more prominent, masculine jaw. The resentment in his eyes when he assesses Arden is unmistakable.

I guess I had my chance at first impressions when I got his sister arrested.

"Sorry I'm late," Arden says, even though he's not actually late at all. "Sorry" just seems to be the right thing to say at this point. Anything else might be deemed as unworthy in Julio's eyes.

And unworthy is exactly what Arden doesn't want to be.

Carly offers a small, anxious smile. She looks exhausted, and like she's been crying. But then, why wouldn't she look rough? She almost had her parents back, and then lost them all over again. How she can hold her head up now is beyond Arden.

She turns to Julio and says something in Spanish, something that ends with "Arden." Julio nods at him, tight-lipped.

Arden reciprocates, swallowing a lump in his throat.

"Arden," Carly says, "this is my brother Julio."

"Tell him it's nice to meet him." It sounds generic, Arden knows.

"He understands you. He speaks English." Julio simply nods at this.

"Cletus was just telling us that the best bet would be to send Julio," Carly says. Arden can tell by her expression she's not comfortable with this.

Arden raises a brow. This wasn't the plan. He looks at Cletus. "And that's a good idea because . . . ?"

"Because none of my connections would be willing to go up against your pa," Cletus says. He sounds winded. He probably shouldn't be exerting himself this much so soon. "And if the wrong people catch wind of it, they'll rat us out."

"Cop code?" Carly says.

Arden and Cletus nod.

"But why Julio?" Arden says. "Surely there's someone else." *Anyone* else. If Carly were to lose Julio . . . Arden can't imagine what it would do to her.

Carly stares into her mug of hot chocolate. "He volunteered. He *wants* to do it."

"He's a man, Carly," Cletus says gently. "A man has to do what he thinks is best."

Carly rolls her eyes, tears threatening the rims of them. "I get it. Manly revenge or whatever. But it's so . . . dangerous."

"I know it's hard. But we really can't trust anyone else to get the job done," Cletus says.

"It's a big risk," Arden says, hoping to come to Carly's defense. "Surely there's someone else who can do it besides Julio."

"Trust me, if there was, I'd be all over it," Cletus says grimly.

Julio taps Carly on the forearm and says something to her in Spanish. When she responds, he shakes his head vehemently. "No," he says clearly. "Me." Then more words spill from his mouth, angry words that Arden wished he understood. Words that upset Carly.

"He says it should be no one but him," Carly says quietly. "That it's his problem."

"*Our* problem," Cletus says, pounding a fist against the table with less-than-convincing bluster. "Your problem is my problem."

"Agreed," Arden says, pulling up one of the metal barstools next to Carly. He stifles the urge to plant even the smallest of kisses on her lips, especially under Julio's glare. "We're in this together." He nods at Cletus. "What else did I miss?"

"We'll need cash. I've got plenty of that," Cletus says to Carly, as if Arden hadn't spoken. He raises a shaky finger at Carly when it looks like she'll argue. "Not another word about it, hmm? I can't think of a better investment than this operation right here."

"He's right," Arden says, nudging Carly. "The old man may not have manners or all of his teeth or his health, but cash is something he's got loads of."

Carly shakes her head. "Fine. But we'll need a story."

"What's wrong with trying for your parents again?" Arden says.

"It's too soon," Cletus says. "And it's a lot of cash for Julio to get together again in such a short amount of time. It'll make your pa suspicious. He's a lot of things, but stupid isn't one of them."

"Then we'll need a story for the cash too," Carly says. She keeps twirling the mug around and around in her hands. Arden wishes he could comfort her somehow, pull her to him. Tell her everything is going to be alright. But Julio watches them closely. And Julio is not a happy camper.

Arden clears his throat. "Maybe he could just try for your father, then," he tells Carly. "It would be more believable if he were trying to just get one over here at a time, right?"

"That could work," she says.

"Do we know if they've made it back to Mexico yet?" Cletus says. "If Dwayne had a hand in their deportation, you can bet he'll be tracing them all the way back home."

"We haven't talked to them yet," Carly says. "All we know is what Mama told Julio when she was still at the bus station."

Cletus adjusts the nose piece on his oxygen line, tucking the connecting tubing back behind his ears. He looks at Julio. "Who else would you want to bring over? Do you have a girlfriend?"

"No," says Julio solemnly.

"Well, you do now," Cletus says. "Something else, though. Moss is a careful son of a gun. Might pat you down. We'll have to be ready for that."

"I'll be ready," Julio says. Arden feels slightly jealous that Julio actually acknowledges when Cletus speaks to him. *Clearly I've got to do something to impress Carly's brother.* He makes a mental note to learn some Spanish when this is all over.

If this is ever over.

"You'll be in danger," Arden says quietly. "Real danger." To say the least. He wants to put a stop to this right now, to talk them out of it, but at the same time, this could work. And if it does, it means that he wouldn't have to worry about getting caught spending time with Carly ever again.

It's just that he's not the one risking it all. Julio is.

But Julio is a grown man. He can make the decision for himself. *He's already seen what my dad can do. He already knows the extent of his power.*

Carly looks at Julio. He fires back instantly, only in Spanish. She purses her lips. "He says 'Lay a hand on my sister and find out what danger really means.'"

Cletus snickers into his sweet tea.

Awesome.

Thirty-One

Arden offers to make me a cup of coffee in what I assume is his mother's fancy coffeemaker (Arden is too manly to have a fancy coffeemaker). I refuse, because I'm too wired as it is, and because something feels weird about sitting back and enjoying a potentially luxurious cup of coffee while watching my brother put his life on the line.

I'll already be watching from the comfort of Arden's room on his computer, which leaves an exotic swirl in my stomach. Our first kiss happened in this house. Also, I pulled a knife on his father here.

This house is full of all things unexpected. Which is not a good thing at the moment. I need everything to go down just as we planned. Or I might pass out.

"Are you ready to go up?" he says. He slips his hand in mine, lacing our fingers together. I've missed his touch, the assurance behind it.

I follow him up the stairs and into his boring bedroom. He messes with the computer to get Julio's live stream pulled up on the screen. When it does, it shows that Julio is already in the cab on the way to meet *El Libertador*. The small camera planted on Julio might go unnoticed by the sheriff, but it stood out like a mangled thumb to me when we placed it on him. Its posing as the single jewel on a gold chain is a gigantic parachute of a red flag to me because Julio is the most frugal person I know, and has never owned anything gold. Not to mention, the jewel/camera is actually the eye of the gold-and-diamond elephant pendant on the chain, which is ridiculous for a man to wear anyway.

But Cletus insists he's used this necklace with great success in busts, and that it's the one necklace cam he never showed off to Arden's father. "It's a classic," he explained.

In any case, Julio actually seems to like wearing the hideous thing. I wonder if he would indulge in gold necklaces if he'd been cast a different lot in life.

The room, this whole operation, seems empty without Cletus running it. But he couldn't steal away from his rent-a-nurse, even for a few hours. Something about him having heart palpitations, which I'm convinced is the direct result from our concocting this kamikaze plan in the first place.

But we went over and over and over it with Julio. He knows what he's supposed to do. Cletus assured us that the sheriff is predictable, driven by greed and power. I get the power part, but not exactly the greed. What more could he possibly want that he doesn't already have?

"You think he's nervous?" Arden says.

I lean back on the headboard of Arden's bed and cross my legs in front of me. No matter what I do, though, I know I won't be able to get comfortable until this is over. But in a sense, it is over, isn't it? I've already lost my parents again, right when they were within my grasp. The chance to meet my little brother and sister for the first time. All these things we've been working for for so long. In a way, a part of my life *is* over. And it makes me want to disintegrate into a puddle of tears.

But I can't. I can't break down until Julio is safe. Until he does what he feels he needs to do. *Please, God, I can't lose Julio too.*

"Yep. He's about to faint, probably." Which is pretty much where I'm at right now. Julio knows the situation can escalate in a matter of seconds; Cletus told him over and over how quickly Sheriff Moss can lose his temper. And I know Julio's worried about it. I saw him praying this morning. I've never seen my brother pray.

"You think he can do this?"

"He's mad enough to." Which is true. He has a crazed, distant look in his eyes, a look that hasn't gone away since our family was deported again. *Again.* I shake my head at the unfairness of it all.

"But can he pull it off?"

"Let's hope so."

Arden unplugs the laptop and carries it over to the bed, motioning for me to scoot over. He nestles beside me, placing the laptop between us for optimal viewing displeasure. From Julio's point of view (the elephant pendant's point of view), we watch the cab driver make turn after turn, just like he did on our first visit to see *El Libertador,* though we know from the address that the meeting point is an entirely different place.

Julio fidgets with the nylon handle of the black cash bag beside him. I would too, if I were transporting twenty thousand dollars. Cletus assured Julio it's mere chump change to him, but I can't imagine carrying around that kind of cash—someone else's cash—wouldn't at least cause a little anxiety.

Finally the cab driver pulls into a parking lot. I suck in a breath. "Here we go."

Julio extracts himself from the car, hauling the bag with him. Once again, he gives the cab driver a wad of cash and asks him to stay. The driver shrugs. This doesn't appear to interest him in the least. I wonder how often he does *El Libertador*'s bidding. We were told to use the same cab company as before. By now they're probably familiar with the odd, abandoned addresses.

Julio's steps on the sidewalk seem to coincide with my heartbeat as he lets himself into a lone brick office building, offset by woods behind it. He walks down a long hallway, passing door after closed door. The building is in major disrepair; large hunks of drywall are missing in places, exposing the wood-frame skeleton of the structure. Wires dangle from squares where I imagine light switches used to be.

Julio approaches suite 154—our final destination—shifting the cash bag between his hands. For a second, he clutches at the elephant on the necklace, blocking our view of his world. It feels suffocating, this darkness. This not being able to see what my brother is doing.

Then he uncovers it again, and we can see.

El Libertador sits in the corner of the room in a metal folding chair, wearing his ugly mask. There is no desk. No other chair.

Julio doesn't appear to know what to do. I don't think I would either, except to stand there mutely, just as he's doing now.

El Libertador doesn't keep him waiting long. "I told you to drop the cash off." His Spanish is impeccable. I hate him for that.

Julio clears his throat. "I . . . I didn't feel comfortable leaving it. It left a bad feeling with me last time."

"I don't care about your feelings."

"I just wanted to make sure you got all your money."

El Libertador cocks his head. "My people ensure that I get all my money. I don't like changes to the arrangement."

Julio's camera moves down, as if he's squatting. For a clipped second, I can see that he placed the bag on the floor beside him. The angle moves back to face *El Libertador*. Julio waits for further instruction.

"Where's your sister?"

"I couldn't bring her. She and I are at odds. She's chosen a path that isn't wise. I had to kick her out of our house. She has to grow up before she can be involved in anything like this again." It stings, because this part comes so naturally to Julio; he actually did kick me out and we actually are at odds.

"You're an interesting man, aren't you, Julio. I wonder why you would go to the trouble of paying me to bring your girlfriend here when I clearly could not deliver on your parents."

We prepared for this line of questioning. The thing that bothers me is that the sheriff brought it up so easily. Like he's baiting Julio. I remember the desperation in Julio's voice when he called me to tell me about our parents. *Can Julio be baited?*

I try to push the thought aside though, because he did just supply some vital information for our bust. He basically admitted to the attempted transfer of our parents. That is a good thing. Is this enough?

But I know it's not. *El Libertador* tried to smuggle our parents. That's all we can prove. We can't prove that *El Libertador* and the sheriff are one and the same. Not yet.

"I know that sometimes things happen that are beyond your control," Julio says calmly. But it's not a peaceful calm. It's a kind of calm that makes me clench the comforter on Arden's bed. I hear deep resentment in the inflection of his tone. "It was a risk I was willing to take. So is this. I know your reputation. I know you'll find a way."

"How is it that you have a Mexican girlfriend, Julio? My understanding is that you've lived here all your life."

Uh-oh. We did *not* prepare for this. "I . . . She's the daughter of a close friend of the family," Julio says, recovering so gracefully I give Arden a triumphant nod. I even let go of the comforter. "We e-mail each other, and talk on the phone." Wow. Even I believe him. And I wish that Julio actually did have a girlfriend. A gold chain, and a girlfriend.

But *El Libertador* is not satisfied. "Where was she born? How old is she?"

Julio is quiet. I feel my heart hammer against my rib cage. His hesitation is audible. "I don't mind telling you these things. It's just that . . . I'm nervous being here. I'd like to get on with it. Please."

"That's a nice necklace you're wearing. Must have been pretty expensive."

I don't like where the questions are going, what they imply. I feel the room getting smaller and smaller around Julio. I wonder what he's feeling right now. "It's fake."

"How did you come up with this much money so soon? Someone

helping you out? How many helpers do you have, Julio?" The questions come like a staccato of shots from a gun.

Again, Julio hesitates for a second too long. "Forgive me, I'm not sure what you mean. I work very much. I also received a bonus from my construction job. Is that what you mean by helper?"

Wow, Julio is a better liar than I am. I scrutinize the mask, wishing I could discern *El Libertador*'s expression underneath.

"Your answers are very quick, Julio."

"So are your questions. And you have a lot of them. Why?"

Arden clicks his tongue. "Oooh," he whispers, as if we're in the room with them. "Dad doesn't like to be questioned. Not smart."

The sheriff proves this fact by standing abruptly. "The questions are mine to ask, not yours." He reaches behind him and produces a small handgun. I cover my mouth with both hands. Arden places his hand on my leg.

The only thing I'm thankful for is that this view of Dwayne Moss shows the prominent scar on his hand—something we'll need to prove his identity. It also shows a great view of the barrel of the handgun, and I have to wonder if all this risk is really worth the payoff. "Now, scoot the bag over here with your foot."

I hope this cures Julio of his smart-mouthing. If I were there, I would be pinching him. Hard. We knew the sheriff would be armed. Arden says he always is. We just didn't think he'd actually draw his weapon—Arden says he never does. Threatens to, yes. Pulls it, no.

What else could Arden be wrong about?

Julio does as he's told. "I apologize," he says. "I didn't mean to offend you." I think he really means it. I think everyone means it when they've got a gun pointed at them.

"Shut up."

It occurs to me then that there's nothing stopping the sheriff from killing my brother at this point. He has the cash. The only witness that Julio was ever there is the cab driver—someone who's undoubtedly in the sheriff's back pocket. To *El Libertador*'s knowledge, it would be a long time before anyone ever found Julio's body.

I don't want to watch my brother die.

The sheriff reaches out, taking several big steps toward us. "Give me your necklace."

Everything goes dark.

Thirty-Two

Carly won't come out of the bathroom. Arden can hear her quiet sobs from the other side of the door. "Carly, I'm so sorry, but we have to go. Dad could be home anytime now."

"Let him come!" Carly shouts. "I'll kill him!"

"You don't know that he did anything." Of course, nobody knows whether he did either. At this point, Arden doesn't know what to expect from his father. He never suspected he'd be the one smuggling immigrants over the border in the first place. *What else don't I know? Is he dirty too, like Pardue? Does Mom know about any of it?*

But the important thing is, they didn't hear the gun go off. All they heard was scuffling. It could mean anything. Julio still could have gotten away.

The black screen on his laptop isn't telling.

"He pulled a gun on my brother! He deported my family, Arden! My. Family. Your dad is psycho. *Psicópata!*"

Arden presses his forehead against the door. "Carly, please. We need to head for Cletus's house. That's our rally point, remember? And if Julio doesn't show, Cletus will know what to do."

What he doesn't want to tell her is that they don't even have enough evidence on his father. He never took his mask off. Arden has talked enough with Deputy Glass to know what is and is not conclusive evidence. And what they have isn't it. Especially considering who they're accusing.

His father could sweep all this under his network of rugs.

Just then, he hears a noise from behind him. He doesn't want to turn around. He knows who makes that sound to clear his throat. *This can't be happening.*

Sheriff Dwayne Moss.

Thirty-Three

The sound of the sheriff's voice pulls me from my self-loathing trance. The actual words send my thoughts chasing after one another on a muddled crash course. I clutch my head in my hands, just in case I'm losing it.

"I'll have a number one, super size, no drink," the sheriff says.

What?

"Carly! Come here," Arden hisses. I nearly break my nose flinging open the bathroom door and stumble into his bedroom. In the dark, Arden's face shows pale in the laptop light. He gives me a grim look.

"What's happening?" I throw myself on the bed and peer into the screen. The camera is facing the driver's seat of a car—the sheriff's driver's seat. *He must have kept the necklace.*

Of course he did. He kept all traces that Julio was ever there. And . . . is he ordering dinner after just murdering my brother?

"Carly," Arden says. "That's our evidence. It ties him to the whole thing. Look. There's the mask next to him in the seat. We've got him."

I nod, breathless. "But where is Julio?" Because this whole scheme doesn't mean anything if Julio doesn't come with it. It wasn't worth the risk. Wasn't worth the danger. Stupid, stupid.

Arden's lips press into a thin line. "I don't know. But look where he's at. That restaurant is five minutes tops from here. We have to go. Now."

◦•◦

The drive to Cletus's house is the longest I've ever been on. My stomach fizzes with churning bile. My foot bounces uncontrollably. If I wasn't clasping my own hands so tightly together, they'd be shaking.

Please be there, Julio. Please.

"It's going to be okay," Arden says, putting a hand on my knee. But the usual Arden Moss confidence is missing from the words. Before I turn away, I catch a glimpse of panic in his eyes. He's looking at the road ahead of us. "There's my dad. Get down!"

I curl myself into a ball in the floorboard, pressing myself under the dash and making myself as small as possible. The sand and general smell of feet invade my nose, sending the urge to sneeze to every nerve in my body. A whimper escapes me. I'm glad his dad drives a car instead of a truck so he has to look up to talk to Arden. This whole hiding thing would be easier if I wasn't shaking like an earthquake, causing a plastic grocery bag in the floorboard to tremble with me.

Arden gives me a warning "shhh." The truck slows to a halt. I hear Arden rolling down his window. Hear him turn down the radio.

I want to open the door and run. I want to open the door and strangle the sheriff. I want to open the door and see Julio in the backseat of his car, alive and well.

I want to confront the world and hide from it at the same time.

I stay scrunched up in place.

"What's up?" Arden says casually.

"Where are you going, boy?"

"Cletus's house." Why would Arden tell him where we're going ohmigod.

"For what?"

"Old man says he has a hot nurse. Wants me to check her out. Why all this father-of-the-year concern? You feeling okay?"

"Be home by twelve."

"I'll think about it." I guess an answer like "yes, sir" would have made the sheriff suspicious. Arden really does have a gift for BS. He doesn't give his dad time to respond. He steps on the gas and the truck jolts forward. When it does, I puke on his feet.

Thirty-Four

"She doesn't like tea," Arden tells Cletus.

"She doesn't have to like it," his uncle says, lifting and lowering a tea bag in a steaming mug of hot water. "It'll settle her stomach."

"She thinks Dad killed Julio." Arden hopes Cletus can discern the question he's really asking here.

Apparently, he can. "No way. Your pa's too chicken." The old man picks up a slice of lemon and violently squeezes it into the cup.

"Well, if you tried to tell me he was too good of a man, I might not have believed you. But that makes me feel a little better." Arden taps his fingers on the kitchen island and shifts his weight on the barstool. "Why do you think he kept the necklace? He hates gold chains."

"Pure greed, if you ask me."

This all sounds too good to be true. "You don't think he suspected a wire?" He glances at the servant's stairwell. Carly has been showering and changing clothes for a solid half hour.

Cletus sighs. "You have to be able to look at things from his point of view. As far as he's concerned, someone like Julio isn't capable of pulling off this kind of thing. He's overconfident, you see."

"So where is Julio?"

"Hopefully laying low."

Arden shakes his head. "Just seems like he would have called by now."

"Has she tried his cell phone?"

"He doesn't have one."

"Then how do you suppose he would have called?"

This conversation is too practical for all the emotions Arden is feeling right now. *Because what if something really did happen to Julio? How will I ever help her through this?*

He remembers what it felt like to lose Amber. He remembers sitting in his room after the funeral while people passed around tissue boxes downstairs. Made themselves plates of food, in honor of his dead sister, who was a stranger to most of them. Hundreds of people showed up. Big names, bigger names, names that meant nothing to Arden and wouldn't have meant anything to Amber. People Arden didn't know and didn't care to know introduced themselves to him at the funeral home, offering condolences or funny anecdotes about her early childhood, when she appeared normal. The preacher extolled all the many admirable qualities of Amber Moss—an impressive feat, considering he'd never met her. At the time, Arden wasn't sure what could be worse than having your funeral attended by a bunch of gain-seeking posers.

Now he knows what's worse: having to attend Julio's funeral with Carly. *Especially if it was my own father who killed Julio.*

He's not sure one human being can actually help another human being overcome something like this. He's not sure he's qualified to be that person for Carly, either.

And how will I deal with it myself? Amber's death broke him. This, though? This will destroy him—and anything left of a relationship he could have had with his dad. Sometimes bridges can be mended, holes can be patched up. Maybe one day, when they're both old, they could find a way to reconcile over Amber. But this? No way. Never.

Outside, it begins to rain on the tin roof of the back porch. In the distance, thunder claps, rumbling through the old kitchen like a guttural groan. "Got a leak out there," Cletus says, oblivious to the hole Arden is digging inside himself. "Need you to come fix it this weekend." He shuffles to the cabinet then, dragging his small oxygen tank on wheels behind him.

Both of them jump when the back screen door opens, then slams shut; the sound of wet footsteps resound through the storm room. Cletus and Arden lean forward, as if doing so will give them a better look at the person heading their way. Arden swears he hears the heavy clod of boots, and wonders whether it was the right thing to tell his father where he was going. Surely he isn't checking up on him in person, not when a simple phone call would suffice.

Carly is just upstairs. He has no time to warn her. She could appear any second and—

Julio steps into the light of the kitchen, soaking wet.

Thirty-Five

I can barely wrap my arms around the box. It's heavy and the edge of it digs into my belly, but since I only have to carry it a small distance, I decide to suck it up and go with it. In Arden's living room I pass Cletus, who's sitting in an elegant leather recliner, looking groggy.

I stop and peer down at him. "You okay?" I ask, letting the box slide down so I can get a better look. I still worry that he'll have a relapse, a second stroke or something, and that it will finish him off. But so far, so good. He doesn't even need in-home health care anymore. He can shuffle around his house without getting too out of breath, and he swears he does his physical therapy exercises every day.

I'll bet.

He rolls his eyes at me. "Girl, you've got bigger things to worry about than old Cletus. Now go about your business."

"Must be exhausting, to oversee such a huge project like this," I tease as I use my knee to push the box back up into my arms.

Cletus isn't able to help much with preparing the giant yard sale Arden's mom suddenly decided to spring on us. But I know if he could, he would jump at the chance to be the first one to move the sheriff's things out of this house.

"She should just throw it all in the trash, if you ask me," he mutters. "That's what I would do." Then he closes his eyes and leans back, dismissing me.

I laugh and carry on.

Arden meets me halfway through the dining room. "Let me get that," he says. "That thing's bigger than you are."

"I got it," I tell him, maneuvering past him.

"*Duro,*" Arden says. He actually nailed the pronunciation that time.

"Your online class already taught you how to say 'stubborn'? I thought you were still learning how to say 'I am not a penguin.'" His Spanish classes are definitely paying off though. When I talk to Mama on the phone, he picks up bits and pieces of what we're saying.

We've still got a few months until we visit them in Mexico. Arden was hesitant to come at first, because he wanted to give us some alone time with our family. But Julio insisted. I'm still shocked about that fact, actually.

Otherwise, I'm so excited I can hardly stand it. To hug Mama and Papi again. To finally meet Juanita and Hugo. I've already got a stash of candy for them I'm taking with me on the plane.

Arden shrugs. "I looked up how to say 'stubborn' on my own. Seems like an essential word to have in my vocabulary, with you as my girlfriend and all. And some cuss words too. You never know when those could come in handy."

"If you cuss in front of Mama she'll make you eat ghost peppers."

Arden gives me a dramatic cringe and grabs a stack of his dad's clothes that were draped on the dining room table. He follows behind me, out into the garage. "What if your parents don't like me?" He keeps his voice low; his mother is standing about ten feet away, sorting through a box of what looks like hunting gear.

I watch her for a moment, appreciating the peaceful expression on her face. She looks older than I imagined her to be, with thin, wispy blond hair and bags under eyes, but I suppose she's been through a lot. Really, she's still going through a lot. She's been turning the house upside down these past weeks, declaring it the filthiest house in the South. The truth is, she's not cleaning so much as she's been removing everything in the house that belonged to Dwayne Moss. She's already sold his truck, and even repainted their bedroom. Arden says she hasn't had this much gumption since before Amber died. We have a theory, Arden and I: The sheriff infused this house with his presence, like black mold, and his mother is trying to remove all traces of it.

And we're happy to help.

I set the box down on the garage floor and extract the suits and dress shirts from Arden's arms, placing them on a pile of other clothes. Then I pull him to me, taking his face in my hands. "They'll love you. They already do. You're their hero."

"But all I did was get you in trouble. Julio is the real hero."

"You went against your dad, Arden, to do what's right. Family is a big deal in our culture. You risked losing yours to help us. That means a lot to them."

"And you mean everything to me." He lowers his mouth to mine but I only allow a tiny peck. I've met his mother just a handful of times since Arden's father was arrested, and I don't want to over-step my bounds with her. She seems to like me though. And I want to keep it that way.

"We've got reporters," his mom says behind us.

The story of the sheriff's deceit rocked not just the insignificant boundaries of Houghlin County, but it reached far beyond. Julio's picture is still being flashed alongside the sheriff's across major news channels as they talk about immigration issues.

The sheriff's activities sparked a media wildfire. On my brand-new, unlisted cell phone I get call after call for an interview. Some-times the reporters are mean. Sometimes they offer to pay me. Sometimes they act like I owe them the interview. They do the same things to Arden and his mother.

We've caused a scandal ourselves, what with the two of us openly dating. America wants our story. The story of two Florida kids who came together under unlikely circumstances, then helped bring down the ringleader of a very lucrative human-smuggling business. I can see the movie trailer for it now. And they better pick someone good-looking—and legit Latina—to play me.

Investigation after investigation has opened up against the sher-iff's office in connection with Julio's allegations. Already, more and more witnesses have stepped forward, claiming to have informa-tion against the sheriff, against *El Libertador*. The FBI is involved, and Homeland Security. This should impress me, I know, but what I feel is that this is happening to someone else, and not to me and Julio and Arden.

People who call themselves experts debate on live television whether or not the laws should be tightened on undocumented immigrants, on whether or not Julio was in the right, on whether or not this will affect the president's policy on the matter. The president of the United States likely knows my name.

Me, the quiet one.

Arden groans. "The No Trespassing signs are up everywhere. They step foot in the yard, you tell me."

His mother nods. "Looks like they're just filming us. I wonder if they would air it if I flipped them the bird." Underneath that fragile exterior of hers, I can see how she and Cletus are related.

Arden chuckles. "Only one way to find out."

And so she does.

Epilogue

Arden pulls into the dirt driveway of Carly and Julio's trailer. He's early, he knows, but he's brought breakfast because he knows how chaotic the airport can be. They have two connections on the way to Mexico, but grabbing a bite in between could be tricky—and who knows what the food choices will be like. Besides, his mother baked them a breakfast casserole and he's determined not to let her efforts go to waste.

He knocks on the door and is greeted by Julio, a mischievous look in his eyes. "*Buenos dias, Arden. Los osos comen pan?*"

Arden laughs. "No, the bears do not eat bread." Julio has been testing him these past few weeks, speaking to him only in Spanish—and trying to trip him up at every chance.

"Carlotta is in her bedroom," Julio says in Spanish, talking slowly so Arden can understand.

"*Gracias,*" Arden says. He sets the casserole dish on the counter. "*Mi madre cocidó el desayuno.*" He's not sure if that's exactly right, but Julio gets the idea.

"*Muy bien.*"

Arden heads down the narrow hallway, his shoulders rubbing on either side of the wood-paneled walls. He finds Carly sitting on her overstuffed suitcase, trying to zip it up. "We're not moving down there, are we?" Arden asks, pulling her up. He plants a small kiss on her lips, then sets to work on her suitcase. "This can't all be clothes, Carly."

She crosses her arms. "Of course not. There are shoes in there too."

But secretly he's glad she has so many clothes. When they first met, she wore the same outfit at least twice a week. It's refreshing to see her indulge in something for herself every once in a while. To act like a normal teenage girl.

"Can I ask you something, and you answer it honestly?" she says, sitting on the bed next to the suitcase.

"I reckon," he says, closing it the rest of the way. He lifts it onto the floor. It weighs a metric crap-ton.

"I know we've talked about this. And I know he'll never ask for it. But . . . do you think I should pay Cletus back for the cash he lost? Julio found out yesterday that because it was confiscated and involved in a crime, the money wouldn't be returned to him."

Every time Arden thinks he can move on from what happened it seems something else is brought up about it. He wonders whether there will ever be a time when he can look back and simply remember what happened, instead of always feeling like he's still in the middle of it.

Arden leans against her dresser, feeling like a giant in this tiny space. "Cletus is a millionaire several times over. Twenty grand is nothing to him."

"But he's a man of principle. On principle, I should pay him back."

"Tell you what. You scratch and save and pinch every penny, then present him with a check for twenty grand. When he laughs in your face, then go buy a car with it. How does that sound?"

She grins. "Can you *believe* that by the end of the day we'll be in Mexico?" Her lip gloss is especially tantalizing at the moment. He sits next to her on the bed, and they lie back. She nestles into the crook of his arm, resting her head on his chest. Nothing in the world could destroy his peace right now. Carly will finally be reunited with her family. He'll get to spend that special moment with her. Life is amazing.

"What did your coach say about you missing football practice while we're gone?" she says.

He scoffs. "He told me to have a good time. What else is he going to say? That I can't go?" The truth is, Coach Nelson wasn't happy about him taking time off during summer practice. But Arden figures someone else can have the limelight this year. Next year, when he's a senior, he'll crack down on his game.

He can't help but think how ironic it is, that his dad is the reason he's back on the team, and now he's not here to see him play—something his father genuinely enjoyed doing. What if it was something they could have reconnected over? Something that would have made them reexamine their relationship at the most basic level and start again?

It's highly doubtful, he knows. His dad is a prick through and through. A horrible father. A horrible husband. A horrible human being, really. But the "what if" part is lost to Arden forever now. Could a man like his dad ever really change? Six months ago, Arden would have said no. But when his father was arrested, when Deputy Glass came to pick up the mighty Dwayne Moss and put him in handcuffs, hauling him to the back of a cop car, Arden saw his father's face. It had been full of shame.

But maybe it's like Deputy Glass—who is now running for sheriff—always says, "They're never truly sorry. They're just sorry they got caught."

Arden supposes only time will tell. And he's okay to leave it at that. Because time is what he's got. That, and Carly.

"Did you get all your homework done and turned in?" Carly is saying, oblivious to his line of thought. "You can't let your grades slip, if you're serious about this football scholarship thing. Plus you've got to get into honors classes next year, in case football doesn't work out."

"Football is going to work out. But, yes, Mother, I did get all my homework done. You should have seen Mr. Tucker's face when I handed it in. I thought he might pass out."

She giggles. "He asked me if I was cheating for you, you know."

"That guy hates me."

"He's just wondering why you're bothering to pass his class all of a sudden."

Arden hoists himself onto his elbow so he can look down at her. He'll never get over those lashes of hers. "I've been wondering the same thing." A lie. He knows exactly the reason he's bothered to do anything productive these last months. Why he's stopped feeling the need to go pranking, why he's been doing his homework, why he's been sleeping at night. And he's looking right at her. This amazing, stabilizing force to be reckoned with, all wrapped up in this deliciously curvy body.

Her gaze lingers on his lips. It's almost too tempting, not to kiss her. She knows exactly what that look does to him. "And what have you decided?" she says, sucking in her breath.

He lowers his head, until their noses almost touch. "That I have a reason to live again. Not just exist. To actually *live*." He lets his mouth brush against hers, once, twice. "Do I have you, Carly?" he whispers. "Do I have you like you have me?"

"Always," she whispers back.

And it's all he needs to hear.

Acknowledgments

I couldn't have done this without my agent/cheerleader/psychiatrist, Lucy Carson. Actually, I'm beginning to realize I can't do anything without her. Even like, shop for pajamas and stuff. As in, "Would these pajamas benefit my book deadline or would they be too stiff and require extra laundering, and therefore, time? What would Lucy do?"

This book (and all of my books thus far) would be a complete and utter failure without my editor/cheerleader/voice of reason, Liz Szabla. Y'all, she leaves notes in the margin like "Um, ew!" and she prevents me from saying inappropriate things about tentacles and keeps the Sasquatch references to a minimum. You guys owe her. Trust me on this.

My work would be steaming crap without my critique partners, Heather Rebel and Kaylyn Witt. They keep me in line, which is not an easy task. They mark up my pages during our critique sessions and call me out when I'm being a pansy or just a plain lazy writer. They endure my morning coffee breath and still sit with me at the café even when I've forgotten to brush my hair.

Many, many, many thanks to who I call the Dream Team, Rich Deas and Anna Booth. They are the geniuses behind my amazing book covers and this one just might be my favorite. After reading the book, you can see just how much they captured the essence of it in the cover. Great job, you two.

I've come to realize I wouldn't be Anna Banks without my publicity team. Molly, Mary, Caitlin, Liz, Nicole—what would I be without you? I will never, ever be able to repay you for all you've done for me. Thank you, times infinity.

Last, and certainly not least in any way, shape, or form, thank you to my readers and fans. I wouldn't be writing these acknowledgments at all if it weren't for you. Thank you to all the book bloggers who spread the word about my work. I lub you guys. Thank you to the librarians who work tirelessly to reach teen readers and thank you to all the teachers who do the same to promote literacy in school.

You all rock. Don't let anyone tell you different.

Love,
Anna

A princess and prince are rivals, vying for the world's
energy source. But when they meet in person,
SPARKS FLY.

Don't miss this thrilling, romantic, and futuristic fantasy from
the *New York Times*–bestselling author of the Syrena Legacy.

1

SEPORA

IF I WERE NOT SUCH A COWARD, I WOULD HURL myself from Nuna's back and plummet to the Underneath below. I would fall with purpose, headfirst on the rockiest part of the land. From this height, it would be painless. It would be swift.

It would prevent war.

But I am spineless, and so I urge my Serpen, Nuna, to fly higher and higher above the morning fog and mountaintops, which float against the sunrise and cast shadows like dark clouds onto the Underneath. Ah, the Underneath, that forbidden bit of land perched just beneath our mountains—mountains that are claimed by individual families or larger clans of families related in some way. Rope ladders sway in the wind all the way down, disappearing into the tall grass in places. If I weren't fleeing my home kingdom of Serubel, I'd be caught up in the beauty of it all, so high, scraping at what feels like the ceiling of the sky and looking down upon the monotony of the life I used to live, running through the grasses, throwing rocks into the River Nefari from the safety of Nuna's back, trampling over the undulating rope bridges connecting each of our mountains.

Yes, any other day, this would be a precious outing, a reprieve from Forging spectorium. Any other day, I would enjoy the freedom of flight, the time with Nuna, the endless possibilities of the morning.

But today will be the last of many things, and I mourn the loss of them already.

My thoughts wander again to far below us, far beneath the early mist and the waterfalls cascading into the River Nefari, to where my body should be sprawled, bloodied and lifeless and mauled. Yet, I tighten my hold on Nuna.

Saints of Serubel, but I am gutless.

Mother would have me believe otherwise: that it takes far more courage to hide, to live a life among the Baseborn class, who live in the poorest corner of our enemy kingdom Theoria. That the living conditions are rough, and the general mood of its residents even rougher. Those Serubelans who live there are not slaves anymore; stark poverty is what keeps them under Theorian control. If they could afford to, they would return to their homeland. If they could afford to, they would become citizens of Serubel again.

But I do not have that freedom. I can never return.

Not as long as Father wants to conquer the kingdoms. Not as long as I have what he needs to do so.

Nuna squirms beneath me as tears slip down my cheeks; she knows my feelings as well as I've come to know hers. She's beautiful, Nuna, even if she is a Defender. Most Defender Serpens are ugly, and not only because of their rugged training scars, but also because they are the color of the green mucus that seeps from noses when someone catches cold. Their spiked tails and thick underbellies resemble calluses instead of the glistening, pearly scales of other Serpens of different uses, and their facial features seem naturally arranged to be fierce, all arched brows and mouths set in an almost humanlike scowl.

But to me, Nuna could never be ugly, perhaps because I've handled her for ten years already, since a time before the weight of my body entrenched a natural saddle along her neck, just behind her head. Grandfather always said that time grew things, like trees and children and affection. Perhaps because of the time I've spent with her, my affection covers over Nuna's flaws. Oh, but it wasn't always so. When I was barely waist-high to my father, he announced that the entire royal family would ride Defenders henceforth to ensure our protection. I remember that day well, even though my understanding of the way of things was only proportionate to my age. I knew the people of Serubel were upset, and I knew it had been Father's doing. Father's decree had come as a shock—a king who felt he needed the protection of a Defender was concerning, especially after a fragile Trade Treaty between Serubel and Theoria had just been penned. It was a cold treaty, but one promising peace—and so why would His Majesty need a Defender Serpen all of a sudden? It put our people at unease, to say the least. But no one in the kingdom could have been more shocked than me, a quiet six-year-old princess, scared of Serpens in general and morbidly terrified of Defenders in particular. Politics were matters for the adults, but riding Defender Serpens was a most pressing concern for a child.

Still, Nuna struck me as different almost from the beginning. Her green coloring runs a bit deeper than the other Defenders, like fern leaves darkened by morning mist, and though she has the necessary scars from training to protect her royal rider, I had seen to it that the wounds were cared for and healed properly, so they are not as pronounced as the other Defenders'.

And when she sees me, I'd swear on the snowy caps of Serubel that she smiles.

Absently, I pet her head now as I spy the edge of the kingdom on the horizon. Where the grassy, rolling fields of Serubel end, that is where the Theorian desert begins. No, that is not entirely true. The kingdoms technically do not border each other; there is the Valley of the Tenantless that sweeps between the kingdoms, a vast, desolate dust bowl full of thickets and thorns and nothing of value and so uninviting and void that neither kingdom will lay claim to it. No one knows why this phenomena occurs, where the bowl comes from, or what keeps it so bereft of life. Why the lush green grass of Serubel gives way to sand, then shriveling plants and prickly thorn bushes. Even the most intelligent of the Theorian scholars cannot solve the puzzle. And so the phenomena is subject to rumors of a curse. Looking down upon the Tenantless from the safety of Nuna's back, I could convince myself of a true curse. But curse or no, I have to cross the valley to get to the Theorian desert—which, in my opinion, might be considered cursed itself.

Who would choose to live in such a dry, desolate place, I wouldn't know.

Perhaps it's fitting that I should flee to an afflicted, bleak kingdom. That if I should live, it will be among the Baseborn class of Theoria. That each day I should break my back for my portion of food and shelter and that I should become a slave to my own hunger and thirst.

Yes, it's fitting, and I want that for myself. I want that for myself more than I want an eternity in the cold recesses of the prison cell my Father reserved for me. I want it more than the worry that he will soon grow tired of my resistance and perhaps trade my cell in favor of torturing me into Forging precious spectorium. I would rather hide in desolation and poverty, whether it be in the Baseborn Quarters or the Tenantless, than be the cause of thousands of deaths in all the five kingdoms.

And saints forgive me, I would rather hide than end my own life.

Nuna recognizes the boundary ahead of us—all Serpens are trained to halt at the sight of it—and she begins to slow, her three pairs of wings catching the wind instead of moving it. I coo into the small orifice that is her ear and bid her to land just before the grass fades into outstretched sand, the first of the overgrown thorn bushes standing guard in front of the rest of the valley.

Nuna cannot come any farther than this. If my father were to search for me, Nuna would be easily spotted, as I'd have to travel by air rather than by foot; she is much too big to navigate the thistles on the ground. Alone, though, I could hide among the thistles themselves, carefully of course, and from above be indiscernible and by ground be imperceptible.

It is the worst way to travel the valley, yet the best possible chance for escape. And so I dismount Nuna at the edge of the bushes.

According to my map, the kingdom of Theoria dwarfs the other kingdoms in size, though it's mostly desert and the population tends to accumulate in Anyar, where the River Nefari widens and cuts straight through. I'll follow the river to this capital city. I'll do as my mother says and I'll embrace this new life. She wants the best for me, Mother. But she also wants the best for Serubel.

And what is best for Serubel is that I never return.

I come around to face Nuna and rub her nose, which causes her tail to whip about in pleasure. Serpens have only wings, no hands or feet or hooves or claws. No limbs to scratch an itch or to self-groom— which makes them especially grateful for a good rubbing down. They enjoy being petted, bathed, touched. Serpens may look formidable, especially Defenders, but with their riders—their bonded riders, that is—they are as gentle as butterflies on a breeze.

And I will miss my Nuna.

I nuzzle the tip of her scaly nose with mine, which would be a ridiculous sight to see, I'm sure. Father would not approve. Even Mother might roll her eyes. And Aldon, my tutor, would sigh and mutter to himself, "Princess Sepora, a lost cause of a princess who treats her Defender as a pet." A pet that is longer than fifteen lengths of me, her head alone three times the size of my body—and so nuzzling really is a delicate matter indeed. But I need this one last comfort, this one last gift of affection from her, before I begin my journey.

She holds very still, careful not to open her mouth and expose her sickle-sharp teeth. I've had many stitches because of her accidental overexcitement, and while I usually do stay away from her mouth, this is a special occasion. "This is good-bye, my lovely friend," I whisper.

The words feel like a bite to my tongue, sharp and painful. Nuna nuzzles back, squirming to get as close to me as possible, slipping on the velvety sleekness of the undisturbed soft sand and losing traction. I step away from her. This is not good-bye for Nuna. She has no idea this will be the last time we see each other. She knows something is amiss, for I've never taken her this close to the border before. But she probably assumes I'll mount her soon, and we'll fly away together.

With my hands, I give her the signal to return to her holding on the far end of the mountains where all the Serpens are corralled. No one must know she's been out this morning. No one must know Mother flew her to my cell to aid me in my escape.

Nuna is not happy with my command and protests with a high-pitched squeal. She's leery of the boundary still, as she should be. I shake my head at her, firmly, and make the signal again. Another tear streaks all the way down to my throat when she slithers backward, away from me. She watches me then, blinking once, as if to give me time to change my mind.

I gesture again for her to go.

I watch after her for a long time as she glissades through the air, leaving me behind. I watch until I can't see her any longer. Then I turn toward the Tenantless. Toward my new life. And I take the first step.

2

TARIK

TARIK MAKES HIS WAY TO HIS FATHER'S BEDCHAMBERS in the farthest wing of the palace, the tension building with each barefoot step. Behind him, Patra pads along quietly, stealthily, the way only a feline could, pausing to stretch and let out an enormous, soundless yawn that brings the muscles in her back taut, the golden sheen of her coat glistening in the candlelight. Despite Patra's great size, Tarik suspects if his giant cat had the notion, she could sneak up on the wind. He waits for her yawn to subside, his lips curling up in a grin.

"You didn't have to come with me," he tells her, and she responds by nudging his palm with her nose, leaning down to do so as it were, since her head nearly reaches the height of his shoulder. Even though it's late in the evening and Rashidi's messenger had put her on alert, she purrs at his side, recognizing that they are going to visit Tarik's father—something they've done together since he was a boy.

They walk past the towering marble columns and the layered stone fountains illuminated with small pyramids of spectorium and, finally, the rows of guards on either side of them leading up to his father's door, swords and shields at the ready. *They can protect my father from any outside intruder*, Tarik thinks bitterly. *But they cannot protect him from the thing inside him, asking him for his life day after day.* Not even the Healers at the Lyceum can figure out what is killing the king of Theoria. Even they, of the Favored Ones, are powerless against this new illness.

The two soldiers standing at the great wooden barrier pull the ornate handles and open it wide for their prince and his feline companion, the hinges creaking loud enough to wake the statues in the massive garden outside.

His father's magnificent bed is at the end of the cavernous room, and it takes Tarik and Patra several more moments to reach it. Taking the steps up to the bed quietly, Tarik motions for Patra to stay behind. She obeys, spilling out onto the floor and resting lazily on her side as she watches him. Rashidi, his father's most trusted adviser, sits on the edge of the bed holding the king's hand. Tarik does not like this rare show of affection from Rashidi, does not want to consider what it must mean for his father's health.

"The Falcon Prince has arrived, my king," Rashidi whispers.

Tarik shakes his head, taking a place next to Rashidi. He cannot recall a single time his father has ever actually called him the Falcon Prince, not since he gave him the title when Tarik was but seven years. "You see into matters with the eyes of a falcon," he'd said. "Knowing discernment when others allow room for ignorance." The name had caught on in the palace and then throughout Theoria, and though he doesn't feel deserving, he could never admit such a thing to a father who had been so proud.

"Let him sleep," Tarik says, absorbing that the great King Knosi, in his weakened state, now takes up so little of the bed.

"I would, my prince, but he has summoned you for a reason," Rashidi says softly.

"The reason can wait until morning," Tarik says, already knowing what the old adviser will say. He doubts his father summoned him at all but rather it was Rashidi's need for tradition, for formalities that brings him to the bedchamber this night. Tarik cannot imagine, though, that his father will even wake, much less speak the decree making his firstborn son the new king of Theoria.

"I'm afraid it cannot, Highness."

"Please, Rashidi. I will never get used to you calling me Highness and meaning it." As the royal family's closest friend, Rashidi had had the displeasure of knowing Tarik when he was a boy. A very rambunctious boy.

The old man laughs. "Perhaps you are not a Lingot after all, my prince. Surely you would know my insincerity."

Tarik snorts. Rashidi wants to convince him that he doesn't mean *Highness*, that he is not officially acknowledging him as a ruler of Theoria. But as Rashidi said, Tarik is a Lingot. He can distinguish a truth from a lie, and right now, Rashidi is telling the truth. He is indeed calling him Highness. And he does indeed mean it.

"My father will recover from this," Tarik says, recognizing the lie in his own voice. Rashidi does not have to be a Lingot to notice.

"No," Rashidi says. "The Healers do not think him to live through the night."

"The Healers have been wrong before." Haven't they? Tarik is not sure.

Rashidi sighs. It is full of pity, Tarik can tell. Sometimes he wishes he didn't have the ability to deduce so much—even from body language. Rashidi is always composed, but tonight, there is an almost imperceptible slump to his shoulders. Rashidi feels defeated. Tarik swallows hard.

"Your father has requested that if he ceases to breathe this night, we will not summon the Healers. You understand what this means, Highness."

"I'm not ready, Rashidi." Not ready to lose his father. Not ready to rule as king of Theoria. At eighteen years old, he has been groomed all his life for kingship. But that was supposed to be in an official ceremony whereby his father would relinquish power to his firstborn heir—an heir that would be at least thirty years old by then, if circumstances permitted. Eighteen years or thirty years makes no difference to Tarik. A lifetime of preparation is not enough to make one ready to oversee an entire kingdom of living, breathing people who depend on the decisions he makes. The risks he takes.

The risks he doesn't take.

"What your mind does not yet know, your heart will make up for," Rashidi insists. "You prove you have the wisdom to rule by admitting that you are not ready to do so. The people love you. Let them support you."

Tarik mulls over Rashidi's words and finds them to be true. The adviser believes the people of Theoria do love their prince, and Rashidi is confident in his ability to act as king. It's reassuring, if only a little, that Rashidi is so steadfast. He is, after all, an advocate of the people first and foremost and adviser to his king second.

"The people do not know me," Tarik feels obligated to say. The people know a boy who takes after his mother. A skilled Lingot. A dutiful son. But they do not know his ability to rule as king. How could they?

Rashidi waves in dismissal. "I well know you, boy. I speak for the people. You'll not disappoint." The truth, or at least what Rashidi sincerely believes to be true.

Tarik places a hand on the linen next to his father's legs and leans on it for support. The king's breaths come in shallow, wheezing whispers, and Tarik is sure it does not help that the air is so hot and so very dry. A trickle of blood seeps from his nose, and Rashidi dabs at it with a damp cloth. The bleeding from his ears and mouth has lessened, but Tarik suspects it's because his father doesn't have much blood left to give.

Rashidi is right. It will not be long now. "What will I tell Sethos?" Tarik whispers. His younger brother, Sethos, just turned fifteen years and is, by far, the most precious object of their father's affections. A son after his father, Sethos is. King Knosi was a great warrior, and so Sethos will be. And so Sethos already is. He studies his craft at the Lyceum with the other Majai Favored Ones. His tutors are pleased with his progress. Father is pleased with his progress. Father will not like missing out on his youngest son.

It is time Tarik summoned Sethos home. He will want to be present when their father dies. It has been difficult enough keeping him away this long. But Father had insisted he continue on at the Lyceum. Father never imagined this sickness would progress so quickly.

Rashidi bows his head. "I will call for him, Highness." A slight pause. Then, "Will you tell the people what took him?"

On this Tarik is torn. It is something he's given a great deal of thought to, and guiltily so. For if he was worried what he would tell the people, he was more certain than he cared to admit of his father's death. All he really knew, though, was that he could not shrug the thought from his shoulders.

"I fear it will cause a panic," he says finally. After all, the kingdom sees his father as the epitome of strength and power, as they should their pharaoh. They may reason that if King Knosi can perish from such a disease, they cannot protect themselves from it. Yet, is that not the truth? If the illness has such far-reaching fingers, surely no one is safe. "On the other hand, if I don't tell them, I fear they won't give this the proper attention it deserves. They will carry on their lives as if he perished from some common illness. What if this new sickness spreads?" His father had just returned from the southern kingdom of Wachuk to negotiate the continued mining of turquoise there. It would be an easy thing to make the people assume he'd contracted something from that place. Wachuk's methods of medicine are primitive at best, and disease is rife there, a fact well-known among the citizens of Theoria.

But the Healers have ruled out any foreign infection. His father has something new, something they've never seen before. Still, if he instructs them, they will speak nothing of it.

"The people need not give it attention so much as the Healers do," Rashidi says. "It would be unwise to circulate news of a plague that our Healers do not have under control just yet."

Just yet. "And if the people begin to present symptoms?" They'd only had a handful of cases and all had been inside the palace walls, easy enough to contain. Easy enough, that is, until his father contracted it. Tarik remembers the day his father suffered his first nosebleed. The king had waved it off, dismissed it as if it were a soldier or a servant, as if such a thing could be controlled with a command. "It's nothing but an inconvenience," he'd said. "Fetch my Healer at once and tell him to put a stop to it." It had taken the Healer two frustrating hours to stop the bleeding. That night, his father had awakened with blood pooling in his ears. From that point on, he'd grown fatigued but refused food to help his energy because he could do nothing but wretch up even the smallest of bread crumbs. Within a week, a sturdy beast of a man who'd personally trained his own guard had wilted into something that resembled a weed with bones.

Tarik swallows.

"By then, the Healers will have found the cure. They always do, Highness."

But it doesn't sit well with him. Hiding something from his people, especially something so lethal, does not seem like the best way to begin his reign as their new king. Not to mention, the Lingots will know something is amiss. There are always ways to bend truths, but they will sense deception coming from the palace. And what message will that send?

"What else do you require from me this evening, Highness?" Rashidi seems aware he is not going to convince Tarik of anything at this moment. He is often shrewd in that way, to know when his usefulness has met its threshold and when to excuse himself. It is obvious now that King Knosi will not be waking up again to do the formal bidding of his most loyal adviser.

Tarik sighs in resignation. "A miracle."

Rashidi leaves him then, alone with his thoughts and worries. Alone with his father for the last time.

DON'T MISS

THE SYRENA LEGACY!

"A refreshing story filled with vibrant characters, feisty humor, and an irresistible romance. This story of star-crossed lovers in a luscious coastal setting brings new life to the age-old myth of merfolk and left me swooning for more!"

—MARISSA MEYER,
NEW YORK TIMES–BESTSELLING AUTHOR OF *CINDER*

SQUARE FISH

FIERCEREADS.COM

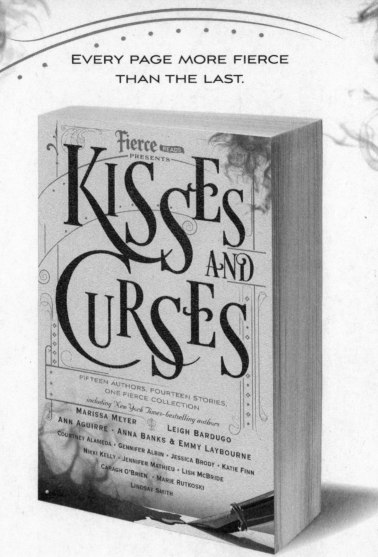